# THE
# GALA

**AMY TACKETT**

# Official Playlist

*Songs to pair with your reading experience:*

"Remembering Sunday" — All Time Low

"The River" — Good Charlotte

"Wake Me Up When September Ends" — Green Day

"Teenagers" — My Chemical Romance

"I Write Sins Not Tragedies" — Panic! At the Disco

"This Is America" — Childish Gambino

"Without Me" — Eminem

"The Anthem" — Good Charlotte

"Sweet Child O Mine" — Guns N Roses

"A Bar Song (Tipsy)" — Shaboozey

"Last Resort" — Papa Roach

"What the Hell" — Avril Lavigne

"Wonderwall" — Oasis

"Ain't No Rest for the Wicked" — Cage the Elephant

"In the Air Tonight" — Phil Collins

"Supermassive Black Hole" — Muse

"Play with Fire" — Sam Tinnesz

To Ruby Dyer, for introducing me to journalism.

To Dan Hollis, for posing the tough questions.

And to Erin Flanagan, for helping me step into fiction.

Thank you all for believing in me. Try not to grade this one too harshly.

# CONTENT WARNING

Welcome to Book One in the Art of Deception. This is a psychological thriller horror novel with adult themes and content, which may not be suitable for all readers. To view a list of content warnings, please visit my website.

Congress shall make no law respecting an establishment of religion, or prohibiting the free exercise thereof; or abridging the freedom of speech, or of the press; or the right of the people peaceably to assemble, and to petition the Government for a redress of grievances.

—The First Amendment, U.S. Constitution

# THEN



*Monday, October 3, 2022*

The glint of a blood-soaked knife hit the light.

*What the—*

"River!" Cole's expression widened in terror as he saw his daughter's bloodied silhouette lying on the floor. "Oh my God, River." He ran to her and dropped to his knees. Her normally tan skin was now pale white, and dewdrops of sweat coated the baseline of her matted black hair. "River, baby? *River!*"

She slid her gaze to meet Cole's, but only for a moment before her eyes rolled back in her head.

"No, no, no. *Rose!*" He yelled for his wife before gently patting the side of his daughter's face.

"Hey, hey. Wake up, baby. Stay with me."

His eyes darted around the room, frantic with panic as he tried to piece together what had happened. There was the knife, but he also saw shards of glass strewn across the floor. His pulse quickened as his gaze followed the trail back to her shattered window.

*What the hell?*

"Dad?" a small voice croaked.

He snapped his head back to her, heart thumping at the sound of her voice. "I'm right here, sweetie." He gazed into her icy blue eyes as she blinked at him, his chest cracking at the sight. "What happened? Please, you have to tell Daddy."

"I—" Her body began to twitch.

Fear shot through Cole's core. "Dammit, River, *stay with me*." He patted his pockets, searching for his phone and cursing when he realized he didn't have it.

"Rose!" He ripped off his shirt, scanning River's body for the source of the wound and wincing when he found it.

*Fuck.*

If he could just stop the bleeding . . .

"Rose, call an ambulance *now*!"

"What's wrong?" He heard her voice—*finally*—from the hallway.

"We need a fucking ambulance." River's body was convulsing now, and Cole relied solely on the adrenaline pumping through his veins to keep him from falling apart.

*No, no, no,* he thought, *not my baby. Please, not my baby girl.*

"Oh my God!" Rose screamed as she appeared in the doorway.

Tears streamed down Cole's face as he tried—and failed—to clot the wound. No matter what he did, the gushing continued. He pulled her close to his chest and wrapped his arms around her before looking up from the thickening pool of blood to find Rose still standing in the doorway, frozen in fear.

"Rosie," he yelled, his cries scratching the back of his throat. "Snap out of it! She needs 911, now." His voice cracked on the last word as he pleaded with his wife to move, to do something.

But it was no use; Rose remained glued to the spot.

*Dammit.*

Desperate, he stood and heaved River's fifteen-year-old body into his arms. "It's going to be okay, sweetie." He pushed past his wife, who flinched when River's flailing arms hit her, and Cole flew down the stairs. "It's going to be okay," he repeated as his tears dripped onto her skin, mingling with the blood. "Daddy's here."

# NOW



Blood, sweat, and tears—those were the liquids that stained Cole's life. The elixir his body forced him to take, again and again, as he relived the horrors from the worst moment of his life, with tonight being no different.

"Fuck!" His body flailed as he awoke from the same gut-wrenching nightmare and gasped for air, his heart beating loudly in his chest.

*Breathe.*

He inhaled a large gulp of oxygen for four seconds, held it for seven, and then exhaled for eight.

*Good.*

After repeating the action several times, he wiped his face off on a nearby T-shirt and then felt around in the darkness for his water bottle, accidentally knocking it over in the process.

He cursed under his breath.

Two years to the day, and this shit still hit the same every night. The sight of her body drenched in blood. The acidic taste of vomit that threatened Cole's mouth. The sheer and absolute terror. It all rushed back just the same.

A rustling sounded at the door, and Cole's English Mastiff, Emmett, pushed into the room and barked at the foot of the bed, waiting for an invitation.

"Em." Cole breathed a small sigh of relief at the sight of his pet and emotional support animal. He had always been Cole's main source of comfort, so when the doctor suggested getting a therapy pet last year, it only made sense to file the paperwork.

Cole patted the sheets beside him and waited as Emmett heaved his two-hundred-pound body onto the mattress. Once settled, the dog nestled his head onto Cole's chest.

It was better than any weighted blanket could have been.

*Breathe. Just breathe.*

His pulse slowed over time, but he shuddered as the images continued to swirl through his mind. Emmett, who knew his owner's habits by now, sensed his discomfort and buried his snout deeper into Cole's chest.

*Breathe.*

Together, they laid like that for several minutes. Then, once Cole's heartbeat had somewhat regulated, he sat up slowly, testing his body's ability to reabsorb the adrenaline.

His throat dry and itchy, he reached for his water again and took a large swig before grabbing his phone to check the time: 5:03 a.m.

"Ughhhhh," he groaned, setting it back down.

His alarm would go off soon, but he dreaded the thought of facing another day. He found it increasingly difficult to get out of bed since River's death, even with the antidepressants his doctor prescribed. Without his daughter's brightness shining in the world, Cole felt . . . hopeless.

Bleak.

Emmett whined, drawing him out of his trance-like state. He snapped his gaze to the dog, realizing he'd climbed out of bed and was waiting by the door now. Cole rubbed his eyes and took a deep breath. "All right, bud. I'm coming."

With as much enthusiasm in his step as a hearse driver on burial day, he forced his body out of bed and commenced his daily routine.

He let Emmett outside and then dragged his feet to the bathroom. He knew he needed to shower—wanted to even—but the thought of bathing, toweling off, and getting dressed again exhausted him.

*Water is excellent grounding work.*

With Dr. Jacobi's words ringing in his ears, Cole sighed in defeat and peeled off his sweaty clothes. Then, he turned on the faucet and waited for the scalding hot water to reach maximum boiling temperature. *Nothing like the painful sting of city water,* he thought. Once he felt confident the water might burn him, he stepped underneath the steady stream and let it wash away the night's horrors.

The rest of Cole's morning followed suit as he argued with himself again and again.

*Brush your teeth—it's not an option.*

*You have to wear deodorant, Cole.*

*Yes, you really need to eat something besides coffee. That's not a food group.*

He grimaced at his demands but obliged, putting one foot in front of the other until his morning routine was complete. Then, with yet another cup of coffee in hand, he slipped onto his back porch and sat in his grandma's old rocking chair. It wasn't comfortable by any means, but going outside and *shocking his senses* was another grounding technique the couples' therapist had taught him.

*Couples' therapist.*

His heart squeezed at the thought. The current status of his marriage, which was hanging by the loose thread of a trial separation, was the last thing he wanted to think about today of all days. Yet, here it was, pounding in his skull like a demon fleeing from salvation.

*I don't think this is working.*

He ran a hand through his loose brown curls as the memories surfaced. They were in the kitchen eating dinner from a takeout container—a regular occurrence since the incident—when Rose had said, "Cole, I love you, but I can't stay in this house going on the way we have been. It's . . . it's too much."

He'd nearly dropped his fork, startled by the comment. "What are you saying?"

"I think . . . I think you know what I'm saying." She'd paused and then added, "I think this"—she motioned at the two of them—"has run its course. I'm tired of pretending otherwise."

Cole's already broken heart had felt like it'd snapped yet again, crumbling into a million pieces. He'd scrambled to come up with words, any words, that would fix what she'd just said, eventually landing on, "We could try therapy."

He remembered the way she'd looked caught off guard, the dramatic lull in conversation, and the obvious confusion in her gaze. She'd asked him to go to therapy before, and he'd scoffed at the suggestion. Paying a stranger to *talk about their feelings* was the last thing he'd wanted, but now? Well, if it meant saving his marriage, he'd do it.

Because he had to.

He loved Rose.

*If only that was enough.*

He shook his head at the memory and scooted the old rocker closer to Emmett, who wagged his tail in response.

Looking up, Cole distracted himself with the dreary fall day that draped his backyard. Above him, a warm myriad of Midwestern red and gold hues blended into the trees, and beneath him, nature's decaying remains covered the ground. He closed his eyes and took in the scent of the damp autumn rain as its residue clung to the sky. Something about its haunting nature was alluring to Cole, and he breathed a gentle sigh of relief as he settled farther into the chair.

Sometime later, Cole felt a familiar warm nudge on his belly. "Hey, Em," he murmured. A single whimper escaped Emmett's jowls, and Cole moved his hand to scratch the dog's ears. "Sup, buddy?"

Emmett barked this time, and that made Cole's eyes snap open, interrupting his nap.

"Shit." What time was it? He scrambled to find his phone, flustered that he'd fallen asleep.

*Three Missed Calls from Nate Cawhill.*

*Two Text Messages from Nate Cawhill.*

He mumbled a slew of curse words as he bolted out of his seat and ran for the front door, wondering what he would say to his boss.

TWENTY MINUTES LATER, COLE rushed into his office at *The Suttonville Chronicles*, where he was the lead investigative reporter. Despite the paper being situated in the heart of suburbia, *The Chronicles* was the second-largest circulating newspaper in Ohio—not to mention it was owned by the nation's leading mass media conglomerate group. Cole had been one of the top dogs among the staff, having only turned down an editor position so he could focus on reporting.

If only he took it as seriously now as he did then.

Cursing as he made his way through the building's entrance, he avoided eye contact with everyone he passed. It was the umpteenth time he'd been late this month, and they all knew Nate would chew his ass out.

Cole shifted his gaze around the room after settling into his desk, eyes roaming for signs of their editor-in-chief. Finally, after several minutes passed without Nate appearing, Cole thought he'd lucked out *again*. He breathed a sigh of relief and sauntered off to the break room for a cup of coffee.

"Thought you'd escape me that easily, huh?" Cole jumped as the refrigerator door swung shut, revealing his boss's glare.

*Shit.*

"Sorry, sir, I had an early interview scheduled with—"

"I don't want to hear it," Nate said, his arms crossed and feet planted shoulder-width apart. "My office. Now."

Cole sighed in response and followed. He thought about how to spin this as he stepped inside the room, taking in the familiar sight of the framed articles and the scent of old, musty books.

"Nate, I'm sorry I forgot to text or call, but I had an early morning interview with the mayor's office that couldn't wait."

Nate eyed Cole, weighing his words. "With whom?"

"His public information officer, Damar Williams." Cole cleared his throat. "Yeah, he had an opening to chat about the arts festival, so, you know, duty calls. Couldn't ignore that."

Cole was fully aware he was rambling too much.

Apparently, so was Nate.

"Where are the notes?"

"Hmm?"

"The notes, Cole. From the interview."

"Oh, um, I took them on my phone."

"Let me see."

Cole sized him up, knowing he'd lost, and let out a long breath.

"Yeah, that's what I thought." Nate stood up from his desk and looked out the window. "I really didn't want to have to do this, Cole, but you've left me no choice."

"Wait, wait, wait," Cole interjected, panicking. "I'm sorry, sir, I really do have an angle on this festival—"

"Enough." Nate turned back to face him. "You're late almost every day, your stories are constantly falling through, and your work isn't as sharp as it used to be. I gave you leniency in the beginning. Hell, we all did, but I can't keep letting these things slide, Cole. I'm going to have to let you go."

Wait a minute. Was Nate, of all people, *firing* him? He was the guy who took a chance on Cole when he'd first graduated, the one who fostered and mentored him into the reporter he is today. And yet he'd said the words without so much as a flinch.

"I—I've been seeing a therapist," Cole started, not mentioning that it was technically a marriage counselor for his not-so-happily-ever-after. "I think it's helping. Please, sir, if you'll just give me a little more time to adjust."

"I've given you more than enough time, Cole. You know our world doesn't allow for missed deadlines and fluff pieces. This is *The Chronicles*, dammit!" He slammed his fist on the desk and then paused, taking a deep breath. "I'm sorry, I really am, but you need to clear out your desk."

Cole felt like he'd been sucker-punched in the gut. He couldn't lose his job—this was the only thing he had left. And what the hell would Rose say when she found out? They only had two months left of their trial separation, and Cole couldn't bear the thought of what would happen if he told her he'd been fired.

*No.* He shook his head to himself. He couldn't let that happen. "Nate, please—" he started, but his boss cut him off.

"I said enough, Cole." He rubbed his eyes before looking back at him. "I'm sorry, but I can't keep making excuses for you. I've protected you for as long as I can, but people are starting to talk. I really am sorry, but please, I need you to clear out your things."

Cole felt the familiar grip on his chest as his lungs involuntarily squeezed shut. *Dammit. Not here.* He worked to steady his breathing as discreetly as he could.

Nate stared at him, as if waiting for a response, but Cole was paralyzed. His body was shutting down and responding to the trauma in the only way he knew how.

*Stop it*, he pleaded with himself, willing his body to listen.

"Cole?" Nate eyed him cautiously.

*Way to go, you lazy piece of shit.*

*I can't believe you got fired.*

*No one will hire you now.*

*Rose is going to leave you.*

*River would be so disappointed. She's better off dead than having a dad like you.*

He gasped as the intrusive thoughts flooded in and constricted his airway. *Where was Emmett?* He needed Emmett.

"Cole?" Nate pushed out of his chair and walked around the desk. "Hey!" He snapped his fingers. "Look at me. What's wrong?"

Cole's eyes widened in shock and embarrassment as the panic attack crashed through him like a heavy tidal wave. He knew from experience he couldn't do anything to stop it—waiting it out was his only option. His pulse quickened as his mind fought to combat the physiological response to his triggers, and the look of pure horror on his boss's face was enough to make him want to curl up and die.

# NOW



An hour later, Cole heaved his body onto a barstool at Gemma's Tavern, one of the local favorites. After the panic attack passed, he'd rushed out of Nate's office without so much as a goodbye.

"Your desk," Nate had called.

But Cole didn't care. Besides a haiku River had scribbled on a Post-it Note when she was eleven and a signed photo of him and Carl Bernstein from his college days, he didn't want any of it. He'd snatched those two items, along with his car keys, and left before anything else embarrassing could happen to him.

He blinked away the memory and raised his finger at Gemma's daughter, Amy. "Can I get a double shot of Jim Beam?"

It was ten in the morning, but considering he'd just been fired and had a mental breakdown in front of his boss—ex-boss—Cole had decided that didn't matter. Drink up, bitches—that's what the kids say, right?

"Sure thing, sugar." She grabbed a glass from under the bar and started to pour. "Just the one, or are we doing a tab today?"

Cole smirked and grabbed the glass, slugging the drink back. "Tab. Another, please."

She obliged and refilled the shot glass before taking his card. "You got it. Ordering any food? Big Nash is in the kitchen today."

Cole considered her question. He wasn't hungry, but Nash made the best damn chicken and waffles in town. Everybody knew it, too. "Sure, why the hell not?"

*Maybe because you just got fired and no longer have an income?*

He scoffed at his internal thoughts and gave Amy his order.

"All right," she said with a smile, "I'll be back in a few to check on you."

"Thank you."

His favorite thing about Amy was she didn't ask questions. It was what made her great at her job.

Cole cringed at the thought—*a job*. The one thing he still had in life, and now it was gone. He scrubbed his hands over his face and slumped his shoulders. How was he supposed to pay his bills? Hell, what would he do for work now? There were other news outlets scattered throughout the neighboring towns and cities, sure, but none of them were as high profile as *The Chronicles*.

And then there was the matter of Rose.

Ever since the separation, Cole had really been trying to do better—to *be* better—for her. He wanted to be the man she needed. And he was getting closer; he could feel it. They were communicating more, she was staying over longer when she came to visit Emmett, and he'd even agreed to Dr. Jacobi's suggestion about individual therapy. But now? It wasn't likely she'd take him back after what had just happened. And Cole knew it.

He sighed and took his second shot. He needed to dull the pain.

After another slew of intrusive thoughts and internal ramblings, Cole asked for a third double shot and a beer to chase it. Amy obliged but not before setting down a fresh plate of crispy chicken tenders and Belgian waffles.

"Here, baby. This will help with whatever it is."

Cole thanked her and enjoyed his pity party of one, savoring every last bite since this would likely be his "last supper" now that he was unemployed.

He sneered again at the thought and dug into his food. Time ticked on as he swallowed the warm bites of comfort food and washed them down with more self-soothing booze. His brain was stuck somewhere between shock and disbelief. He'd never been unemployed a day in his life, not since he turned sixteen. Cole had a strong work ethic, and he was passionate about his career. He loved the news and everything the industry stood for, even if some people bashed the media. He knew he was an honest journalist, committed to presenting the world with unbiased facts, no matter how ugly.

*Ugh.*

He needed to remedy this and fast. He pushed the now-empty plate to the side and pulled out his phone. It was Thursday, which meant he had a week before their next marriage counseling session. He shifted in his chair, a new thought forming in the cusp of his mind. If he could find work before then, maybe Rose never had to know. He narrowed his eyes as he considered this new idea. Was it realistic?

With his résumé, possibly. But he'd have to settle for a smaller paper—or a different role.

Regardless, though, this wasn't the worst idea he'd ever had. If he worked quickly (and let go of his pride), then in theory, he could find another job before she ever knew he'd been fired.

Cole was, after all, the top investigative reporter at *The Chronicles*.

*You mean you used to be.*

He shut down the thought and grabbed his phone from the table, pulling up his LinkedIn app. He tapped on the jobs section and typed in a few keywords, but the results were all so strange.

A Multi-medium Finalist? What did that even mean? Cole scrunched his eyes in confusion, clearing the blurred words as they danced on the screen.

Multimedia Journalist.

*Oh.*

That made more sense.

Shit. He probably needed to Uber home.

Sighing, Cole closed the app and clicked on the familiar rideshare one instead. If he was going to do this, he needed to sober up. He typed out his destination and waited for someone to accept his ride. Then, he flagged down Amy to ask for the check and cashed out as he waited for "Noah" to arrive.

*"D-D-DAD," RIVER'S VOICE SQUEAKED out.*

*Cole felt a rush of air and butterflies leave his chest at the sound of her voice. "I'm right here, baby." He stroked her hair again and tried to mask his fear to be brave for her.*

*"Dad, I—" Her voice broke off again as another violent convulsion roared through her body.*

"AHHHH!" Cole's voice broke the silence in the air as his throat ached from the scream. "Fuck!"

Tears began to stain his face as he clutched his chest.

*It was just a dream. It was just a dream. Just a dream.*

Except it wasn't. It was his worst fucking nightmare, and he *lived* it. Again and again. Every damn night.

*It's what you deserve for not being there.*

A dog whine interrupted Cole's frantic thoughts. Emmett was sitting at the edge of the couch, waiting for his owner's command to comfort him.

"Em, come here, boy." He wrapped his arms around the dog and then buried his face in his fur. Emmett was the only thing that made the pain stop rattling in his chest as he worked to control his breathing. "This shit never ends, bud."

The pup licked his face in response, desperately trying to soothe Cole's heartache.

*I should've been there.*

The thought haunted Cole, and he shuddered, shielding his eyes from the warm stream of sunlight that beamed through the window. *What time was it?* He checked the clock on the microwave and groaned at the 3:45 p.m. time stamp. It had been noon when the Uber driver dropped him off, meaning he'd been passed out on the couch for almost four hours. *Shit.* That was four hours he could've been searching for a new job, which he needed *before* he saw Rose next week.

Chastising himself, he stood up and stretched before heading into the kitchen. He needed a fresh pot of coffee and a massive painkiller to get through this next part.

*I'm going to have to let you go.*

Nate's words rang in his ears. He still couldn't believe that just a few hours ago, he'd been fired. And by Nate, of all people.

The timer on his coffee pot went off, drawing him back to the task at hand: a job.

He needed to find a job.

Fast.

"All right. Surely it can't be that tough, Em," Cole said, looking at the dog. "I can do this."

Emmett tilted his head in response.

"What? You don't think I can?"

The dog blinked.

He blew out a breath and shook his head. He had to stop having conversations with his pet. They never worked in his favor.

"Okay," he said, this time to himself, "let's see what I can find . . ." His voice trailed off as he sat down at his kitchen table and opened his laptop, his eyes glazing over the listings.

*Senior MMJ*

*Multimedia Journalist (Sports)*

*Reporter/Photographer*

*Entry-level Producer*

*Evening News Anchor*

*Features Editor*

*MMJ/Reporter*

Cole sighed and took a sip of his coffee. Investigative jobs were hard to come by in this area, and he knew that, but physically seeing the lack of opportunity drained him. This was not how he envisioned his life at thirty-eight.

"What do you think, Em, Features Editor or Senior—"

Cole's continued conversation with his dog was interrupted by a knock at the door.

*That's weird.*

Cole didn't have visitors. Not since Rose left, at least.

*Rose.*

His heart throbbed as the panic set in. Maybe she'd heard about him getting fired. But who would have told her? His mind raced as he thought of who she could possibly be in contact with from work. Marcy from accounting had been in her book club once, but she was in her late fifties and didn't like to text, which was part of the reason why she left the book club. "Too many dings throughout the day!" she'd said to Cole once when he asked her about it at work. "I just want to read books, not novel-length group texts!" She had a point, he remembered thinking.

Another knock sounded from the front door.

*Shit.*

His palms sweated, and he stood up, trying to determine how he'd explain being home in the middle of the day. He was out of PTO days, and she knew he was on thin ice as is.

With a new sense of dread, Cole chugged the last of his coffee and slowly made his way to the door. Once there, he took a deep breath and opened it, preparing for the worst.

Only, it didn't come.

Because Rose wasn't there.

No one was.

"Hello?" Cole looked around, expecting to see someone lingering in his driveway or on the sidewalk, but still, no one was there.

*What the hell?*

He took a few steps onto the outdoor landing and put his hand on his brows, shielding his eyes from the sun to see if he could get a better look. "Anybody out here?"

When no one responded, he swiveled around, annoyed he'd been taken away from his task. Damn kids. Didn't they know he had a crisis to figure out?

Just as Cole was about to head back inside, he noticed a black envelope tucked into the old wreath on his door. He reached for it and then hesitated, looking around again.

Was this a joke?

Or worse, divorce papers? His eyes widened at the thought.

No, no, maybe it was his severance package. News stations were old school, right?

Curiosity getting the best of him, Cole snatched the envelope from the door and examined it.

A jet-black, eight-by-eleven-inch envelope stared back at him. No address, no name.

"Hmm." Cole raised an eyebrow and looked over his shoulder. Then, he returned his gaze to the parcel and flipped it over, a reflective gleam catching in the sun. Confused, Cole stepped out from the awning and scrutinized the package under the sunlight.

At first, he couldn't make out what he was seeing, but then, a large "Z" appeared on the package, and the hairs on his arms rose.

"No," Cole breathed.

He jerked his head around again, his beady eyes anxious to catch anything out of place. *It couldn't be.*

Could it?

All hesitancies aside, he ripped open the package and came face-to-face with what looked like an invitation. "Holy shit."

# THEN



*Saturday, June 8, 2019*

"Happy birthday to you! Happy birthday to you! Happy birthday, dear River, happy birthday to you!" Cole beamed as he watched his daughter blow out all twelve candles on her pink tie-dye cake and then grimaced when he saw one of the boys staring at her chest.

He cleared his throat and shoved his way past the kid, asserting himself beside River and kissing her head. "Happy birthday, baby doll." He smirked as he watched the boy's eyes widen and then dart away.

*That's what I thought.*

"Daaaaad," she said under her breath. "You're, like, totally embarrassing me right now."

"Sorry, hun," he said, locking eyes with the boy yet again for good measure. "It's just not every day your little girl turns twelve."

"Babe," Rose warned, tugging at his arm. "Leave the poor kid alone."

He grunted and turned to face his wife, moving as a swarm of teenagers hovered around the cake, all waiting for their turn to cut a piece. "I still don't understand why you agreed to let her invite boys. She's twelve, not twenty."

Rose laughed and rolled her eyes. "And I had my first kiss at eleven, babe. Come on. We'd be naive to think nothing goes on at this age. I'd rather her hang out with boys here, under our supervision, than sneak around and do it."

Cole still didn't like the idea of all these grimy boys seeing his little girl in a bikini. She hit puberty over the spring and was starting to develop, much to Cole's chagrin, and he wanted nothing more than to shove a baggy T-shirt over her and keep her locked up in the house forever.

*If only.*

He sighed, walked over to the cooler by the pool, and grabbed another beer. He didn't drink much these days, but he needed something to help distract him from all the pubescent hormones at this party.

Popping off the lid and taking a swig, he settled into one of their zero-gravity chairs and flipped through the channels on their outdoor TV screen. River had insisted on playing something called *Riverdale*, but no one was paying attention—especially with the teen bop music playing over the loudspeakers. Cole turned on the captions and surfed his way to the news stations.

Some odd minutes later, he looked up and saw his mother glaring at him under her sun visor. "You really shouldn't be drinking at your daughter's birthday party, Cole. I mean, what kind of example are you setting for her?"

"Nice to see you, too, Mom." He flipped his hat around backward and took a long pull from his drink out of spite. "You missed her blowing out the candles."

Janet Sloane straightened her posture and looked away. "Your father was busy meeting with the Walker brothers about a potential investment deal. Sorry we couldn't make it sooner, but you know how these things go."

An awkward silence filled the air. Cole had never been close with his parents, which he didn't mind, but seeing the way they dismissed River always unsettled him, right down to his bones. He flexed his jaw and decided to turn his attention back to the TV, not wanting to make a scene. "You can put the presents over there."

Janet hesitated but inevitably walked away, leaving Cole alone with the afternoon news, just how he liked it.

He watched as the new weekend anchor from WZAS fumbled her way through the opening headlines. Not that Cole was one to judge. He was terrible on camera, which was why he wrote for the paper but still. It was hard not to notice when someone was jittery during a live broadcast.

*"Hey, Rebecca, sorry to cut you off there, but we have a breaking story rolling in live from New York."*

Cole sat up straighter now as he watched the camera cut to his friend Elijah and then to a live feed from their more prominent partner outlet in New York City. The captions were delayed, but that didn't matter. Cole saw everything he needed on screen.

*"Apparently, local NYC residents woke up this morning to a sea of helicopters flooding the Upper New York Bay. Authorities arrived on scene after multiple reports were made but not before the chopper's inhabitants splashed various paint colors on our nation's beloved Lady Liberty. Before fleeing the scene, they also dropped a large, rainbow banner that read, 'How proud are you, America?'"*

A wave of adrenaline hit Cole's veins like a stab of ice.

*"Authorities are still investigating the matter, but New York City Chief of Police Daniel Bronson said he believes an artist named Graham Zanella may be responsible."*

"Zanella," Cole breathed.

He'd heard the name before, at a Black Lives Matter protest he covered last year. He remembered, because it was odd, but it was only mentioned in passing. He didn't have a chance to follow up with anyone about it at the time.

His phone vibrated in his pocket, and he pulled it out to see Nate calling.

"You seeing this shit?" he spat, before Cole even had a chance to say hello.

"Yeah. I think I've heard the name before."

"Shit on a stick," Nate grumbled. "All right, looks like you're going to the Big Apple this weekend. You up for it?"

Cole looked over his shoulder at River, who was laughing in the pool with her friends. "Um, well, I'm sorta in the middle of my daughter's birthday party." He paused and glanced at Rose, who was sitting across the lawn making small talk with his mother. "Can it wait until Monday?"

Silence filled the line, and Cole panicked at the thought of missing the story. He was the preferred man for the job, but that didn't mean there weren't others eager to swoop in and take his place.

"What time is the party over?" Nate finally asked.

Cole rubbed his hand over his face. Technically, there was no end time. The invites they sent out said to stay as late as you wanted, and some girls were even spending the night. He couldn't leave Rose alone with everyone, could he?

"Sloane!" Nate barked after a beat too long.

"Not until late," he sputtered.

Another pause, and then he said, "I can let you take a red-eye if you promise to be on-site first thing in the morning. That's the best I can do. Otherwise, I'll have to give it to—"

"I can do it," Cole answered, cutting him off. "Just text me the flight info, and I'll be there."

# NOW

## Thursday, October 3, 2024

*Dear Mr. Sloane,*

*I am writing to inform you that you have been cordially invited to participate in my next event: an art gala slated for Thursday, October 31, 2024. I understand you've been trying to find me for quite some time, and I'm pleased to say you have my attention.*

*Before you can attend, though, you must complete three tasks. My team will send you information for each one, and you must complete them to advance to the next level. Then, if you succeed, my team will reveal the final event's location, where we'll have the opportunity to meet.*

*I understand this is outside of my usual antics, but I do hope you'll accept my invitation.*

*Are you ready to play, Cole?*

*-Z*

Cole read the invitation three times before he let out a breath.

*What the hell?*

An exclusive art gala.

A series of events.

All from Zanella.

And Cole had been . . . invited to participate?

He needed to lie down.

This must be a prank. Barry down at the news station must be behind this. Because there's just no way this was real . . . right?

Cole reread the invite and frowned. *A gala.*

He shook his head and contemplated throwing it away—and calling Barry to cuss him out, but then he did something peculiar.

He turned it over.

And saw a QR code.

"What the hell?" Cole said and stared at it briefly before tearing out his phone. Even if this was a prank, he had to see what it was—due diligence and all.

Fumbling with the lock screen, Cole scanned the code and watched as a dark graphic loaded. Then, after what felt like an eternity, his eyes widened, and he felt his reporter senses tingling. There, on the front page, was a hooded figure holding a sign that said, "Let the games begin." Cole clicked on it, despite his better judgment, and a video appeared on the next screen.

"Holy shit."

He hit play and watched as a person dressed in all black appeared on screen. Their face was hidden behind a white mask, but Cole assumed it was a man due to the individual's tall, muscular build. Cole squinted, trying to place where the video was taking place, but he couldn't see anything beyond a plain, brick wall.

At first, nothing happened, making Cole's palms sweat. He waited with baited breath until finally, the figure moved.

He bent down out of the camera's view, and when he stood up, he held an art palette. Cole watched as the masked man dipped a paint brush in black and turned to start painting on the wall behind him.

At first, there was no sound, the movie eerily similar to a silent film, but then, a Siri-like voice began narrating.

"Hello, and welcome to Zanella's next event. You have been chosen to participate in this life-altering experiment due to your unique talents, skill sets, and abilities." The voice continued as the figure opted for a light blue paint. "As you know, you must complete three tasks to receive the final invitation. Instructions for each event will appear here, starting with the first."

Cole's heart palpitated, nearing dangerous levels.

"We will meet at 4427 Vineyard Grove, Hampstead, Ohio, Saturday at 8:30 p.m. All you have to do is document what you see. Tell the story in your own words and get it out to the masses. We look forward to seeing what you do."

Document what you see? Get the word out to the masses? "There's no way," Cole said in a hushed voice, his mind reeling.

Graham Zanella was an *underground* artist, meaning no one knew who he was or what he looked like, only that he was a mysterious and disturbing individual who orchestrated unhinged live art performances throughout the East Coast.

One that Cole had tried—and failed—to track down for the better part of two years.

Cole shuddered as the memories of Z's performances washed over him: Black men and women sitting still as statues outside the White House, their bodies painted in blood; a variety of battered women stacked on top of one another and positioned into a giant X on the streets of Boston, while techno music blared in the background; the sick immigrant children who were on display in a large, clear quarantine box outside of a hospital in Florida. Zanella was the mastermind behind all of it.

His art knew no boundaries.

And apparently, neither did Cole.

His obsession with Zanella had cost him everything.

Cole wiped the sweat from his brow and looked at his phone. He'd promised himself he wouldn't go down this rabbit hole again, not after what happened with River. He couldn't.

And yet—

He clicked play on the video again, rewatching it for details he may have missed. When nothing new turned up, he quickly navigated to a second screen and typed the address into his search bar. Hampstead was more than an hour away, and he wasn't very familiar with the area.

*Mazie's Drive-in Movie Theater* populated at the top of the results.

"Shut up," Cole said. "A movie theater?"

He scrunched his eyes as thoughts started racing through his mind. What the hell did Z have planned? A screen takeover, a live-action scary movie scene. It could be *anything*. Cole felt ill.

He grimaced, wondering what he was supposed to do with this information. He'd just been fired and had no outlet to run the story.

*Fuck,* he cursed internally. *Think. Think. Think.*

He rubbed his temples until, finally, a thought occurred to him.

*Nate.*

He needed to tell Nate.

Yes, that's exactly what he would do. He would tell Nate, and if he was lucky, he could potentially get back in his boss's good graces enough to get his job back and cover the story on Saturday. Rose never had to know he had lost his job.

His brain moved on autopilot as he rushed inside to grab his jacket and then pulled his phone out to order another Uber so he could pick up his car. This could fix everything. *No,* he corrected himself. *It* would *fix everything.* He turned to lock the door on his way out, but then another thought occurred.

*The final act.*

Zanella's invitation said he could only attend the final act if he completed all three tasks. That meant there was more. Z had an entire series of artistic events planned—AKA, Cole had an entire series of stories he could pitch and run with front-page bylines.

That's what he really wanted. Plus, his boss would be more apt to hire him back if he had an ongoing, active part in the investigation rather than a one-off lead. His wheels started spinning as he considered covering the story on his own and then taking it to Nate.

But could he really do this? After everything that had happened?

"Dammit," he breathed. "I need to think."

Emmett trotted over and wagged his tail.

"I need to head out for a little bit." Cole spoke directly to the dog. "You gonna be okay by yourself?"

Emmett whined in response.

Cole blew out a breath and headed for the kitchen, grabbing Em's leash and throwing on a ball cap. "All right, come on, bud. Let's go see Jayce."

# NOW



*Thursday, October 3, 2024*

Twenty minutes later, Cole waltzed into the local marketing firm, Rival, with Emmett in tow. He needed to speak to his best friend, because Jayce knew everything about Cole's past.

The incident.

Zanella.

*All of it.*

He approached the front desk, ignoring the woman's disdainful look as she noticed the dog. "Hey," he offered. "I'm here to see Jayce Ryles. Is he available?"

The woman tore her eyes from Emmett, finally addressing Cole. "He's in a meeting."

Cole looked at his watch and frowned. It was nearly five o'clock. Was Jayce really in a meeting this late? "Okay, well, do you know when he'll be out?"

Her wrinkles furrowed in response. "I don't. Can I take a message for you and your . . . companion?"

Cole tapped his foot and checked his watch again. "You know what? I'll just wait. Thanks."

She sighed in exaggeration and phoned someone upstairs. "Please tell Mr. Ryles someone is here to see him at his earliest convenience."

"Thanks," Cole repeated, more coolly this time.

Where was the young, quirky brunette that used to sit at the front desk? She always loved Emmett and was super kind. This woman seemed like she was overdue for an enema.

He shuddered as he shook off the mental picture and then found a seat in the lobby. While he waited, he tugged off his worn Springhill University hat, the black one his grandpa had gifted him when he was just a little boy, and ran a hand through his messy brown waves. His blood was boiling with a mix of anticipation and anger as images from the video looped in his mind.

For Cole, Zanella was the source of so much angst, so much heartbreak, and devastation. Could he really face the artist after all this time?

*No.*

He shook his head. It wasn't right or fair to dishonor River's memory like this. What the hell was he thinking even considering this? A wave of shame washed over him, and he felt nauseated. He stood up to leave, a decision made, when a large, booming voice echoed, "Cole Sloane! How goes it, you fine gentleman?"

*Dammit.*

Jayce slapped a hand on Cole's shoulder and pulled him into a hug.

"Hey, man," Cole replied. "Sorry, I didn't mean to waste your time. I was actually just heading out."

"Nonsense!" Jayce bellowed. "Kathleen, I'm heading out for the night. Enjoy your night." He nodded to the spinster, who glared at the pair of them angrily.

Cole shook his head. "Oh, no, that's really okay. You don't have to do that."

Jayce raised his eyebrow. "What's the matter, bud? Afraid I'll steal Emmett away from you?" He scratched the dog's ears and gave him a big hello. "Let's go. I'll take you to my favorite place."

"Bloody. Extra bloody." Jayce slammed his menu shut and gave it to the waitress. "As rare as the health department will let you."

The server giggled, and Cole watched as Jayce winked at her.

"And for you, sir?" she asked, turning her attention to Cole.

"Just a plate of hot wings will be fine, thanks. And a tall Miller." This conversation definitely called for a drink or two. "On second thought, can I also get a shot of your barrel whiskey?"

The waitress nodded and then took their menus, leaving the men alone.

Cole took a deep breath, preparing to apologize again for the interruption and reassure him nothing was up, when Jayce slapped the table and said, "Cole Sloane comes to my office on a Thursday afternoon, with his dog nonetheless, and then orders a beer and a shot as soon as we sit down for dinner."

"Yeah, about that—"

"You got back together with Rose, didn't ya?" Jayce interrupted, offering Cole a sly smile.

"Oh," Cole said with a smile that didn't reach his eyes. "No, that's not it. She and I . . . uh, I don't know what we are, honestly."

Jayce eyed him and hitched his lip. "Cole, you devil. Did you sleep with someone?"

"What? No." Cole shook his head. "Dude, this isn't about a woman."

"Oh." Jayce looked disappointed as he sat back and took a drink of water.

Cole cleared his throat, fidgeting in his chair. "Yeah, I don't know why I came to your office. I'm sorry. I shouldn't have bothered you. It's nothing."

Jayce leaned forward and put his arms on the table, a curious expression on his face. "What's up, man?"

Cole hesitated, unsure of what to say. He could lie and make something up, but Jayce always knew when he was lying.

"Come on, you can tell me anything."

*Spit it out.*

"Fine," Cole finally breathed, "but fair warning, it's about Z."

Jayce's eyes widened as his brows shot to the top of his head. He nodded and then leaned in closer as Cole launched into the invitation story. When he was finished, Jayce let out a long breath and ran his hands through his hair. "Damn, dude."

"I know," Cole responded. "I came here to ask your opinion, but then I decided just to ignore it, maybe tell one of my old colleagues." The words tasted bitter on his tongue. Could he really give this story away? An ache raced through his chest at the thought.

Jayce nearly spit out his drink. "Wait, what? You can't be serious."

"Yeah," Cole said, shaking his head. "I . . . I think I am."

"Cole, you have the opportunity of a *lifetime* to finally get the exclusive with this guy. The same guy you were chasing for years, may I remind you." Jayce paused for a moment as the waitress sat their drinks on the table. "You can't just give that shit up. You have to participate."

"No." Cole tore off a piece of the complimentary bread and handed it to Emmett, who was patiently—but also not so patiently—waiting. "I can't. I can't do that. Not after what happened . . ." His voice was soft.

Jayce paused at that and set his glass down. "Dude, are you really still harboring guilt for that?"

Cole gulped as a lump formed in his chest. "You know damn well if I hadn't been traipsing all across the country trying to find that man, she'd still be here."

"I do not know that," Jayce argued. "And neither do you. What happened to River . . . it was awful. The worst tragedy a parent could go through, but it wasn't your fault." He paused, allowing the words to sink in. "And it wasn't Zanella's. You have to forgive yourself, and him, if you ever want to move on. You have to learn to start living again, man."

Cole looked down, fighting the tears that threatened to give away his hardened visage. The mention of her name on anyone else's lips—it was still too much at times.

"I just . . ." he finally started. "I just wanna . . . rip his throat out sometimes, you know? Like if I hadn't been so fucking obsessed with him . . . I don't know." His voice broke on the last line, and he covered his face.

*Deep breaths. Deep breaths.*

After a moment, he regained his composure and looked back up at Jayce. "I failed her."

Jayce looked at him now, all signs of playfulness cast aside. "I don't believe that for one second, and neither should you."

That was exactly what he believed.

Because it was true.

If he'd been home, if he'd protected her better, then he could've saved her from—

"If anything," Jayce rattled on, interrupting his thoughts, "you need to do this *because* of River. She would have wanted this for you. She loved you." He looked directly at Cole as a soft smile settled on his lips. "You were her superhero—always apt to chase the bad guys. Stop letting this be your kryptonite."

Cole wiped his hands over his face and scratched his five o'clock shadow. A conflicting ache grew in his chest as he wrestled with his demons.

Because he wanted to do this.

He knew he did, and that's why he was so ashamed of himself. Because after what happened, after losing his baby girl, he should hate Zanella.

And he did, to some extent, but as Rose always said, there was something about this guy Cole just couldn't shake.

*Rose.*

His eyes widened as a new reality crashed over him: Rose actually *did* hate Zanella.

"What?" Jayce raised another eyebrow.

"Rose," Cole said, a sense of dread filling his lungs. "There's no way she'd be okay with this."

"Oof," his friend said through a buttery bite of bread. "I didn't think about that."

"Yeah." Cole drummed his fingers on the table and chewed his bottom lip, mulling it over.

Rose wouldn't be happy; he knew that. But . . . what if this saved his job? Cole didn't stand a chance with her if he was unemployed, and this plan was better than his original idea to find fast employment elsewhere.

This was more logical.

Or, so he thought.

He needed another opinion.

"I was fired," Cole blurted without thinking.

"You got *fired*?" Jayce's mouth dropped open.

Cole cleared his throat, ignoring the sting of embarrassment he felt in his chest. "Yeah. This morning."

Jayce wiped his face with a cloth napkin, scrambling to keep up. "What happened?"

Although he hated to, Cole admitted the truth. "I deserved it. I was late again this morning, and Nate finally snapped. Said he couldn't keep making excuses for me." He scratched the back of his neck and then reached for his beer.

"Holy shit, dude," was all Jayce could muster.

Cole nodded knowingly. "Yeah."

"Rose isn't going to be happy about that, either."

"Obviously." Cole sighed. It was a shitty situation either way. He sat forward and tried to shift gears. "But I was thinking, if I go to the first event and then pitch it to Nate, he'll have to give me my job back. And then Rose never has to know about that whole debacle."

Jayce twisted his lips to the side. "Maybe, but then you still have to deal with the fallout of her reaction when you tell her about Z."

A thought unlocked in Cole's head. "Unless I don't."

He watched as understanding flooded Jayce's face.

"And how would you manage to pull that off?"

Cole shrugged. "I don't technically have to tell her everything I'm doing while we're separated."

A grin spread across his friend's lips. "You sly, sly dog."

Cole's head was spinning now. He hated the idea of deceiving Rose. She was the only thing left in his life that mattered. He cared about his job, sure, but she was what helped dull the pain—better than any pill or drink.

Which is why, in the end, it had to be this way.

He had to hide this from her if he had any shot of regaining employment and winning her back.

"This is my best option," Cole said definitively. "The *only* option."

Jayce squinted at his friend, a small smile playing on his lips. "So, are you saying what I think you're saying?"

"Yeeeeah . . ." Cole answered slowly as he thought it over. The fallout could be terrible, but the payout? It could be worth everything. "Yeah, I think so." He felt the tightness ease in his chest, if only just the slightest.

"Well, all right, then," Jayce said with a wide grin. He slugged back his own beer and then said, "Let the games fucking begin, baby."

# THEN



*Thursday, August 27, 2020*

"Hey, babe," Cole said as he walked through the front door and threw his keys on the nearby sofa table.

It was just past three in the afternoon, and he was riddled with excitement about the night.

"You're home early," Rose commented from the kitchen.

Cole strode over and kissed her on the cheek, a teasing smile forming on his lips. He didn't usually get home until five or six, especially during this time of year. Between the local university's rush week scandals resuming and the ongoing sex trafficking issues in the state, Cole was up to his eyeballs in work.

"I know," he said with a wink. "Is River home?"

Rose raised an eyebrow. "Just went upstairs. Why?"

Cole's face broke out into a shit-eating grin, and he yelled, "Riv! Can you come down here for a second, honey?"

He listened to the sound of her door opening and then shutting before her feet padded down the hallway and stopped at the top of the landing.

"What?" She was still in her school uniform from the private Christian school Rose had insisted they send her to.

"You feel like hanging out with your old man and mom tonight?"

36

She ran her hands through her jet black hair and shifted on her feet. "I don't know. Maybe." Glancing back and forth between Cole and Rose, she added, "Why?"

"I got us free tickets to the Cosmos game!"

Rose and River groaned in unison.

"Seriously, Dad? You know I hate baseball." River pounded down the stairs and grabbed a muffin from the open cake dome on the kitchen island.

Cole hadn't noticed the fresh-baked blueberry smell when he first walked in, but now he was wondering how he'd missed it.

"Come on! It'll be fun," he began, following in his daughter's footsteps and grabbing a pastry. "We haven't done anything as a family since the stay-at-home orders were lifted."

"I don't know, hun," Rose said, "that's all the way in Cedar Pines. It'll take an hour with the city's traffic."

Cole popped a bite in his mouth and mumbled, "Which is exactly why I came home early." He knew this would be a tough sell when he accepted the tickets from his coworker, but it was also an opportunity he couldn't pass up. "Come on, we could all use a night out, especially with school starting back, Riv."

"Do we have to wear masks?" Rose asked.

Cole let out an exasperated sigh. "Yes, but we can't let that stop us from living our lives. This damn virus has already taken up half our year." He paused and looked at River. "Plus, I hear the pitcher is 'like, totally cute, this season.'" He said the last part with a high-pitched voice and a fake hair flip.

"Oh my gosh, Dad, stop!" A dark crimson color bloomed on River's cheeks.

Rose laughed. "I mean, I guess it could be fun, but we should eat before we go. Those prices are ridiculous at the concession stands."

Cole yelped and pumped his fist. "Yes! That's what I'm talking about." He glanced back at his not-so-little girl now. "What do you say, River Bug? You can even pick the place."

River rolled her eyes, and Cole smiled, knowing he'd won her over with that comment. "Fiiiine," she said with an exaggerated tone, "but I want tacos." She popped another piece of muffin in her mouth and said through full cheeks, "And only the good kind from that Mexican place we like."

*That's my girl,* Cole thought. "Deal!"

One lime margarita, a dozen tacos, and an expensive parking ticket later, Cole, River, and Rose strode through the entryway at the Cosmos stadium. The heat was thick in the late-summer air, and the masks didn't do them any favors. Cole was already sweating bullets, but he didn't let that deter him from what was about to happen tonight.

"Dad, can I get some popcorn?" River's voice broke through his thoughts.

"River, honey, we just ate, and the popcorn here is like fifteen dollars," Rose answered before Cole could.

"I didn't hear you complaining when you ordered that thirteen-dollar margarita," she mumbled.

"Excuse me?" Rose stopped dead in her tracks.

*Oh boy,* Cole thought. "Ladies, let's just have a good night." He glanced at River first and said, "You need to apologize to your mother," and waited while she grumbled a quick apology. "Okay, now, I think we can swing a bucket of popcorn, just this once."

"But, Cole—" Rose started to interrupt him as River squealed.

"Rosie, she's not asking to do drugs or buy a designer gown. It's fine. We can afford it." He pulled a twenty from his wallet and handed it to River. "Here, you wait in line with your mom. I'm going to go find our seats."

Smiling, River threw her arms around Cole's neck. "Thanks, Dad!"

She bounced off to the nearest concession stand, and Rose followed, rolling her eyes as she twirled her finger at Cole, insinuating their daughter had him wrapped around his finger, which, to be fair, she did.

River had always been a daddy's girl, and Cole cherished their relationship more than anything in the world. He recognized their bond was special—so what if he gave in every once in a while? She was a good kid, and at thirteen, he didn't have many years left with her before she went off to college and dated some tattooed loser named Axel or Fox. He had to cherish this time while he could.

Making his way through the stadium, he found their seats in record time. With the pandemic still fearmongering the entire country, attendance was at an all-time low. Not that he minded, though. This would give him all the more advantage tonight. He inhaled the familiar scents of dirt, freshly cut grass, and leather as he settled down in his chair. This view would be perfect.

River and Rose joined him after a few minutes passed, and Cole wrapped his arms around his wife before placing a soft kiss on her temple.

"You're going to have to do more than that for undermining me in front of her," she whispered.

Cole suppressed a laugh and eased into a half-grin. "Yes, ma'am." He would do anything for this woman, especially when she wore baseball jerseys.

They settled in for the opening pitch, and the first two innings passed without much action. The score was still zero to zero, with both teams having struck out. The Cosmos weren't known for being the best, but neither was their opponent, the Boston Tigers.

After the third and fourth innings passed much the same, Cole started to feel antsy. His source had said tonight, right? He checked his phone, second-guessing himself.

"Hey." Rose twisted in her seat and nudged him. "Do you see that?"

Cole's eyes snapped to the ball field, heart pounding. Was this it? He scanned the diamond, then the outer field, but saw nothing out of the ordinary. "See what?"

"That," River answered, pointing to the audience just above the home team's dugout.

Cole followed her gaze and felt his insides light up. What had once been a seemingly normal crowd was now an entire section of people in hospital gowns, and none of them wore masks.

*Yep,* he thought, *this is it.*

"This is what?" Rose looked at him now.

*Shit.* Had he said that out loud? Judging by the way she was looking at him, that was a definite yes. *Fuck.* He looked at her now with earnest eyes, a silent apology written in them.

"Did you know this was going to happen?"

"I—" His words were suddenly lost in a chorus of voices as the mock patients began singing "Take Me Out to the Ball Game."

Cole turned away from his wife, thankful for the interruption. He watched as the players and audience members alike gaped at the group, confusion settling over the stadium like a bad heat wave. Where had they come from? How many were there? What was the goal here? He pulled out his phone to jot down the questions in his notes, but Rose snapped her fingers at him, demanding attention.

"Cole! Answer me!"

He slouched his shoulders in defeat. "Yes, I got a tip this morning that Z may be here."

Rose glared at him. "So, that's why we're here? Not because of family time, but so you could cover a story?"

He scratched the back of his head as he battled with what to say. Meanwhile, the Zanella actors were getting louder with each passing breath. "Technically, we're here for both."

"Are you kidding me right now?"

*Fuck.* Cole knew she'd react this way if he'd been honest about the lead, which is precisely why he was hoping to pull this off as a coincidence. "I'm sorry, honey. I should've told you."

Rose opened her mouth to respond, but River cut her off. "Dad! Look!"

He snapped his attention back to the stunt at play and gawked. The participants were now spreading out into the stands, mixing with the other attendees and deliberately *breathing* in their faces. Cole's brain scrambled as he struggled to choose between staying and apologizing more or whipping out his phone to record the event and search for Zanella.

Eventually, the high of the chase won out.

"I'm sorry, Rose," he said. "I've gotta go. He could be here." He leaned down and kissed her cheek again, despite her rising anger, and took off. "Riv, stay with your mom!"

"But I wanna go with you, Dad!"

Cole's heart throbbed at her words. He paused for a moment but then said, "Sorry, River Bug, it may not be safe. Stay with Mom. I'll meet up with you guys later!"

He turned around just as the screen monitor blacked out, and a deep, male voice came over the loudspeakers.

*"Herd immunity: noun. Resistance to the spread of an infectious disease within a population that is based on pre-existing immunity of a high proportion of individuals as a result of previous infection."*

Cole leaped down the stands, almost falling more than once.

"Since a vaccine does not yet exist, we have brought patients here tonight to help you achieve natural herd immunity. Welcome to the new era of chicken pox parties, ladies and gentlemen."

*Oh, fuck.*

Cole watched in bewilderment as the patients broke out into a charged run and rushed the field, making the security measures at this event laughable. He turned off his camera for a moment, just long enough to shoot Rose a quick text.

**Hubby:** *You guys should leave—I had no idea this was what he had planned. Don't worry about me. I'll take an Uber. Going to be a long night.*

Rose responded almost instantly.

**Rosie:** *Enjoy sleeping on the couch.*

# NOW

*SATURDAY, OCTOBER 5, 2024*

THE NEXT FEW DAYS passed in a blur as Cole prepared for Saturday's event. After having dinner with Jayce, he still felt uneasy about his decision but was convinced this was the right move. He would cover the story on his own and then pitch it to Nate the second he had something concrete in his hands. There was no way he could turn down an exclusive, inside account of whatever these games were.

When Saturday finally arrived, Cole awoke from his usual nightmare with a feeling he hadn't experienced in a long time—a twinge of hope.

He set the day in motion with his typical routine, but this time with a little pep in his step. He couldn't explain the high he felt at the idea of finally meeting Zanella. Chasing him was like the hit of a familiar drug Cole just couldn't quit. Except this time, the stakes were higher, giving him a valid excuse to chase that euphoric experience and pursue the story.

The day dragged on as Cole anxiously out-waited the clock, and finally, at 7:00 p.m., he let Emmett out one last time, grabbed his jacket, and headed out the front door.

"Wish me luck, Riv," he whispered under his breath.

An hour later, Cole pulled into the drive-in, opting for a space in the back near the exit. He needed a quick getaway if things got ugly.

He was too anxious to sit still, so even though it was early, he got out of his car and surveyed his surroundings. To his left was a young group of what Cole assumed to be college kids, and to his right, he saw an elderly couple setting up beach chairs. He glanced back at the movie screen, suddenly realizing he didn't even know what was playing.

*Huh.*

He wrinkled his brow, looked around, and then felt his heart drop when he found what he was looking for.

*The Exorcist—Showtimes: 6:30 and 8:30 p.m.*

"You've gotta be kidding me," Cole muttered under his breath. *That fucker would pick a satanic cult movie to drive his next act.*

What had Cole gotten himself into?

Shaking off the unease, he set out for the concession stand, hoping some popcorn and soda would distract him—and clear his head. He got in line behind a large group of pre-teens, wondering what parent in their right mind would let their young kids come to this. Cole and Rosie never let River see anything that was R-rated when she was that young.

He shook off the thought, not ready to go down that negative spiral tonight. He needed a clear head if he was going to stay focused on Zanella.

Cole paid for his snack and drink and then turned around to walk back to his car. He had no idea what Z was planning tonight, but given the timing, location, and horror movie selection, Cole knew it couldn't be good.

"Cole? Cole Sloane?"

Cole's ears perked at the sound of his name, and he swiveled around to see who the voice belonged—

"OOF!" His thoughts were lost in a shower of raining popcorn and soda as his body smashed into someone else's before they both tumbled to the ground.

"Ohmygosh!" the familiar voice squeaked. "I am *so* sorry! Are you okay?"

Cole pushed himself up, brushing the dirt off his knees before offering a hand to the woman he knocked over. "I'm fine. Are you okay?"

"Yes," she breathed, accepting the hand. "Ugh, again, I am so sorry, Cole!"

*Cole.*

That's when he remembered the girl sounded familiar, and his eyes snapped to hers.

"Luna?"

"Yes, yes, it's me. The office klutz. And apparently, now the movie drive-in klutz." She straightened her top and ran her fingers through her choppy blonde hair. "Oh, and now I've ruined your shirt!"

Cole looked down, noticing the soda and butter stains for the first time.

"Here, let me get you some napkins." Luna dashed off to the counter before he could stop her, returning a beat later.

She half-frowned, half-smiled as she shoved large quantities of recycled napkins into his shirt, trying to soak up the impossible stain. "Shoot, it's not coming out!"

"Here, stop." Cole grabbed her hand. "It's fine, really. What are you doing here?"

"Oh." Luna bit back a small smile as crimson stained her cheeks. "I was supposed to be on a date, but . . ."

Her words trailed off, and Cole followed her gaze back to the college-aged group that had set up camp beside him.

He let a small smirk escape his lips. "Didn't feel like babysitting?" he asked with a look of amusement on his face.

Luna rolled her eyes and shoved Cole's arm. "He obviously lied about his age on the dating app, okay?" She rolled her eyes and ran her fingers through her hair. "What about you? What are you doing here? I haven't seen you since . . . well, you know."

Cole did know. Luna was a photographer at the paper, one of the only ones he liked, as a matter of fact. She was quirky and annoying as hell, but her work was good.

"Just . . . seeing a movie," he responded casually.

Luna eyed him. "Uh-huh. You with anyone?"

"Nope. Just me and my now-stained tee."

"Oh, sheesh. I really am sorry!"

Cole offered a polite laugh, noting how she shifted on her feet and messed with the flannel tied around her waist. "It's okay. I'm just messing with ya. I have a spare in my car. I think I'm parked beside your 'date,'" he said with air quotes.

Luna gave him an annoyed glance. "And here I was going to offer to walk with you."

"Hah!" Cole actually chuckled that time. "Here, let's go. Can't have you walking alone at night when *The Exorcist* is about to play."

"I'm perfectly capable of walking by myself, thank you," she retorted.

"Touché."

Cole gestured for her to lead, and he followed.

"So," she asked after exactly three seconds of silence, "what are you really doing here? Are you . . . meeting your wife?"

"No, just . . . needed to get out of the house." Cole wanted to trust her but didn't know if he could.

"You don't really strike me as the guy who gets out of the house to watch horror movies at a drive-in alone." She raised an eyebrow.

Cole cleared his throat. "Maybe that's exactly who I am."

Luna stopped walking and surveyed him. "Wait a second. Is that a notebook sticking out of your pocket? Cole Sloane, are you reporting on a case?" Her mouth dropped open as she awaited his response.

"Shhh!" Cole glanced around, nervous someone had overheard.

"Ooooooh, you are. Okay, spill! What's the tea?"

"What's the what?"

Luna rolled her eyes again, clearly over his senile tendencies, and Cole found himself wondering how old she was. Twenty-seven? Twenty-eight? She was certainly younger than him.

"The tea! The scoop! What's the story, Cole? Tell me."

"Keep your voice down," he urged. "I'm just . . . following a lead is all."

"Here? What kind of lead could be here?" Her words were hushed yet urgent as she spoke.

Cole took in a breath, deciding how much to divulge, when her eyes lit up, and he watched the answers click into place.

"You're following, Z, aren't you?" she asked.

Cole groaned.

"I knew it." Luna jumped up and down, spilling some of her own popcorn while doing so.

"Shhh! You have to keep your voice down. I'm serious." It was Cole's turn to run his fingers through his messy, dark brown hair. "Come on. Let's talk in my car."

Luna squealed under her breath and then followed Cole back to his black Jeep Wrangler. After they were both inside, Cole rolled their windows up, glanced around one last time, and then launched into the full story. When he was done, Luna's eyes were wide with fascination.

"Let me see," she demanded.

"What?"

"Let me see the video. The website!"

"Oh." Jayce hadn't asked to see the video when Cole told him. Was it weird that Luna was asking? No, she was a journalist, too. It was just in their nature to be nosey. "Okay, fine, one sec." He pulled up the website on his phone, handed it to her, and listened as she replayed the video he'd now seen a hundred times.

"Woah," she breathed when it was done. "Did you tell Nate about this? He's going to freak."

"No." Cole shook his head. "Not yet. But I will. Just as soon as I have the story tonight. I was worried he wouldn't believe me if I showed up empty-handed."

Luna's eyes softened. "Oh, right. Makes sense . . ."

Cole checked his watch as her voice trailed off, ignoring the awkward silence that hung in the air. "You should really get back to your date. I won't be able to keep an eye on you once Z starts his act."

Luna scoffed. "Okay, one, why do you think I need a man to protect me? And two, heck no! I'm not going back to frat row when I could help you cover a breaking story."

*Oh, shit.*

Cole hadn't considered she'd want to tag along. He couldn't let her put herself at risk; it was too dangerous. "I don't think I was supposed to tell anyone. It may disqualify me if he finds out."

"Oh, please," Luna counters. "You received a magical invite from the elusive Graham Zanella telling you to come to a first-hand account of his live-action art show and to report it. You seriously think he didn't expect you to bring a photog? I mean no offense, Cole, but images aren't your strong suit."

Cole blanched at her words. "That's not completely—"

A large beeping sound interrupted him. He looked around, panic setting in as he realized it must be starting.

He looked back at Luna, who had a gleeful, determined face, and said, "All right, let's go."

She squealed and drummed her feet. "This is going to be so epic."

Cole slammed his door, eager to watch whatever was about to unfold. "Make sure you have 911 at the ready, just in case," he told her.

"On it." She pulled out her Nikon DSLR camera from her backpack, which doubled as a purse, and strapped it around her neck before pulling out her phone to hit record.

Cole snapped his gaze back to the scene surrounding him. Nothing initially seemed out of order, other than the siren, but then a large pillow of fog slowly rolled in from behind the movie screen, reminding Cole of his favorite scary movie.

*Here we go.*

He jotted down "fog machine" and "siren" on his notepad, not wanting to miss a single detail. Glancing back up, he gazed at the crowd, noting their reaction as several individuals climbed out of their hatchbacks and rose from their chairs.

"Aye, is this part of the movie?" one of the neighboring jocks yelled.

"Worried it'll make it harder to get your dick wet?" another teased.

The horn continued to bellow in the background, and then the screen turned off, leaving an unsettling darkness. Cole felt the goosebumps rise on the back of his neck.

*What are you doing, Z?*

A murmur rippled through the crowd, but Cole couldn't see why. He pressed up on his toes, desperate to know what was happening, but there were too many people. Without thinking, he climbed on top of his Jeep, nearly falling in the process.

His pulse quickened as he leaned forward and squinted, trying to make out what everyone else was seeing. It took a moment for his eyes to adjust, but once they did, he could vaguely see two—or maybe three—shadowy figures standing beneath the screen.

"Can you see anything through your camera? If you zoom in?" He looked at Luna, who was standing on the hood of his Jeep.

She placed the device in front of her right eye and adjusted the lens. "No." She shook her head. "It's too dark and far away. I can't get a good angle from here."

Cole started to suggest they move closer, but then he jumped as the movie screen roared to life, blaring through what must have been overhead speakers instead of car radios.

Only, *The Exorcist* didn't play—it'd been years since he'd seen the old possession movie, but he remembered it well enough to know this wasn't it. He chewed the inside of his cheek as a Bible verse rolled across the screen, and he listened as the same Siri-like voice he'd heard in the original video recited it.

*"Matthew 8:32: He said to them, 'Go!' So, they came out and went into the pigs, and the whole herd rushed down the steep bank into the lake and died in the water."*

A scream erupted, and Cole snapped his head to the right, searching for the source.

"There! In the front row by the entrance." Luna pointed to a woman who was dressed in all white.

"Come on. Let's move." Cole jumped down and grabbed Luna's wrist the moment her feet hit the ground. He ran with speed and intent as he weaved their way through the crowd.

The woman's cries continued to echo all around, and when Cole finally reached the front, he saw why.

The shadowed figures from before, which Cole now realized were men in hooded executioner masks, had picked her up and were strapping her down to a cot lying beneath the screen. The color drained from his face as he processed what was happening.

He scrambled to think, but a loud noise sounded overhead just then as scenes from the original movie began playing in the background. They moved at warped speed, sending chilling screams and ominous sounds into the air. Cole shivered but grabbed his notepad again and scribbled notes by the light of the movie. When it snapped off a moment later, he internally cursed before shoving the paper back into his pocket and opting for a voice memo on his phone instead.

Quickly, he hit record and then returned his attention back to the scene at play, careful not to disrupt as he pointed the device at the actors.

"This woman has been possessed by an evil spirit!" one of the masked men yelled. "And we are here to cleanse her troubled soul from the ways of this world!"

The woman erupted in another violent shriek, sending chills up Cole's spine. He couldn't remember the last time Zanella had enacted a religious form of art, if ever.

"We have come before you tonight by the mighty hands of God to deliver this woman from evil and to send the demons within her back to the pits of hell!" another executioner yelled. "Who among us is a believer—brave enough to cast out the devil himself?"

Cole looked around, wondering if what happened next would be part of the act, or if they were really asking for fucking volunteers from the audience.

No one responded at first, and an uncomfortable silence settled among the crowd. The faces around Cole resembled a mix of gleeful anticipation and delayed horror, as they, too, tried to determine if this was real or fake.

Finally, a female voice broke the group's trance. "I will do it."

Heads everywhere snapped, and Cole watched as a woman in her mid-forties hesitantly approached the scene.

The third masked person cocked their head and offered an outstretched hand. "The Lord said there would be one among you. Bless you, kind woman, for helping us manipulate this beast and restore this poor lady's soul."

Frozen in both fear and fascination, Cole took slow, steadied breaths, readying himself for whatever was about to happen.

"What is your name?" The woman from the audience approached the possessed woman.

"*Babies*," she hissed back.

An involuntary shudder vibrated through Cole. These actors were fucking good. Almost too good.

"And why have you taken over this woman's body?"

"Wouldn't you like to know, *Rebecca*."

The woman, who Cole now understood was Rebecca, stopped in her tracks, her eyes widening, if only for a moment.

"Yes, I know your name, too," the demonic woman giggled.

Rebecca straightened her spine and looked back at a man from the audience. He nodded and moved to follow her.

"You have no place here, Babies. Jesus Christ is my Lord and Savior, and under his name, power, love, and authority, I command you to leave this woman's body and flee to wherever it is Jesus Christ would send you to, never to return again!"

The audience stilled, waiting for the actor's reaction, and approximately two nanoseconds passed by before the woman's high-pitched shriek hit the air.

"What the fudge?" he heard Luna squeak beside him.

He turned to look at her, a question in his eyes, but then the steady hum of a new sound whirling above drowned out the noise around him. Luna's hair began whipping around her head, and Cole heard more cries erupt from the audience as terror set in.

*What the hell? Is that—*

He shot his gaze to the sky, confirming his thoughts.

*A helicopter.*

Adrenaline rushed through him as he contemplated what to do next. Zanella had used helicopters in his acts before, and Cole knew from experience that usually meant he was dumping something.

He turned to Luna and spoke quickly. "We need to go."

She wasn't listening, though. Instead, she had her camera in hand, ready to capture whatever horrors awaited them. "This is going to be such a good shot."

An uneasy feeling settled over Cole as the aircraft drew closer. All around him, trees swayed madly in the wind, and loose chairs blew out of sight.

He looked back at Luna, ready to insist they run, but it was too late.

Her camera was high and aimed as the helicopter's door flew open, the sound of squeals erupting.

And that's when all hell broke loose.

# NOW



"Shit." Cole watched as dozens of bloodied pigs plummeted to the earth, taking people out one by one.

"Luna, let's go!" He tugged her elbow, pulling her out of her trance. "We need to find shelter!"

She nodded in agreement, pausing to snap a few more photos before turning to follow Cole.

"Get out of the way!" a man boomed.

"Mommy!" a young girl screamed.

"Move, dammit!" another person yelled.

Cries echoed all around them as chaos ensued.

*Graham fucking Zanella*, Cole thought. The man was a bloody psychopath. No pun intended.

"Over here!" He jabbed his finger at the restrooms, where people had started to huddle under the building's awning.

Together, the pair ran under and took a moment to catch their breath.

"This is wild," Luna managed.

"No fucking kidding," a bystander said.

"Ma'am, my name is Cole Sloane, reporter," he cut in, not wanting to waste a second. "Would you be willing to comment on what you saw here today?"

"I don't know! I just saw bloody pigs falling from the sky at my local drive-in theater. You tell me what I fucking saw here today!" The woman shuddered and wiped her palms on her jeans. "This is some fucking doomsday shit my grandma warned me about."

"I believe this is the work of Graham Zanella, an underground artist who facilitates live art performances," Luna said.

"A live art performance? Girl, this is the enemy's work! You better go home and start praying, start sheltering in place, because the damn end of times just knocked on our fucking doorstep."

"What's your name, ma'am? And can you spell it for me?" Cole was still recording on his phone and wanted to capture every detail.

Another scream pierced through the air, and the woman darted away, an apologetic look on her face. Cole snapped his head around and saw the possessed actor from before now riding one of the large boars.

"In the name of Jesus, I command this to stop!" She cried at the top of her lungs as the creature bucked her off and scurried away.

"Miss! Miss!" Cole ran after the woman, hopeful for an interview. "Miss, Cole Sloane, reporter for *The Chronicles*. Could you give me a comment about what just happened here tonight?"

The woman kicked off her shoes and ran from Cole.

"Miss!" He took off after her, in pursuit of the story. "Miss, please? Are you with Zanella? Why did he choose a religious act?" Cole wheezed as he tried to regulate his nervous system, all while dodging the crazed boars. "Are there more to come?"

The woman turned and threw a small Bible at Cole, which he dodged just in time. When he jumped back to his feet, he watched as the woman dove into the back of a white van and then took off into the night.

He cursed as he picked up the book and shoved it into his jacket pocket.

"Cole!" Luna's voice cried through the air.

He swiveled around, searching for her sandy blonde hair in the sea of chaos.

"Over here!"

Cole spotted her then, waving a hand as she tried shoving off a half-dead pig from her body.

"Luna!" Cole ran after her then, panic setting in. He knew he shouldn't have let her get involved. How could he have been so selfish?

"Get off of her, you fucking beast!" Cole shoved the creature off and threw the Bible at it, scaring it away.

"Are you okay?" He turned back to Luna, assessing the situation.

"I'm fine," she snarled. "Just couldn't get that dang thing off me." She started to stand but almost immediately fell back down.

"Here," Cole grabbed her around the waist and offered a shoulder for her to hold onto. "I've got you."

"The book!" she said.

"What book?"

"The one you threw at the pig! Is that from the woman?"

Cole's brain snapped into place as his mind started working again. "Oh, yeah, one sec!" He quickly retrieved the now-battered Bible and tucked it back in his jacket.

Then, he hurried back to Luna and let her lean on him as she stood. Somewhere in the distance, Cole heard police sirens, and he knew in his gut the event was over. He contemplated staying to talk to the cops, but looked at Luna's ripped, blood-stained clothing and thought better of it. He'd call them later.

"Come on," he said. "Let's get out of here."

"Are you okay?" Cole asked again for the dozenth time once they were inside his Jeep.

Luna winced as she rolled up her jeans, inspecting her left leg where the pig had landed. "I think so," she finally said. "I'll know more tomorrow."

"Let me take you to a hospital."

"What? No way. This story is hot. We've gotta take it to Nate."

Cole looked at her in disbelief.

"You're serious?"

"As a mother-flying pig."

Cole looked at Luna in utter confusion before breaking out into laughter.

"What?" Luna objected but then fell into the same hysterical laughter.

"That expression made no sense."

"Yeah, well, whatever. The point is we have to go." She pulled her camera off from around her neck and started looking at the photos she had captured.

Cole put his hands over his face, trying to calm his body and brain. "That was insane."

"No kidding," Luna started, "but enough of this. We've gotta go." She clicked her seatbelt into place and looked at Cole.

"Okay, okay," he responded before turning the keys over in the ignition and throwing on his own seatbelt. He started to pull out of the parking spot but paused. "What about your car?"

"Just bring me back later," she answered like it was no big deal.

"Right," Cole responded. "Cool. Let's go." He pressed his foot down on the gas pedal and high-tailed it out of the parking lot.

Much to his surprise, they sat in silence for most of the car ride. Cole didn't know about Luna, but his mind raced with images of the bloody pigs raining from the sky, along with the possessed woman screaming during the play.

Surely she must've been part of the act.

She wasn't really possessed.

Cole wondered why Zanella had chosen to focus on a religious aspect, and he mentally racked his brain for any snippets he could remember from his childhood growing up in church. He'd never paid much attention, but this much he did know: you don't play with demons.

He shuddered at the thought and decided to focus on the drive again instead.

Nearly an hour later, he pulled into *The Chronicles'* parking lot and helped Luna hobble to the entrance. It was nearing midnight by now, but they both knew it was best to tackle the story while it was fresh.

"What the hell are you two doing here?" A female voice boomed through the hall as Cole and Luna made their way to the editorial room.

"Jada, is Nate here?" Cole spat.

"You know damn well he isn't here at midnight on a Saturday." The night editor raised a perfectly arched brow. "Cole, weren't you just fired?"

Cole rolled his eyes. "Yes, technically, but Jada, we—"

"I don't wanna hear it, Sloane." Jada held her hand up, cutting him off. "You've caused enough trouble here as is."

Cole rubbed his face in frustration.

"Jada," Luna stepped in. "We have a story to pitch, and I think you're gonna wanna hear it. It's about Zanella."

Jada hesitated at the remark and raised her brow. "Graham Zanella?"

"Yes," Luna responded. "Cole received an invitation to attend a gala of some sort and potentially meet him, but first, he has to complete three tasks. The first one was tonight. We just came from the old drive-in where he hosted a performance." She paused, grabbing her camera from her bag once again. "Here, just look at my camera. I have photos. It's all there." She handed Jada the device. "And I have more on my phone, too. Video footage of the whole thing."

Jada looked at the camera with a skeptical expression but turned it on nonetheless. Cole held his breath as he watched her click through the images, anxious to get started.

"An invitation, huh?" She looked at Cole.

"Yes. It's all true. And I can prove it, but right now, we've really gotta get this story out before someone else scoops us."

*Please say yes.*

Jada turned back to Luna again, who gave her an earnest look.

"Fine," she finally breathed. "But this better be good."

"Eek!" Luna squealed. "You're the best. Let's go, Cole!"

The furrow in Cole's brow softened. "Thank you, Jada," he said as he reached for Luna, ready to help her hobble off again.

On the way back to their desks, Cole said, "You start editing photos and get some videos ready for social—I'll write."

"On it. I can't wait to see the headlines! 'Only When Pigs Fly,' or 'Snorts in the Night,'" Luna rambled as she mimicked headline motions with her hands.

Cole tuned her out and got to work. His career was at stake, so this needed to be good. No, scratch that. It needed to be a true "Hot off the press! Extra! Extra! Read all about it!" moment.

Thankfully for him, Z made that easy.

# NOW



Sunday, October 6, 2024

**Popular Underground Artist Makes Scene at Local Drive-In Theater**

*By Cole Sloane, Investigative Reporter*

*Patrons experienced more than they bargained for during a late-night screening of "The Exorcist" last night at Mazie's Drive-In Movie Theater.*

*"We believe this to be the work of Graham Zanella," Whipner County Sheriff Rio Gonzola said. "Our team is working hard to find the artist and ensure the safety of citizens and animals alike."*

Cole sat in Jada's office, bouncing his leg as he watched her read the article. He needed her to believe in this story—to believe in him.

After what felt like an eternity, Jada finally laid down the paper and locked onto Cole's gaze. "This really happened?"

"Yes. All of it. You saw the pictures on Luna's camera."

She looked at the photographer, analyzing her bruised, swollen leg and the blood stains on her jeans. "And that?" she motioned.

"A pig landed on me. Son of a gun came out of nowhere."

Jada winced. "Good grief." She shook her head and then looked around at the skeleton crew staff. "All right, listen up, people! We've got a breaking story to cover. The entire front page will need to be reworked, and I want a big push on social. We've only got a few hours, so let's get to work!"

"Yes!" Cole let out a sigh of relief and pumped his fists in the air. "Thank you, Jada. You won't regret this."

"I better not, or Nate will have my ass, too."

Cole high-fived Luna and then set to work.

After a meticulous run-down with the copy editor, designer, and social media specialist, Cole finally felt like he could breathe. He had no idea what came next or when Zanella would contact him again, but for now, he was celebrating the small victories.

At a quarter-past five, he finally rounded up his belongings and offered to drive Luna back to her car, exhausted from the previous day's events.

"Come on," he said, pushing open her door, "you need some rest."

"Me?" Luna raised an eyebrow. "I think you need some rest, sir."

Cole rolled his eyes. "I meant because of your leg."

Luna considered his response. After a beat, she said, "Yeah, I guess you're right. Let's go before Nate realizes the guy he fired is going to have a byline in today's edition."

Cole's chest tightened at the thought. Nate had to give him his job back after this.

Surely.

*Ugh.* He didn't want to think about it.

Once they were in the car, Cole realized how tired he was. It was a struggle to stay awake behind the wheel, even with Luna's constant stream of dialogue. The girl was nice, but damn, she could talk.

"Hello, earth to Cole!" Her voice snapped through his thoughts, clearing his head again. Case in point.

"Sorry, I'm just really tired. Do we have to talk? Maybe I could just turn on the radio."

Luna shrugged her shoulders. "Fine. Suit yourself."

"Thanks." Cole offered her an apologetic smile and then turned to the local news station.

After approximately thirty-two seconds of silence, Luna said, "Are you serious?"

"What?" Cole spared her a side glance.

"You listen to the news?"

*Doesn't everyone?* Cole thought but didn't say. "Of course I do."

Luna's features twisted into a questioning look. "But you're a reporter."

"Precisely."

She sat back and laughed. "So, I would assume the last thing you'd want to do after being newsy all day is listen to more news. That's like a retail worker going home and being excited to fold laundry."

Cole sighed. "I like to be in the know, okay?"

"I think you need a life, Cole."

*No kidding.*

He opened his mouth to respond but was cut off by a breaking news alert blaring through the anchor's voice.

Luna's eyes widened. "Do you think this is it?"

"Turn it up," Cole ordered as he merged onto the highway.

"Yes, master," she said in mock frustration.

Cole rolled his eyes and listened.

"I'm sorry to cut in, guys, but we just received word that Graham Zanella was in our very own town last night—Mazie's Drive-In to be more specific."

"No way?" the original reporter asked.

"Yes, it appears he made quite a scene, reenacting his own version of *The Exorcist* with a group of actors claiming to be possessed before—and get this—live pigs started falling from the sky."

Luna's eyes snapped to Cole's. "How do you think they know already? We haven't even published."

"I don't know . . ." He paused, trying to come up with a logical explanation. "Remember the woman who came forward from the audience? I wondered whether she was part of the act. Maybe she was invited, too."

Luna twisted her lips to the side, her brows furrowed. "Yeah, but if she was supposed to report it, then why intervene? That's, like, Journalism 101. You don't involve yourself in the story."

"Maybe her task was different than ours," Cole said.

"Wait, so you think Z tasked everyone with something different?"

Cole shrugged. "It's possible."

"Hmm." Luna sat back, considering the idea.

Now approaching the exit, Cole signaled his blinker and merged to get off the freeway. How long had he been gone? He checked the time and cursed under his breath.

"What?" Luna stared at him.

"My dog, Emmett. I've gotta get home and let him out. He's not used to me being away this long."

"Awwwwwww! You have a dog?!"

Cole cringed at her enthusiasm. "Yes."

"Can I meet him?"

"What? No."

Luna didn't even blanche. "Oh, come on! I love dogs. And they love me."

Cole pulled onto the old gravel road that led to the drive-in. "I mean, maybe, sometime. Yes, sure."

She squealed in her high-pitched voice. "Yay! I can't wait. What kind is it?"

"A mastiff." He turned the car into the lot and made way for the only remaining car: a red VW bug.

*That would be her car,* he thought.

"Ohmygosh, even better! My aunt had one once. The big dude drooled all over me. It was great."

"Uh huh," Cole murmured as he pulled in beside her toy car.

He pushed the gear into park and took a moment to observe the aftermath of last night's artistic destruction. Given the circumstances, it wasn't as bad as Cole expected. Police tape was plastered throughout the vicinity, and some residual pig blood coated the ground, but all the flyaway objects had been cleaned up and returned to their place. In fact, if Cole didn't know better, he'd think it was merely Halloween decorations.

*If only.*

He placed his hand on the car door's handle, ready to assist Luna, but then remembered her leg. "Wait, are you going to be okay to drive?"

"Oh, yeah." She brushed her hands to the side. "I drive with my right leg, so all's good."

Cole cleared his throat, suddenly a little uncomfortable. "Okay, well, promise me you'll get it checked out?"

Luna smiled, a fire sparking behind her green eyes. "Yes, don't worry about me. I'll be fine." She hobbled out of her seat and fished out her keys. "You just worry about finding the next clue from Z. I am SO in for the rest of your tasks."

"Wait, I never said you could—"

She slammed the door, before he could finish the sentence.

# NOW



*Sunday, October 6, 2024*

*"Dammit, River, stay with me. Rose! Where's the fucking ambulance?"*

Cole shot out of his bed and screamed.

*No. Not again.*

He took a deep inhale and worked to stabilize his breathing. One would think by now he'd be used to the night terrors—the awful imagery that haunted his dreams.

But he wasn't.

No matter how many times he relived that moment, the pain would never dull.

Never cease.

*Deep breaths in, and deep breaths out.*

Cole had things to do today; he was sure of it. If he could only regain control of his breathing, he would remember.

*Zanella.*

And that's when it hit him.

Images of last night's events flooded his head, washing away the horrific core memory of his daughter.

Time—what time was it?

He searched for his phone and found it under Emmett's sleeping body. The dog had curled up in bed with him this morning when Cole got home, obviously missing his master's company.

*1:02 p.m.*

*Three missed calls from Nate Cawhill.*

*Four text messages from Nate Cawhill.*

"Shit," Cole muttered.

He didn't even bother to open the text messages but instead took a deep breath and hit the call button.

Now or never.

On the third ring, a husky, out-of-breath voice answered, "Well, it's about fucking time. Do you wanna explain to me why your name is all over my publication today?"

"Nate, I'm sorry, but there was no time to wait. I went to Jada, and she agreed. We had to get the story out before someone else did."

"And you didn't think to call me? Instead of trying to go behind my back?"

"That's not how it was—"

"Enough! We'll discuss this in my office. Tomorrow morning. Eight o'clock sharp."

*Wait a minute,* Cole thought. "Does this mean what I think it means?"

"It means you have a lot of fucking explaining to do. Tomorrow. Eight o'clock, Cole. Don't be late." He hung up the phone, and Cole's world exploded.

He was going to get his job back.

He could afford his bills and not have to start over somewhere else, and Rosie wouldn't even have to know.

*Rose.*

Cole had almost forgotten about her in the midst of everything.

He checked his phone again, noting the time. She would likely be home from church by now, probably making a grocery list and getting ready to go to the store. That had always been their routine when they lived together.

If he hurried, though . . .

"Em, buddy, you wanna go see Mommy?"

The dog's ears perked up, and he wagged his tail in response.

Twenty minutes later, Cole rang his mother-in-law's doorbell, with Emmett drooling beside him. Their separation was nearing four months, and he was desperate to win Rose back. With the renewed hope of being employed again, plus all the progress they'd made in couples' counseling, he felt confident she would finally consider coming home.

*As long as she never finds out you're pursuing a Zanella story again.*

He waved the thought away, willing it to go back to the recesses of his mind.

This would work.

This *had* to work.

Just then, a curtain from the closest window caught his eye. He turned and saw his father-in-law, Bob, glowering at him through navy blue spectacles.

The man had never liked him.

Cole cleared his throat and offered a sheepish wave, hoping to someone above that Rose was home.

"Emmy!" Cole's attention snapped back to the door as Emmett took off.

There, standing in a fitted pair of leggings and his old, gray Springhill University sweatshirt, stood Rose. Even in something as simple as that, she still took his breath away.

"Hey," he near-whispered.

She looked up at him through scarlet curls as Emmett knocked her over. "Hey, Cole." She returned her gaze back to the dog. "And hey, Emmy, boy. How are you? Momma missed you."

Cole admired the way she cradled the dog's floppy jowls. It was so attractive.

Everything she did was attractive to Cole.

"I'm sorry I didn't call or text first, but I was kind of hoping we could talk, without a therapist present if that's okay."

Rose stood up, wiping the slobber and dog hair off her. "Sure. Wanna come inside?"

Cole glanced over her shoulder and saw Bob was still lurking. "I was kinda thinking we could get a coffee down the street at that new place that just opened, or maybe go back to the house?"

Rose followed his gaze and suppressed a laugh when she saw her dad. "Sure. Coffee sounds great. Let me grab my shoes."

Cole's heart beat faster as he smiled to himself and waited for her return.

A minute later, Rose emerged from the house and offered Emmett a treat. "Such a good boy."

She rubbed his ears and looked at Cole.

He hesitated for a minute, the words getting stuck in his throat. "Umm—"

"Coffee?"

"Right." He nodded and looked away. "Let's go."

Cole set off down the street, totally not nervous at all about telling his wife he was possibly lifting out of the fog of depression, and that he definitely wanted her back—all the while omitting the very reason *why* he was feeling this way.

Nope, not nervous at all.

They walked in silence until the pair rounded the corner, the coffee shop appearing in plain sight.

"So," Cole started, "what's this place called?" Someone was standing in front of the sign.

"Boom, Roasted."

Cole couldn't help but laugh. "Are you serious?"

"Dead," Rose said with an answering laugh. "I guess the owner is a huge fan of *The Office*."

Cole's shoulders dropped as he felt the tension ease at their familiarity. "I mean, it is a great show."

"The best," she agreed.

Shaking his head, Cole handed her Emmett's leash. "Here, you grab a table outside and stay with him. I'll get us drinks. Iced vanilla coffee with almond milk still your go-to?"

Rose smiled and gave Cole a soft look. "Yes. Still my go-to."

Cole felt his cheeks flush, and he took off and got in line.

*I can do this*, he thought. She would be happy he was feeling better, right?

The person behind him cleared their throat, pulling Cole from his thoughts.

"Sorry," he murmured and then proceeded to place the order, pay, and move down to the drink pickup area.

"Cole!" a barista shouted a few minutes later.

He nodded thanks and then picked up the drinks, fully aware he was stalling.

"Deep breaths. You can do this," he mumbled under his breath and then headed back to their table.

"That was fast," Rose said, taking her beverage.

He sat down beside her and contemplated his next words as sweat ran down his neck. Was it supposed to be hot today?

"So," Rose said, curiosity lingering in her voice.

"So."

They looked at each other in awkward silence for what felt like an eternity, but in reality, was approximately forty-two seconds.

"I—"

"What—"

The pair laughed, and Cole ran his hands through his hair. "Sorry. This is a bit awkward, isn't it?"

Rose offered a slight grin. "Just a little."

*Focus, man.*

He took a deep breath and tried again. "So, I have some news."

"Yeah?" Rose raised a single brow.

"Yeah, and I think you'll be happy for me, for us." Cole paused and cleared his throat. "It's actually about work."

"Oh?"

"Well, kind of, yes. I got a new lead, a new story to investigate, actually. And it just . . . feels really good to be working on something again, like old times, you know? I've been feeling . . . better, mentally speaking." The words spilled out of Cole, causing simultaneous regret and relief.

Everything he'd said was technically true, but his pulse throbbed as the guilt laid heavily on his chest.

When he finally lifted his gaze to Rose, a knot formed in his chest as he noted the subtle way she tucked her hair behind her ear—the same way she'd always done when she was feeling shy or nervous.

"A new lead, huh?" she said at last.

"Yes, a local one."

*Also not a lie.*

Silence once again filled the air, and Cole thought he might vomit.

"And you're feeling better?"

He nodded in response. "Yeah, I think I really am." The gravity of Cole's words hit him as he realized something else. "My night terrors have slowed down."

Rose's eyes widened, shock registering on her face. "Really?"

"Yeah," he started. "I mean, I still have them, but . . . they've slowed. Aren't as frequent. Or as intense." He sat back in his seat and grabbed his drink, a small smile settling on his lips.

Maybe the doctors had been right after all.

Healing *was* possible.

"Oh, Cole." Rose reached across the table and grabbed his hand, pulling him forward in his seat. "That's wonderful to hear."

She smiled at him, and Cole felt his chest contract.

This was going well, better than he expected.

"Thanks, Rosie." He squeezed her hand, relishing the feel of her touch.

"I mean it," she said. "I'm really happy to hear you're doing better. I know you've had a hard time with all of this." A serene look washed over Rose's face. "She would be happy for you, too, you know."

Cole's eyes snapped to his wife's as a familiar pang throbbed in his chest.

Rose's expression wavered, if only for a moment. "River would be happy for you. She admired you so much, Cole—looked up to your work in every way."

He closed his eyes and broke her gaze, a pool of tears threatening to stain his cheeks. His chest ached at the words, the pain still so unbearable underneath it all.

"I miss her so damn much," he whispered. Rose placed her other hand on him, and his inner dam broke, the tears cascading down his face. "I miss her every second of every day, Rosie."

Rose leaned forward and placed her forehead against Cole's, tears now leaking from her eyes, too. "I know, hun. I do, too. So damn much."

Emmett whined and nuzzled his head between their laps, sending each a small sense of comfort.

They remained like this for what felt like both an eternity and no time at all, leaning into the other for support. The counselor told them grief would come in waves, and despite his earlier sentiment, this one was a fucking tidal pull.

Finally, after Cole regained his composure enough to speak clearly, he said, "It's not just her I miss. I miss you, too, Rosie. I miss us."

He felt her breath hitch at that. She opened her mouth once, closed it, and then opened it again. "I miss you, too."

That was all Cole needed to unleash the tether on his restraint. He leaned in and pressed his lips to hers, cherishing the feel of his wife. She hesitated at first but slowly started to move her lips in unison with his.

Cole felt fresh tears fall between them as he deepened the kiss, accepting every ounce of solace she gave him and not caring who saw.

Because this was his comfort.

This was his home.

He was about to pull away and ask her to go home with him when a voice interrupted them.

"Cole? Rose?"

He blanched at the sound, and she broke away, stealing his heart in the process.

He listened to her clear her throat. "Um, David, hi."

Cole groaned.

Leave it to his brother to interrupt this moment.

"Bub, what's up, man?" He locked eyes with his little brother, urgently trying to send a message before it was too late.

David's eyes widened as he registered his brother's gaze, and then he looked back to Rose. "Oh, um, sorry. Didn't mean to interrupt. You guys just surprised me is all. I was curious who the love birds were on my patio. I was about to tell you to get a room, but then I realized who you were."

"Wait a minute," Cole said.

"What do you mean *your* patio?" Rose asked.

A smile cracked across David's face. "Didn't Mom and Dad tell ya? This is my coffee shop."

Cole actually laughed at that statement. Because of course it was. And of course his parents hadn't told him. David had always been the favorite.

Cole grunted. "Figures."

"Don't be jelly, big bro." David looked between the two of them again and then cleared his throat. "Anyway, I didn't mean to interrupt. Carry on. Enjoy the drinks. Just don't leave us a bad review." He winked and then spun around, heading back inside.

"Did you really not know he owned this place?" Rose questioned, her facial features still twisted in shock.

"No clue." Cole scoffed and then ran a hand through his messy hair. "But it doesn't surprise me. You know David, and my parents."

"Yes," Rose said, smiling shyly. "I sure do."

An awkward silence settled around them once again. Cole cleared his throat and took a sip of coffee, stalling.

*Ah, fuck it.*

Now was as good a time as any, he figured. Taking a deep breath, he looked back at Rose and said, "Do you think we could, maybe—"

"I should really get back," she cut in.

Cole slumped his shoulders in defeat, realizing the moment had passed. "Oh, um, yeah. Yeah, same."

He watched as she slurped the rest of her coffee and then gathered her things.

"I just have a really busy day tomorrow."

Cole nodded. "Yeah, me too."

"But I really am happy to see you doing so well, Cole."

"Happy enough to . . ." He let the question linger.

Rose tucked another red strand behind her ears. "You know what the therapist said. We should give it the full six months before making any rash decisions."

"This isn't rash, Rose," he pleaded. "You have always been what I want—what I need. I don't need another two months apart to tell me that."

She closed her eyes before responding. "We'll see how things go over the next few weeks, okay? I don't want *our* stuff to cloud your progress. I want you to keep getting better, Cole. We both need to just keep working on ourselves, before we jump back into this."

Cole's heart softened. It wasn't what he'd hoped for, exactly, but she hadn't shut him down completely.

"Okay then," he said. "A few weeks."

# NOW

*Monday, October 7, 2024*

"You can do this," Cole said under his breath as he checked his watch: 7:52 a.m.

*Not late.*

He took in a few deep breaths and texted Jayce, filling him in on everything while he waited for Nate. Cole was confident he'd secured his position back, but his nerves rattled all the same. Everything was riding on this.

"Hey, stranger." A familiar voice disrupted his thoughts.

"Luna, hey," he said as he checked his watch again.

She raised an eyebrow. "Nervous?"

A laugh boomed from Cole's chest. "Is it that obvious?"

"Just a little."

He rubbed the back of his neck and put his phone in his pocket. "I just really need him to say yes to this."

"I'm sure he will. I mean—" She paused to gesture at the paper. "You already published a breaking story yesterday—and that was *after* he fired you. I think you're good."

Cole nodded. She was right—he knew that. He just needed to hear Nate say it for his own peace of mind.

"Speaking of Z," she cut in again, "have you gotten any more instructions about the next challenge?"

"No, not yet—"

"Sloane! Let's go," a sharp voice interrupted.

"Shit," he breathed, "sorry, Luna. Talk later, okay?" He turned on his heels and headed into his ex-boss's office. Anxiety swirled inside of him as he once again sat across from the man who signed his paychecks.

"Nate—" he started.

"I don't like that shit you pulled, Cole."

*Ah, fuck.*

"I know, I'm sorry, sir. It's just that it was so late, and Jada said you weren't in, and time really was of the essence. You know what they say—the news never sleeps." Cole mentally punched himself for that one. His mother's words rang in his ears, *desperation isn't a good look.*

Nate cocked his head and sat back in his chair. "No, you idiot, not that. I'm pissed as hell you didn't come to me *before* the event. We could've leaked that shit early and went live from the social pages—hell, even partnered with the station!"

*Wait, what?* Cole's head was spinning.

"You mean you're not mad I went to print?"

"Oh for heaven's sake, no." Nate waved his hand as his voice carried. "I care about the story, Cole. You know that."

"But, you fired me?" His face twisted in confusion.

"Yeah and don't make me do it again." Nate stared him down, another unspoken message traveling between them. "Now that we've established that," he said, leaning back in his seat, "tell me everything about this mysterious invite. Jada briefed me, but I want the full details from you."

Dumbfounded, Cole cleared his throat and launched into the whole story. Once he was finished, Nate leaned forward with a curious look in his eyes.

"Fascinating."

Cole shook his head in response. "I know. Like I said, it's the weirdest shit. I thought it was a prank at first from one of the guys here, but it's all legit. Or seems to be anyway."

"And you haven't heard from him since?"

"No, not yet. I'm hoping something happens today, though. I mean, the story's gaining traction at all the major outlets."

"Hmm." Nate drummed his fingers on his desk in thought. After a moment, he finally said, "Maybe we need to go bigger."

Cole eyed him suspiciously. "What do you mean?"

"I mean," Nate started, "maybe we need to go live now with an interview."

Cole blew out a breath. "I mean, I can try to go back today and find an employee who was an eyewitness and see if they'd be willing to go on camera."

Nate shook his head. "No. I meant an interview with *you*."

"Me?"

"Mhmm."

Cole stared at him in disbelief. "I don't want to be on camera. That's why I write—despite print being a dying field."

Nate rolled his eyes. "Cole, he sought *you* out and gave very specific instructions to report on the story. We may have missed out on the opportunity to livestream the event, but we can have one of the field reporters from WZAS do an exclusive with you for the evening news tonight. And I can have our social team livestream it from our pages in real-time."

Cole considered his words for a minute. He really did not want to be on camera. But on the other hand . . . "It could help the story go viral if we get the art community to tune in."

"Exactly." Nate smiled and slapped his legs. "I'll call Jason down at the station—you connect with Greyson."

"Uhh . . ." Cole searched for the right words. This was all happening so fast. Did he really have his job back? "Right, sure. On it."

He stood up to leave, but then Nate said, "And Cole? I was serious. Don't make me fire you again."

He cleared his throat and nodded. "Absolutely. You have my word."

Nate nodded his head in dismissal and then raised his phone to his ear, no doubt calling Jason. Cole walked out without another word and headed back to his old desk in complete and utter shock.

"Well, that went better than expected," he mumbled to himself.

AN HOUR LATER, HE sat in the conference room with Luna and Greyson, the social media manager.

"Weren't you, like, fired?" Greyson asked with a vicious grin and half-raised eyebrow.

Cole sighed, remembering exactly why he never talked to this guy. Greyson had held a grudge against Cole ever since he called out an error the kid made on his first day. Cole hadn't meant to embarrass him, but Greyson could never let it go.

"Didn't you, like, just get your degree?"

Greyson was still too green to have that much bite, yet here he was, twisting every one of Cole's nerves.

"I'll have you know, Cole, that I'm coming up on my five-year reunion soon, and I really don't appreciate the attitude. Okay, Grandpa?"

Cole's eyes crossed as he struggled to maintain his composure.

"Okay, Grey, first of all," Luna cut in, "Cole isn't that much older than us, and secondly, from what I hear, grandpas are kinda your type. So, if this is all some master manipulation way for you to hit on Cole, I think you're barking up the wrong tree, because he doesn't play for your team, sweetie."

Cole almost sputtered his coffee as Greyson's cheeks flushed.

"Now, now, children," Nate said, interrupting their debate as he walked in. "No need to get your gym shorts in a wad."

Cole continued to cough while Luna stifled a giggle.

"What is it you needed, sir?" Greyson finally managed.

"I'm glad you asked." Nate slapped him on the back and then filled him and Luna in on the details. When he was finished, he added, "Jason's on his way over now. Cole, he said you guys could run through a few practice questions since we'll be livestreaming the interview on our pages."

"You're putting *him* on camera? In front of a live audience?" Greyson asked, revealing a slight twang to his voice.

Cole shot him a look.

"Yes, that's what I said. So, Greyson, I'll need you to send out a post and a couple of stories letting our audience know we'll be going live today at one. Then, borrow a few phones to set up a livestream from Facebook, Instagram, and TikTok. I want this everywhere."

Greyson pursed his lips but then said, "Yes, sir. I'll get right on it. But may I remind you it's not my fault if we go live and he flops."

"Greyson," Nate said with a sharp tone.

"I'm just saying." He waved his hands and feigned innocence.

Nate turned his attention to Luna for the first time. "We'll need some behind-the-scenes images, and then I want you to snag a couple of Cole and Jason after the interview as well."

Luna nodded and smiled. "You got it, boss man."

"Perfect." Nate clapped his hands together. "Let's make some viral news magic, team!"

Cole and Greyson groaned in unison while Luna squealed.

The next few hours went by in a flash as everyone prepped for the interview. When it was finally time to go live, Cole did his best to maintain his composure and retell the events as factual as he could. As a trained journalist, he knew Jason would have his own angle, but Cole didn't want his opinions to muddy those of the viewers. This was Zanella's story, after all—not his.

When they were finished, Cole breathed a silent sigh of relief and headed back to his desk to decompress. He'd always hated being on the opposite side of interviews.

"Wanna grab a drink?" Cole looked up to see Luna had returned yet again, only this time with a hot pink raincoat, clear umbrella, and messy bun.

Had her hair been up all day?

*Why are you looking?*

"You deserve a drink after that, is all I meant," she sputtered after a beat of silence.

Cole scrambled to fix his face, realizing he'd been staring. "Uh, yeah," he stumbled. "I can always go for a drink."

It was at that exact moment he realized he'd never pictured Luna as someone who drank. "You mean alcohol, right?" He stood up from his desk and scrutinized her.

"Hah!" Luna snorted. "Yes, Cole. I mean alcohol. I'm not a psychopath."

Cole let out a low chuckle. "Sorry, you just don't really seem like the drinking type. What do you get, like a Bahama Mama? Wine cooler?"

Luna mocked feigned horror. "Cole, we're not in preschool anymore. I like anything that bites." She winked and made a fake biting noise, causing Cole's eyes to grow wide as his cheeks flared red. "Hah! You should've seen your face. I'm kidding, of course. Well, sorta. I like sweet and spicy drinks—cocktails, mostly. The bigger question is, what do you drink? I'm guessing you like imported beers—Irish ales, probably."

Cole's mind was still momentarily paralyzed from her earlier commentary. He tried to shake the image of her biting and focus on their conversation. She'd said something about beer—what was it?

"Cole?"

"Hmm?"

"Am I right? Do you like fancy beers? Shoot, or maybe I'm wrong. Maybe you like liquor. Oh! I bet you like scotch. The overly expensive kind that tastes like cigarettes."

That comment caught his attention. "Scotch does not taste like cigarettes."

"Hah! I knew it."

Cole rolled his eyes. "Whatever. Yes, I like beer and scotch, but I'm a reporter, so I mostly stick to the cheap stuff." He held the door open for Luna and slid out after her. "Where are we going?"

He watched as she ducked her head under the awning and peeked into the sky. "Well, it's not raining yet, but it's supposed to soon. So, either somewhere in close walking distance, or you're driving."

Cole scanned the streets and took in his surroundings. To the left was an old dive bar called Lucy's, which was flanked by bikers and hipsters alike, and to the right was a popular chain restaurant bar followed by an Irish pub.

"I'm in the mood for Guinness," he finally said. "Let's hit the pub."

Luna giggled to herself. "I love being right."

"Hmm?" Cole cocked an eyebrow.

"Nothing," she said, pulling her raincoat tighter. "It's just that I originally said I bet you liked Irish ales. I was correct. I like being correct."

She took off before Cole could respond, so he did the only thing he could: follow her. Together, the pair set off down the street, carving their way through the maze of late afternoon employees who were all likely doing the same thing they were. Once there, Cole opened the door for Luna, waiting to usher her inside, and then headed for the bar.

"So," Luna said as she shook off her iridescent, hot pink jacket, "have you heard anything from Zanella?"

Cole shook his head in disappointment. "No, still nothing."

"Well, Greyson said the videos had a good viewership, so hopefully, something will happen soon."

"Yeah . . ." Cole drummed his fingers as he scanned the menu, allowing his voice to trail off.

He was certain Z would contact him again, right? But how? That was the question creeping into Cole's subconscious as he tried not to bubble with anxiety.

"Have you checked the website?"

Cole wrinkled his brow. "Hmm?"

"The website—anything new on there?"

The website! Cole had completely forgotten amidst the chaos. Scrambling, he reached for his phone in his pocket and then pulled out the invitation to once again scan the QR code. "I can't believe I forgot," he said as the loading screen buffered. Maybe this was it, and it'd been here all along.

"Lemme see!" Luna shouldered against Cole, bouncing in anticipation.

When the page finally loaded, though, a large black screen popped up with a password-protected box.

"Shit," Cole murmured.

"What do they mean the website is locked? How will you access the clues?" Luna took the phone out of Cole's hands and hit the refresh screen once, twice, thrice, all to be met with the same message.

Cole dropped his head in his hands and let the reality sink in. Of course the website wouldn't work. That would have been too easy, and if there was one thing Cole knew, Zanella didn't do easy. "I need a drink."

Luna slid his phone back to him. "Well, now what?"

Cole shook his head as he flagged down the waitress and ordered a beer. He waited for Luna to place her order, too, and then said, "I don't know." He paused, racking his brain to remember if Z had left them any breadcrumbs.

As a reporter, he was always looking for things unsaid—pieces of information that didn't add up, but this felt like a roadblock he didn't know how to navigate. Everything he thought he knew about Zanella had been dumped in the air and twisted around. Cole was stumped, and he didn't like it.

"I wonder what it will be like," Luna's voice cut in.

"What?"

"The final act. I mean, I know it's supposed to be a gala, but, like, will it all be tied together? The first one obviously had themes of religion. I'm scared to know what the final event will be if *that* was the first."

Cole considered her words as he reminisced on Saturday night's events. He shuddered at the thought of the bloody pigs. "How did he get those pigs in the helicopter?"

"No clue," Luna said, smiling at the waitress as she set down their drinks. She took a sip of her apple cider sour and pursed her lips. "Whose blood do you think was on them? I hope he didn't actually harm any animals for that."

Cole sighed. "I don't know. It's hard telling with him, honestly." Shifting gears, he asked, "How's your leg?"

He listened as Luna rambled on about being accident-prone her whole life, and he let out a genuine laugh when she told him a story about almost drowning because she dove underwater and swam to the ladder, only to get her head stuck under a guy's crotch.

"You've gotta be kidding," he said through a smile as he raised the glass to his lips.

"Dead serious," she responded. "It was so humiliating—and scary! I couldn't figure out what my head was stuck under, and I was desperately trying to break free to the surface. When I finally escaped and got fresh air in my lungs, I was absolutely *mortified* knowing I'd basically been banging my head between some boy's legs." She shuddered and slurped down the rest of her drink. "He and his friends were all laughing at me. It was awful."

"He probably thought you were trying to give him head," Cole joked without thinking.

Luna's mouth dropped open. "Ohmygosh, I was, like, twelve!"

He laughed at Luna's theatrics, noting the blushing color that stained her cheeks. "You know," he started, digging into their cheese fries, "I was a twelve-year-old boy once. I can almost guarantee that's exactly what he thought."

He popped a fry in his mouth and gave her a knowing look.

"I regret telling you that." Luna covered her face with her hands. "It's only fair now if you tell me an incredibly embarrassing story."

He met her eyes and noticed they weren't green like he'd originally thought. They were blue—just like River's.

He felt a sobering rush of cold air glide across his skin, and he stiffened.

Luna looked at him and frowned. "You okay?"

"Yeah." He shook his head quickly. "Just feeling tired. I should probably head home."

"Oh, okay, yeah. It's been a long week." Luna grabbed her rain jacket from the back of her bar stool and stood up. "I should be heading out, too."

Cole opened his mouth to respond, but he felt his phone vibrate in his pocket. Normally, he would ignore it, but it could be Rose. And after the conversation they had yesterday, he didn't want to risk missing it.

He pulled it out of his jeans, frowning when he realized it was just Jayce responding from earlier.

*Jayce: Atta boy! Knew you could do it.*

He rolled his eyes at his friend's antics. He knew Jayce meant well, but sometimes he was too much, even for Cole.

Sighing, Cole started to click the lock button, but just then, his eyes widened at the sight of a second text.

From an unknown number.

"Holy shit," he whispered, swiping it open.

"What? What?" Luna jabbed her shoulder into Cole's, eager to see what sparked his attention.

**Unknown:** *Congratulations on passing the first task. Your reward awaits you at the theater.* — Z

Cole looked up at Luna as he felt the familiar sense of adrenaline pumping through his veins.

She gave him a knowing smile and said, "Your car or mine?"

# NOW



An hour later, Cole, Luna, and Emmett crammed into Cole's Jeep and headed back to Mazie's Drive-In. Cole had only meant to make a pit stop at his house to let Emmett outside to go potty, but Luna had insisted they bring him.

"Are they playing any movies tonight?" Cole asked as he merged onto the interstate.

"Mmmmmm, lemme check." Luna finished scratching Emmett's ears and then pulled out her phone. "Yes, it looks like they have one showing tonight for *Casper Meets Wendy*. Must be kids' night."

Cole's heart ached at the thought as he remembered taking River there while she was growing up.

"Ooooooo, that means their concession stand will be open," Luna said with wide eyes and a smile.

"Are you serious?" Cole side-eyed her.

"Uh, yeah. In case you've forgotten, we didn't exactly eat dinner, and I'm not in the business of having liquid meals."

Cole rolled his eyes at her antics and focused back on the road.

"What are we looking for when we get there anyway?" Luna asked, not noticing—or rather not paying attention—to his annoyance.

"Anything out of the ordinary. Z likes to leave his signature on all his work, so maybe there's a hidden message written somewhere or another QR code to scan that will unlock the website."

Emmett barked, and Luna turned back around in her seat to pet him. "Don't worry, big guy. I'll share my popcorn with you." The dog licked her nose in response.

Cole looked at the pair in his rearview mirror and smiled. It'd been a while since he'd met anyone who'd loved on Emmett the way he and Rose did.

*Rose.*

Cole suddenly blanched at the thought. He'd gotten his job back without her ever knowing he'd been fired—true—but he needed so much more to go right over the next few weeks before she'd consider coming back to him.

And Luna—oh, fuck, what would Rose think about Cole spending so much time with her? She knew Luna was a colleague, but Cole suddenly felt inappropriate at the close proximity they shared.

"Earth to Cole?" Her familiar voice wedged into his thoughts.

He cleared his throat and shifted in his seat. "Sorry."

"You're being weird," she observed.

"Am not."

"Are too."

"Whatever," he responded and then leaned forward to turn the radio on. "I haven't listened to the news yet today."

"Total weirdo," Luna mouthed to Emmett.

Cole rolled his eyes and accelerated the gas pedal, eager to get to their destination and out of this confined space before his chest started closing in on him again.

After learning about a shooting at a local university bar, a domestic spat that ended in a man's eyes being shot, and a new bakery that's slated to open next month, Cole turned down the volume as he rolled his vehicle once again onto the now-familiar gravel road.

"Thank God," Luna said. "That shiz was depressing."

"They talked about sweets."

"Yeah, a real treat. Icing on the cake, if you will."

Cole shrugged. "News is news."

He opened the door and then helped Emmett exit the back.

"Good boy." Cole scratched his ears and hooked the leash to his collar. "Let's see what we can find."

"You take the back area. I'll get the front half," Luna said as she climbed out.

Cole smirked, knowing all too well that's where the concession stand was. "At least investigate the booth while you're eating."

"Can do!" Luna hopped off with a look of hunger in her eyes.

*Focus.*

He drew in a deep breath and closed his eyes.

*Just breathe.*

He still didn't know exactly what he was looking for—only that he'd know it when he saw it. That's how Z always worked. You never knew what to expect from him, and that's how he liked it.

Cole scanned the back half of the theater, mentally dividing it into sections: the restrooms were off to the left, the screen was positioned front and center, and the operations building was nestled about one hundred feet back to the right. It wasn't likely Zanella would've placed any clues on the screen. It'd be too visible and likely cause damage. He ruled that out and then turned his attention to the bathrooms.

Definitely less discreet, but also *gross*. Cole made a face and shuddered.

The operations building. He'd start there.

"Let's go, boy." He clicked his tongue at Emmett and started walking that way.

Once he was about halfway there, though, Emmett paused and started sniffing, veering Cole farther to the right and toward the wooded acreage.

"Come on, bud. This way." Cole tugged at the dog's leash, but he didn't budge. Instead, Emmett started dragging him farther into the woods, his nose glued to the ground. "Em!" Cole tried but failed once again to veer the dog back to his path. "Where are you going, bud?"

Cole was so focused on not tripping over his own feet that he nearly ran smack dab into a tree when Emmett made an abrupt stop.

"Shit! Emmett, what are you doing?" His voice now commanded attention.

The dog whimpered in response and led Cole around the tree to the backside of the trunk.

And that's when Cole saw it.

There, plastered against the rough, grainy bark, was a dead baby pig stabbed to the tree with a solid black knife.

"Fuck me," Cole breathed.

# NOW

*MONDAY, OCTOBER 7, 2024*

"Is that—"

"A dead baby pig," Cole said, nodding his head.

"Cheese and rice," Luna squealed.

Cole had no idea how he hadn't smelled it before now. Hell, how had no one smelled it—discovered it? It was a fucking decaying animal, for Christ's sake.

He shuddered and then remembered his phone. He scrambled to pull it out of his back pocket—because people who put cell phones in their front pocket were psychopaths, River had once told him—and pulled up Z's website.

"Try 'pig,'" Luna said.

Cole blinked, the sarcasm spitting out before he could stop himself. "Wow. Hadn't thought of that. Thank you so much for your help, Luna."

She rolled her eyes, obviously not deeming him worthy of a response.

He blew out a breath, tapped on the password icon, and did, in fact, type: pig.

*Access Denied.*

Right, because that would be too easy. Cole let out a frustrated sigh and tried again, this time using a capital letter. When that still didn't work, he proceeded to try a plethora of combinations, all of which did not unlock the website—even Luna's personal favorite: WhenPigsFly.

He sighed in defeat and racked his brain, trying to remember if Zanella had any boar or pig imagery in any previous events.

"Hey, Cole," Luna's voice cut in.

"Yeah?"

"I think I found the password."

Cole looked up now, giving her his full attention.

"There." She nodded toward the bloody mess. "On the knife."

Confused, Cole scrunched his eyes. "I don't see anything."

Luna heaved an exaggerated breath and threw her hand out to yank his shirt up over his nose. "Walk closer. You'll see what I mean."

Eyeing her, Cole took a cautious step toward the animal and tried not to suffocate from the rotting flesh scent that entered his nose.

What the hell was she talking about?

Just when he was about to open up his mouth to protest, a glint on the blade handle caught his attention. Cole cocked his head and leaned in closer.

Black-on-black lettering was inscribed on the handle that read "BABIES."

Cole felt a shudder creep up his spine as he remembered the name of the demon from the first act. He turned back to look at Luna and arched an eyebrow.

"Well," she said, "type it in! Try it!"

Cole waited a beat, hesitating for reasons he didn't quite know, and then shook off the eerie feeling and typed in the password.

*Access Granted.*

A sly smile spread across his lips. "We're in."

Luna squealed and yanked Cole's arm, dragging him away from the rotting carcass. "Lemme see! What's it say?"

Cole's body was buzzing with adrenaline as he waited for the screen to load. What would the story be this time? And would the task be the same—to report on another act? His chest bubbled with anticipation.

Finally, the screen loaded, and Cole was met with the same dark-hooded figure as before. He let out what probably sounded like a moan, which raised an eyebrow from Luna, and clicked play.

"Congratulations on completing your first task, and welcome to the next round of the games," the Siri-like voice boomed as the person reappeared, painting the same mural. "With your help, we have successfully gained America's attention and piqued the curiosity of Christians and atheists alike. Citizens are questioning their core beliefs all over the country, and regardless of what side of religion you're on, we are starting a conversation."

Cole's heartbeat sped up. Zanella had never publicly spoken of his intentions or meanings behind his work, so this was crack to a news junkie like Cole. "Now that we've addressed religion, let's force them to take a closer look at their political beliefs. It is an election year, after all."

*Oh, shit.*

The video continued. "For your second task, set your alarms for bright and early Saturday morning for the Springhill University homecoming parade. The festivities will begin at eleven o'clock. Your mission is the same: to document and report what you see. You may need time to digest the events, though, so if I were you, I'd escape to the bonus floor of Owens Hall immediately after. You never know who may be lurking."

The screen faded to black, and Cole and Luna blinked at each other.

"Dude," Luna said, "he wouldn't."

"Oh, but he would."

"Does this mean we might actually meet Z?"

Cole's heart skipped a beat as he registered the thought. "I . . . I don't know. I mean, it sounds like it."

Luna grabbed the phone from his hands and hit play again, rewatching and leaving Cole to his thoughts.

What the hell was going to happen at this parade?

And how would the student body react?

*Wait, the student body.*

"It's meant to rile the left side," Cole blurted.

"What do you mean?" Luna paused the video that she was now rewatching for the second time.

"He's bringing up politics in an academic setting. You know that demographic tends to lean left. He has an agenda—of what, I'm just not sure."

"That's not true," Luna countered.

"Well, we won't know for certain until the game, but I definitely think it's a strong possibility."

"No, I mean what you said about the demographic being left-winged," she said with authority. "Just because someone is in college or connected to university life doesn't mean they're automatically a Democrat, or Republican for that matter. If anything—" She paused, mulling over the words. "It's the time in most people's lives when they begin to question their political beliefs for the first time, because they realize they can. You'd be surprised how many deviate from the belief system in which they grew up."

Cole rubbed his temples and considered her words. Luna may be a strange, perky, pain-in-the-ass at times, but she had a good point.

"You're right," he finally said, wheels spinning. "I'm just trying to figure out what the hell is going to happen."

"Let's figure it out over a meal. I dropped my popcorn when you called me, and I am *starving*, Cole!"

He rolled his eyes but then heard his stomach rumble, too. Fast food wouldn't be too time-consuming or inappropriate, he figured.

"I'll drive through Taco Bell, but that's all. I've gotta get Emmett home. It's past his bedtime."

THE NEXT FEW DAYS passed by at a snail's pace. After Cole bought Luna tacos and dropped her off Monday night, he'd texted Nate immediately with a simple: *Next task is Saturday.* Then, he confirmed he'd brief him on the specifics Tuesday morning. He was supposed to meet Rose later that day for therapy, but she canceled at the last minute saying something had come up. Dr. Jacobi didn't have any availability to reschedule, which meant they'd just have to wait until their next appointment. Cole had groaned in agony as he dealt with the disappointment of not seeing her *and* awaiting the parade.

It was a tough week, to say the least.

When Saturday morning finally came, he dug out his old Badger sweatshirt and tugged on his favorite pair of jeans. He considered putting a hat on to tame his dark, unruly curls, but he opted for hair gel today instead. When he was finished getting ready, he looked like the stereotypical Midwesterner football fan, which made blending in easy, just the way he liked it.

Cole hadn't been to a Springhill game since River was thirteen. That was the age she'd deemed it no longer cool to hang out with her parents on the weekends and swapped their usual tailgate tradition for moody dates with her room. Cole's heart ached at the thought of returning without her, but he knew he had to do this.

For himself.

And Rose.

He could do this one hard thing for their future.

It was worth it.

Cole grabbed his keys, wallet, and phone before heading to the door and pausing to give Emmett one last head rub.

"I know, buddy. I wish I could take you with me, but there will be too much food and too many distractions for you today."

The dog perked his ears.

"I'll bring you home a special treat. I promise." He said goodbye, promising to be back later, and walked out the front door, ready to tackle whatever Zanella threw his way.

He'd been waiting years to meet him.

Could today really be the day?

# THEN



*Saturday, September 23, 2006*

"B-A-D-G-E-R! Badgers! Badgers! Springhill U Badgers!" Rose rolled her arms up in the air as she finished the cheer, and Cole busted out laughing in the silence of her RA dorm room.

"You gonna do that in the stadium?" he teased.

"Maybe." She placed a hand on her hip and cocked an eyebrow. "Are you saying you wouldn't enjoy seeing me move like that all night?"

"Oh, I would very much enjoy watching you embarrass yourself." He laughed as her mouth fell open in mock annoyance.

"Whatever. You're just jealous." She giggled and then smoothed out her outfit. "But, seriously, how do I look? Is this spirit-y enough?"

They were getting ready for the university's homecoming game, and Rose had insisted on going all out since it was their senior year. Cole honestly didn't care what she wore. As long as she took it off for him at the end of the night, he'd be happy.

"You know what I think, babe." He gave her a knowing look and winked. "You look beautiful."

Satisfied with his response, he watched her blush and then bounce over to the mirror to finish putting on her makeup.

They'd been together for nearly two years now, and still, Cole couldn't get over how lucky he was to call her "mine." When he first saw her in their Intro to Marketing course, he'd instantly been drawn to her scarlet-colored hair, freckle-dusted skin, and dark brown eyes. It had taken him almost the entire semester to work up the nerve to ask her out.

But thank God he did.

"Babe?" Rose's voice cut through his thoughts like a honey-edged sword.

"Hmm?" He blinked at her, trying to remember what she'd been saying.

"I asked if you wanted to take another shot before we go?"

His eyes widened as he took in the sight of *his woman* holding a bottle of cinnamon whiskey with a shot glass balanced between her breasts. "Uh-huh. Yep, yep." He scrambled to his feet and nearly knocked over a chair in the process. Rose squealed as he scooped her up and planted her on the nearby desk, his hips pressing between her thighs as she wrapped her legs around him. "Absolutely, I do."

A gasp escaped Rose's lips. "Cole Sloane, did you just quote *The Office* to me?"

He laughed and then bit his lip. "I'm sorry, you've got me hooked on that show. I have the new season air date written in my planner."

Rose moaned. "You know I love it when you talk dirty to me."

Cole laughed again and then slipped the bottle of liquor out of her hands and twisted the cap open. "Well, in that case, you better get your tickets."

She furrowed her brows but only for a moment before asking with a mischievous grin, "What tickets?"

Cole poured the liquid into the shot glass, splashing some onto her exposed cleavage, and then whispered, "To the gun show."

Rose let out a soft, sultry laugh, and Cole used his tongue to lazily suggest they blow off the tailgate.

They didn't make it to the game until the second quarter.

# NOW

*SATURDAY, OCTOBER 12, 2024*

"Cole, you gotta try these chicken wings."

It was only a quarter after ten, and already, Luna had grazed food from approximately half a dozen tailgaters.

"I'm not hungry." He checked his phone for the time again, only to discover less than a minute had passed—10:16 a.m. Clearly, he was anxious to get started.

"What do you mean you're not hungry? It's prime brunch time, my dude." She licked the sauce from her fingers and then dug into another flat.

"I already ate." He looked again: 10:17 a.m.

"Yeah, but Cole, people are just giving away free food! I've never seen anything like it."

He twisted his face in confusion. "Wait, have you never been to a tailgate?"

"Nope," she said as she smacked her lips. "Parents didn't allow me to. And I never had any interest as an adult. I don't really like sports ball things."

*Ahh*, Cole thought. *That explains it.*

When he'd met Luna at the student center this morning, he couldn't help but notice her . . . ensemble. She was dressed in a black sweatshirt that read "SPORTS" with nothing else on it, paired with a pink-and-white, tye-dye ball cap that said, "Saturdays are for the girls."

He had to give her an A for effort, he supposed.

"Just try not to steal any more food or drinks until after the parade. I'm worried you'll get sick." He thought back to his own days as an SU student and shuddered at all the vomit-clouded memories. Thank God he'd learned how to handle his liquor.

"Don't shame me," Luna said as she paused at a tent to crack open a complimentary seltzer. "I can't believe it's acceptable to drink before noon—and in the streets, no less!"

Cole threw up his hands in surrender and returned his attention back to his phone. Their banter had killed exactly four minutes—only forty more to go until the parade started.

"Are you going to livestream this for Nate?" He looked at Luna and her pile of chicken wing bones.

"Nah," she said. "I think he was worried about capturing underage drinkers on camera. I mean, he didn't say that, technically, but he acted super weird when I asked. And after the headache the dean gave us after running that story last year, I'm assuming he's trying to avoid additional strife."

Cole rolled his eyes. They were journalists, not lobbyists. He hated the way Nate would bend when faced with university pressure. "Figures."

Luna shrugged. "I could stream it from my personal page, I guess, but I think he'd throw a fit about that, too."

"Nah," Cole grumbled, "not worth it. Just clean your fingers off so you can take photos. I'm going to take notes on my phone and then try to find a couple interviews after the fact." He had a sick feeling flooding his gut the more he thought about what was to come.

*Please no more dead animals, Z.*

Luna stuck her tongue out at Cole before finishing her snack, wiping her hands, and tossing her garbage in a nearby trash can.

Cole rolled his eyes and then led her through the familiar parking lot as they wove their way through a sea of baby blue, navy, and gold. The parade would be coming down main street, led first by the cheerleaders and band. Then, a mix of sororities, fraternities, and other clubs would come through, followed by the dance team. Last would be the football team. The players and coaches always dressed in suits and ties to march down the street and then through a tunnel of fans as they made their way inside the stadium. Coined the "Badger Walk," it was supposed to get them excited for the game, but Cole suspected it was more for the fans' benefit than the players.

After another tailgate crash, a porta-potty pit stop, and an awkward run-in with an old professor, Cole guided Luna to the front of main street with a few moments to spare. He steadied himself, taking a deep breath and trying not to let the ghosts of his past haunt him today.

"Hey," Luna said, grabbing his hand, "it's going to be okay. We got this." She squeezed it, and Cole nodded a silent thanks, the touch of her skin against his sending a new wave of emotions through him.

Before he had time to dissect them, though, the familiar sound of the school fight song boomed through the streets, and his heart stammered. "Here we go," he said under his breath.

The adrenaline raced through his veins, his entire body on edge. What was going to happen next? He cringed at the possibilities.

Regardless of whatever it was, though, he knew one thing for certain: it was going to be bad. He could feel it in the marrow of his bones.

The final beats of the school anthem faded out as the band marched past Cole and Luna, and they turned their attention to the first float that rolled by. It was full of the university's cheerleaders, just as Cole had suspected. He squinted and surveyed the space-themed vehicle, looking for signs of Zanella.

A female cheerleader roared over a megaphone. "Springhill Badgers are *out of this world*! Who's ready to blast off into space today?"

The male squad members all mimicked cocking and loading a gun as they pointed T-shirt cannons into the air. Cheers erupted everywhere, and Cole jumped.

*Breathe. It's just T-shirts.*

*And a bunch of drunk college kids, but what could possibly go wrong?*

He shook off the thought and tuned his senses back into the moment. The spaceship had passed, and a sorority float full of martians on the moon consumed his view. The crowd was still chaotic, and music boomed from the overhead speakers. Cole could barely hear himself think.

"Look." Luna shook Cole's arm, and he snapped his attention to her.

"Hmm?"

"Over there." She nodded to the other side of the street where the university's mascot, Hayden the Honey Badger, was dressed up in a similar martian costume. "Maybe one of Z's guys is in there. Isn't the mascot usually *on* a float?"

Cole cocked his head and considered the thought. It would be a great disguise. But what was he going to do?

"Maybe we should go over there," he said.

"What, by crossing the street?"

"You got a better idea?"

Luna opened her mouth to respond, but just then, a loud bang roared through the air. Cole jumped, but the audience continued to cheer.

"They've got fucking *fireworks in space, man,*" a drunk guy yelled from behind him.

Another bang went off, and Cole searched the sky. He couldn't detect any remnants of a spark.

"I don't think those are fireworks," Luna said, her eyes now locked on the next float.

Cole's heart dropped to the pit of his stomach. He turned to follow her gaze, and sure enough, it was, in fact, not a firework but a man dressed in all black holding a gun.

An AR-15, to be exact.

"Oh, fuck.

# NOW

*Saturday, October 12, 2024*

COLE'S HEART HAMMERED OUTSIDE of his chest as he tried to figure out what to do.

*Boom!*

Another shot blasted into the sky, and this time, it elicited a few screams as others noticed the man in black.

*Boom! Boom! Boom!*

More open fire hit the air, and that's when Cole spotted the second shooter.

And the third.

And the fourth.

And the—

"Crap!" Luna said, her eyes wide in terror. "There are dozens of them!"

Cole panicked as the realization set in. There was a shooter on every float, all dressed in black from head to toe and harboring the same weapon. Another round of shots filled the air, and that's when the hysteria set in.

"HELP!"

"Somebody call 911!"

"The dude's got a fucking gun!"

"I want my mommy!"

Cole froze at the sound of the little girl's scream. He turned and looked at her, his chest tightening at the sight of her pink bow. River had one just like it at that age.

*"Hi, Daddy! Look at my pretty hair."*

The memories of her as a toddler came flooding in.

*"Mommy fixed it for me. Do you like my bow? I chose a pink one."*

"Cole!"

He snapped his eyes to Luna, who was snapping photos left and right.

"Mommy!" the little girl screamed again, causing Cole's heart to ache.

Where was the child's mother? He couldn't leave her here like this.

"Cole, come on!"

He took a sharp inhale and then ran to the child.

"What are you doing?" Luna screamed.

"She's lost!"

Luna looked like she wanted to argue, but as the chaos grew around them, she audibly groaned, tucked her camera behind her, and followed Cole.

"Hi, sweetie," Cole said, crouching down. "What's your name?"

"Daai—sy!" She screamed in between sobs as tears soaked her face. "I want my mommy!"

"We need to get her to shelter," Cole yelled over the onslaught of bullets.

"Here, I've got her," she said, stepping forward and unwrapping her camera strap from her neck. "You take this. Snap some pics if you can, but most of all, stay safe."

Cole nodded and placed the camera over his shoulder before turning back to the girl. "Daisy, this is my friend Luna. She's going to take care of you and make sure you're safe and find your mommy, okay."

"O—kaaaay."

Luna smiled at Daisy and stretched out her arms. "Is it okay if I hold you?"

Daisy shook her head "yes," and with that, Luna scooped her up and headed back toward the student center, quickly lost in the shuffle of everyone else.

Cole turned his attention back to the street, which was now filled with aliens and martians alike; students everywhere had fled their floats and were infiltrating the crowd.

*Boom! Boom! Boom!*

His head throbbed from the noise, but he needed to act fast. He quickly considered his options, trying to figure out how to cover this without getting hit, but then a thought occurred to him: it wasn't likely the shooters would harm anyone since they were part of Zanella's act. They were here to make a statement, not *kill* someone. That wasn't his M.O.

At that sudden realization, Cole finally felt his feet move as he sprung into action. He ran back to the edge of the sidewalk, crouched down on one knee, and started taking photos with Luna's camera.

"Get out of the way, idiot! There's open fire!" someone screamed as they knocked into Cole.

"I believe this is part of a performance act from Graham Zanella," Cole said in a rush. "Would you be willing to go on record—"

The wind rushed out of him as the man shoved him in the chest, desperate to get away. "Are you crazy? Move!"

"Please, they're shooting at the sky—not at us!" Cole screamed after the stranger, but it was a lost cause.

*Shit.*

No one would believe him right now. Hell, he wouldn't either if he were them. It was impossible to think logically, given the circumstances.

Cole shook his head and jumped back to his feet. He'd worry about interviews later. For now, he needed to figure out the bigger picture.

He looked around and observed how, even amidst the chaos, the floats continued to move, which likely meant the drivers were part of the act.

*Boom!*

"Fuck!" His ears rang at the onslaught of more bullets.

He needed to get to higher ground if he wanted a better view, preferably before he went deaf.

He surveyed his surroundings, his heart beating wildly. Across the street was a bank with a large set of stairs. It was high enough, but he'd have to cut across the street, and that would be difficult. He spun around in search of a better option. To the right, something glinted in his eye, and Cole did a double-take as he spotted the bronze statue of the school mascot.

It wasn't perfect, but it was much closer.

It would have to do.

Cole raced off toward the statue, dodging terrified drunkards left and right as screams pierced the air. He had to figure out the end game if he was going to cover the full story.

Now at the base of the statue, Cole swung the camera back around his neck and started climbing the massive honey badger. One step, two steps, three—

"Shit!"

His foot slipped, and he nearly fell off but regained his balance just in time. He took a deep breath and then continued, eventually heaving himself on top of the sculpture. "Okay, let's see what you're doing, Z." He cupped a hand over his eyes and squinted into the midday sun.

In front of him, the parade was still moving, and he gawked when he saw the masks each shooter now wore. One by one, the floats rolled by, the faces of U.S. presidents staring back at him. Cole watched in awe as the Biden, Trump, and Obama impersonators waved at the roaring crowd, guns still in hand.

He snapped a few photos and then pulled out his notepad, writing furiously.

Then, he looked back at the parade, contemplating his next move, when a loud siren echoed over the campus speakers. Cole screamed as the sound pounded against his eardrums.

*What the fuck is happening?*

He lifted his gaze once again to the streets, observing the crowd's behaviors.

And then he heard the familiar electronic female voice:

*"A well-regulated Militia, being necessary to the security of a free State, the right of the people to keep and bear Arms, shall not be infringed."*

"The Second Amendment," Cole breathed.

And that's when it all clicked.

Zanella had said politics. This was an act to draw attention to gun violence—to school shootings and mass murderers, and the country's ongoing battle concerning the matter. How do we protect our rights *and* the safety of the innocent? Cole could see the headlines now.

He jumped back down to the ground and whipped Luna's camera around to start taking photos of the people around him.

Because this wasn't about capturing the act.

No, this was about documenting the crowd's reaction. Zanella wanted to tell a story through the eyes and behaviors of those who fell victim to the violence. Of this, Cole was sure.

He understood the assignment.

# NOW



*Saturday, October 12, 2024*

"I can't believe you scratched my lens!" Luna inspected her Nikon with a frown. "This stuff isn't cheap."

"Sorry, next time there's a parade full of shooters and open fire for a public art statement about gun rights, I'll try to be more cautious."

"That's all I ask, honestly."

Cole rolled his eyes and checked the time. It had been an hour since the sirens blared, and he and Luna were now sitting in the middle of an art studio at the top of Owens Hall. Even though Cole had been a student here, he'd never heard of this space, so it took them a while to find it—especially with the mass hysteria of the crowd and local police outside.

"What time did the video say he'd be here?" Luna asked, still messing with her lens.

"It didn't," Cole said. "Just that we should come here afterward to decompress—and that someone might be lurking." He narrowed his brows as he inspected the bare room yet again.

A few paintings sat up against the floor-to-ceiling window sills, with a bucket of brushes crusted in the neighboring sink. Cole wondered when the last time this space was used.

"Well"—Luna stood up and dusted off her pants—"I'm tired of waiting. I don't think he's coming, and I'd much rather *decompress* with food. Plus, didn't he say you'd meet at The Gala? I think this was just a trick."

Cole thought about what she said. It was logical, yes, but Z wouldn't have told them to come if he didn't have a plan, right? "Just five more minutes, please." He looked at her with an earnest expression in his eyes.

Luna tapped her foot. "Fine, but then I'm going to José's and ordering a very large margarita and downing all the free chips and salsa I can, before we head back to the office."

*That wasn't a bad idea*, Cole thought.

He opened his mouth to respond, but then he heard it: footsteps in the hallway. His eyes snapped to Luna, whose mouth had dropped open.

"Do you think it's him?" she mouthed.

Cole shrugged his shoulders and raised a finger to his lips, miming a "shush" sound. He took a cautious step forward and held his breath as the footsteps neared the doorway and then stopped.

Was it Zanella? Or just a student who'd stumbled upon them at the wrong time? Cole's chest throbbed as his mouth went dry.

It had to be Z. It had to.

The footsteps resumed, and Cole's body buzzed with adrenaline. He looked at Luna one last time, and when he refocused his attention on the door, a pair of emerald green eyes stared back at him.

Cole's heart stammered, but before he could even open his mouth, the stranger said, "Who the bloody hell are you blokes?"

And just like that, Cole's shoulders slumped, defeat settling deep in his bones. "You're not Z."

"You got that right, mate. I thought I was meeting him here, but apparently not."

"Ohmygosh!" Luna gasped, her reflexes taking over as she grabbed Cole's arm. "I know who you are—*Solstice Blackwood*!"

The stranger smiled at her, a devious grin taking over his features.

Cole's eyes widened in recognition. "The rockstar."

*That explains the wardrobe,* Cole thought as he scanned past the man's face and took in his appearance. The singer wore a lime green feathered top hat—which only slightly hindered his wild, long black curls—a beige-colored fur coat, and black leather leggings with combat boots.

"At your service, mate. But please, call me Sol." He tipped his hat at the two of them and continued. "And you two are . . . ?"

"I'm Luna Monroe," Luna said, shaking the rockstar's hand without an ounce of shyness, "and this is Cole Sloane. We work for *The Chronicles*."

Cole offered a quick guy nod, his mind reeling as he remembered covering a story about Sol last year. He was the headliner at a week-long indie rock festival near Yellow Springs and had fallen off the stage during the first night. The entire event was canceled after Sol was rushed to the hospital in an ambulance.

"How's your leg?" Cole asked as their eyes locked again.

"Ah, doing much better, thanks, mate. I seemed to have had a little problem last year with a little too much blow, but I'm walking the straight and narrow now. Yes, I'm now Sober Sol, that's what the fans call me." He strode farther into the room and picked up one of the paint-crusted brushes from the sink.

"I can't believe you're here!" Luna was still fangirling, despite the enormity of the circumstances.

"But *why* are you here?" Cole asked. "I don't get it. You're not a journalist."

"Oooo, are you crashing like me?" Luna placed a hand on her hip and continued talking. "I wasn't technically invited, but I ran into Cole at the drive-in and kinda crashed his plans for this whole thing."

"Hah!" Sol threw his head back and laughed. "A party crasher—I bet Z loves that. But no, I was invited, I'm afraid. The bloody invite showed up at my band rehearsal one night."

"Wait," Cole said, "so were you also at the—"

"The drive-in," Sol finished for him. "Yes, what a bloody mess that was, no pun intended."

"But we didn't see you there." Luna gave him a confused look.

"Well, of course not. You think I'd show up like *this* to a place like *that*? I was incognito."

Sol's voice faded into background noise as Cole's thoughts spiraled. He should've known Z wouldn't be here. Not yet, at least. His reveal wouldn't be until the end, at the final act—Cole knew that.

But it didn't make it any less disappointing.

Finally, Cole said, "I still don't understand what's happening."

Sol's lip twitched upward. "Now you riddle me this. A rockstar, a journalist, and a photographer who crashed walk into a bar." He stopped and winked before cracking a taunting smile. "No, I can't do that one. It's too obvious. You Americans and your repetitive jokes. You gotta try sumthin' new every once and a while."

Luna scoffed. "What, they don't make century-old jokes in England?"

"Or Australia," Sol answered. "That's where my mum lives. Dad's from the U.K." He walked to the windows and observed the city's wide-eyed view, twirling the paintbrush in his fingers. "Anyway, the way I see it is easy. Z has hand-selected only the very finest storytellers for whatever the hell this shitshow is that's going on."

"Storytellers?" Cole asked.

"Yes, yes. Think about it, mate. A journalist. A songwriter. Z is telling a story, and he wants us to capture it."

A million follow-up questions fired in Cole's synapsis. "That may be so," he said, "but the question remains: why now? And why us?"

Sol shrugged his shoulders. "That's to be determined, still, eh?" He winked at Luna, whose cheeks were crimson red.

Cole watched the silent interaction between them but then quickly dismissed it. "So, who else is coming then?"

"You think there are more?" Luna looked at him now.

"Don't you?" Cole rebutted.

She thought for a moment before responding. "Maybe they didn't complete the first challenge."

Sol adjusted his hat and took off his fur coat, revealing an oversized, black Metallica t-shirt. "Or, maybe they weren't ready to meet Zanella yet. I, myself, was pretty spooked after those blokes shot off their guns. And look at me. I don't scare easily." He threw the coat over his shoulders and popped his neck. "I imagine the others are still out, hiding in their cars, or phoning mummy and daddy asking, 'Is this really worth it?'"

Cole started to answer him, but just then, a ping sounded on his and Sol's phones. They looked at each other for five nanoseconds and then scrambled to check their notifications, Luna nudging her way into Cole's personal bubble yet again. "Is that him?"

"Crikey," Sol said. "It better be."

Taking a deep breath, Cole swiped open the text message from the provocateur.

**Unknown:** *Have you met your teammate yet? Everything's better when you have a friend. How about a little bonding time to get to know one another better? I've prepared a special for you at Forrest Fox Brewing Co. Go, have one on me, and see what secrets you can unveil. — Z*

"Forest Fox Brewing Co.?" Sol asked.

"Teammate?" Luna blurted.

"It's the local brewery," Cole said, answering Sol first before turning to Luna. "It sounds like he's paired us up, which means there are definitely others. He must've sent us all different directions for after the parade."

"Aye, well, that solves the problem then, doesn't it, mates?" Sol's mouth transformed into a lopsided grin, and he slapped his hands together. "Z wants us to loosen up a bit and have some fun, all while making a buddy! Always so considerate, that one. Now how do we get to the brewery?"

Cole and Luna made eye contact again, a silent hesitation passing between them.

Finally, Luna shrugged her shoulders, and Cole caved.

*What's the worst that could happen?*

# NOW



"We'll have the special, please," Sol said, ordering for the whole table.

"Aren't you supposed to be sober?" Luna asked.

"Ah!" Sol brushed her off with a wave of his hand. "As long as I don't hit the hard stuff, my publicist doesn't get too upset."

Cole wasn't sure that's how sobriety worked, but who was he to judge? He cleared his throat and said to the waitress, "I'll take a shot of your barrel whiskey, too, please."

"Absolutely, sir." The server smiled at him and nodded a quick yes before heading back to the bar. Once she was gone, he pulled out his phone and saw a text from Nate.

**Nate:** *Nice work. Let me know how tonight goes.*

**Cole:** *Will do!*

He slid the device back into his pocket and stared at the late autumn sunlight as it gleamed through the brewery's stained glass window. It was nearing five o'clock now, just on the brink of happy hour. After they'd received the texts, Cole and Luna agreed to meet at the bar after busting out a quick work session. Nate wanted a full report ASAP, and Cole was happy to oblige.

Now mentally and emotionally tapped out from the day's festivities, he needed a strong buzz to help him sort through this next part.

"So," Luna said, breaking the silence as usual, "why do you guys think Z had us come here?"

Sol took a large slurp from his water before responding. "Must be a clue about the password for the next event, I suppose. I just hope this time isn't as dreadful as the last. Can you believe that bastard killed a baby pig? His mum outta raised him better than that."

Cole opened his mouth to respond, but a new thought occurred to him then. "Give me the menu." He yanked it from Sol's hands.

"Blimey, Cole! They've got dozens of other menus in this place. You don't have to go off stealing mine. The food may be shit, but I'm hungry, mate."

But Cole wasn't listening. He was busy scanning the drink menu on the back. "The drink. What was the name of the special?"

"Oh, fudge, we didn't ask!" Luna's eyes widened in understanding.

Cole scanned the menu again and again but didn't see anything marked as a special. "Hey!" he yelled, throwing a finger in the air at their waitress. He hated when people did this, but desperate times called for desperate measures.

"Sorry, sir, your drinks will be right out."

Cole shook his head but couldn't speak fast enough.

"What was the name of the special we just ordered?" Luna interjected.

"Oh," the woman said, sighing in relief, "tonight's special was invented by the owner. It's called Momma's Milk. It's our twist on a White Russian. It's quite good really. I think you'll all enjoy it."

She continued rambling about the drink, but Cole wasn't listening. He, along with Sol, were busy frantically trying to load Zanella's website. After a painstaking ten seconds, the familiar black screen appeared, and Cole tapped on the password box. He typed in "mommasmilk" as quickly as he could and hit enter. He held his breath, and Luna knocked into his shoulder, eager to see what was happening.

*Access Granted.*

"Yes!

"Bravo, mate!" Sol clapped a hand on the back of Cole's shoulder and then brought him in for a hug. "Bloody brilliant! Miss, I'm gonna need a double round of drinks for the table! We have cause for celebration!"

Cole cracked a genuine smile, the first in a long time. Just one more task. That's all that stood between him and Z. His spine tingled.

Snapping his attention back to his phone, Cole tapped on the screen and waited for the Siri voice to load.

"Hello, and welcome to the third task. If you're watching this, it means you successfully completed the second challenge and have unlocked access to the third."

Cole glanced at Luna, the anticipation rising.

"Our latest act ignited a new wave of conversation, and the political polls are all over the place. And to that, I say, well done."

The video had zoomed in on the masked man's hands as he continued to paint the infamous brick-wall mural—a mural that Cole could still not make out.

"For your final task, you must be available Friday night from nine until whenever the job is done. The fallout will be extreme, and your content may be taken down, so live coverage will be most effective. You will be visiting Scare Minerals Scream Park, the legendary haunted cave at 37 North Pioneer Road in Suttonville, Ohio. Document the entire journey from start to finish, and you will pass. We look forward to seeing what you do as we challenge the current social climate in which we live. Godspeed."

The video clicked off, and the three looked at each other in silence.

"Woah," Luna breathed.

"Yeah." Cole nodded.

"Looks like we're having a sleepover, mates!" Sol concluded.

THREE HOURS LATER, COLE and Luna had somehow made their way to the dancefloor with the rest of the crowd. After breaking his sobriety streak—which Cole later found out was only six days—Sol hopped up on stage and offered to perform, winning a gushing response from the audience. The brewery usually had live music on the weekends after the twenty-one-and-over crowd settled in, so the manager didn't protest.

"You dance like an old man!" Luna shouted over the music.

"I AM an old man, Lu!" Cole yelled back as he cracked a smile.

"Did you just call me Lu?"

"Would you rather I called you Stu?"

Luna burst out in laughter so hard tears started to form in her eyes. "I've never seen you like this, Cole!"

"Me neither!" He headbanged to Sol's questionable yet popular music and mimicked an air guitar solo.

It was safe to say he hadn't been this drunk *and happy* in a while. Sure, he drank frequently, but he was toeing a dangerous line tonight.

*Fun Cole* was emerging, for crying out loud.

This could not be good.

"Hey, Luuuu," he slurred, "check this out!"

Luna watched in horror as Cole jumped on stage, gave the audience a "rock-and-roll" hand gesture, and jumped backward into the audience.

"Cole!" she screamed.

But he didn't hear her. He was floating on a cloud of carefree, rock-and-roll bliss.

Until he wasn't.

Approximately thirty seconds after diving into the air, his daydream abruptly stopped when the meager crowd dropped him, and he face-planted into the floor.

*Fuck.*

He was going to regret that tomorrow.

"Cole!" Luna screamed again as she scrambled over to him. "Are you okay?"

"I'm fine, I'm fine." He waved off her help and then slowly made his way back to a standing position. "Really, I'm fine—"

His voice broke as his knees buckled, and he started to fall again. Luna caught him just in time and offered her shoulders for support.

"You're bleeding."

*What?*

Cole thought he'd heard her say he was bleeding, but that couldn't be right. He touched the side of his forehead and winced.

*Oh.*

Maybe she was right.

"Come on, Grandpa."

Cole didn't argue as Luna shouldered some of his weight and led them toward the back. His vision was starting to blur, and he couldn't quite make out where they were going until they were there.

"Here," she said as she sat him down on a bench and walked to the sink. "Let me help clean you up."

"Are we in the . . . bathroom?" Cole winced as pain shot up his neck and throbbed in his head. Yup, Fun Cole definitely came to fuck things up. He silently chided himself.

"Yes," Luna said. "You got any better ideas?"

Cole shook his head and grumbled a line of expletives as another wave of pain rattled through him.

He was absolutely going to regret this tomorrow—if he could remember it.

Returning with a damp wad of towels in her hand, Luna said, "Next time you get the sudden urge to crowd surf, maybe don't." She offered a teasing smile and then started dabbing at the blood on his forehead.

"Duly noted." At first, he winced at her touch but then fell into a moment of ease as he inhaled the scent of her perfume.

What was that? Berries? Oranges?

"You smell nice."

He didn't mean to say it out loud.

Luna's cheeks flushed. "Um, thanks."

Cole watched as she continued to clean his injury and suddenly realized how close they were. He hadn't been that close to any woman other than Rose in years.

He'd be lying if he said he didn't enjoy the way heat radiated from her body.

"There," she said, interrupting his thoughts. "Good as new."

"Thanks." Cole smiled at her, his eyes lingering for far longer than they should've. He was still married—he knew that. But the alcohol mixed with their close proximity, and the head injury—can't forget that—were messing with him.

It also didn't help that she was gorgeous, with her freckle-dusted nose, gentle smile, and well-kept figure.

But he wasn't supposed to notice that.

His eyes fell to her lips, then back to her eyes, and for a moment, he considered leaning in and seeing what happened.

"Coley, my bud! Are you all right?"

He jumped at the now-familiar, foreign voice, almost knocking Luna over in the process. Sol banged into the restroom, sweat dripping from his face.

"You took a nasty spill, mate."

Cole cleared his throat. "Yes, yeah, I'm good. All good here."

"That's gonna hurt tomorrow, buddy." The rockstar walked over to the sink and splashed cold water on his face. "Come on, let's have another drink to numb the pain."

Grateful for an escape, Cole rose but stumbled to his feet.

"I don't think you boys need another drink," Luna said.

The three grumbled as they made their way back to the table, where a plate of nachos sat untouched. Cole's mouth watered with excitement.

"Foooooood." He fell into his seat, eager to stuff his face with the soggy goodness. "Lu, pass me the hot sauce."

"Here, let me get it for you, mate." Sol picked up the bottle of pepper sauce and launched it at Cole from the other side of the table.

"Sol!" Luna yelled.

A crash sounded as the bottle landed on the floor beside them. Cole looked down and blinked, trying to determine what had just happened, and that's when he saw the red liquid trickle out.

A waitress was rushing to their aid somewhere in the background, but Cole couldn't tear his gaze away from the blood. It was seeping everywhere, and his heartbeat raced.

A hand brushed by his foot, and Cole flinched at the touch.

"Sir? Are you okay?"

He looked at the woman and opened his mouth to respond, but the words got lost in the back of his throat when he saw River looking up at him.

*Oh, God.*

Cole's entire world shut down in an instant.

"River! Baby!" he screamed. "What happened? Tell Daddy what happened!"

Cole launched himself forward and scooped his daughter up in his arms, panic mode setting in.

"Rose! Call an ambulance." His eyes darted around the room, desperate to know what happened. "Where the fuck is Rose? Someone call an ambulance *now*!"

Fear consumed his lungs, and he started running for the door.

"Hey, let me go," River screamed, batting a hand at him. "Put me down! What the hell are you doing?"

"Baby, we have to get to the hospital." Cole pushed his way past the strangers who were now staring at him.

Luna's voice cut in through the chaos. "Cole, what are you doing? That's our waitress."

Cole paused at her words. He looked at the woman in his arms and felt the oxygen leave his lungs; it was not his daughter.

He immediately dropped her, and that's when his world went black.

# THEN



"It's called post-traumatic stress disorder, more commonly known as PTSD."

Cole stared at the doctor in disbelief. "Isn't that just for, like, war veterans?"

He'd been having trouble since . . . well, since what he now referred to as *the incident*, but he wasn't expecting this. He eyed the man, hoping he'd heard him wrong.

"Actually, no," Dr. Talbot said. "It can happen to anyone who has experienced a traumatic event. In your case . . ." He paused, giving Cole a serene look. "I'm not surprised at all, to be honest."

*Great,* Cole thought. "So what, I'm just fucked then? On top of having to go through it once and dealing with the normal amount of grief, I'm just stuck reliving the worst day of my fucking life?" His fists were clenched now, his voice rising with each word.

Dr. Talbot took his glasses off and set his clipboard down. "I understand this is a lot to take in," he started, "but with the proper medication and psychotherapy, we can manage the symptoms. It won't be easy, but it will improve over time if you're committed to treatment."

*Medication.*

*Psychotherapy.*

*Treatment.*

The words swirled around in Cole's head, simultaneously overwhelming and frustrating him. He didn't want to be broken. He didn't want to take medication. And he especially didn't want to go to fucking therapy where he answered questions like, "How does that make you feel?" Talking about her and what happened—it was too much. Cole shuddered.

"And what'll happen if I don't?"

"Well." The doctor sighed. "Your symptoms will likely intensify. The episodes will become more frequent, the nightmares will be never-ending, and you'll likely experience worsening symptoms of depression and anxiety."

Cole snorted and dropped his head in his hands, letting his inner demons take over. This was all so *fucking* unfair. All he wanted was to hold his baby girl again—not deal with this shit. A single tear started to slip out of the corner of his eye, and he coughed, clearing his throat, and wiping it away with the heel of his palm.

"All right," he said, sighing in defeat. "I'll try the meds first, I guess."

Dr. Talbot smiled. "Great. I really think this will help you, Cole. You did a good thing coming here today. I know it's not easy to ask for help."

Cole nodded, but he was already mentally somewhere else as the broken image of his daughter's bloodied body reappeared in his brain.

# NOW

## Sunday, October 13, 2024

*"River!"* Cole screamed as he launched forward in his bed. He clutched his chest, struggling for air as the remnants of his nightmare clung to him.

"Hey, hey, it's okay. Just breathe, hun."

Cole jolted at the sound of another voice entering his room.

"Rosie?" he breathed.

She nodded with a soft smile. "Yes, it's me. I'm here, and you're okay." Rose slipped an arm around him as she sat on his bed and cradled his head.

Cole felt his soul break into a million pieces as he nuzzled his head into her hands and let the tears fall.

*That fucking dream,* he thought.

It was so real, more real than usual, and yet he couldn't shake the feeling of why.

And then he remembered the bar last night.

"Oh my God," he said, sitting up. "The bar. The woman. What the hell happened?" His eyes popped open even wider as the fragmented memories seared into his brain.

"You had an alcohol-induced PTSD episode. Luna called me from your phone after you blacked out, and I came and got you." She paused, slipping a strand of hair behind her ear and chewing on her lip. "Cole . . . she mentioned something else, too. Two things, actually."

*Oh, shit. Shit. Shit. Shit.*

The hazy bathroom scene flooded his brain.

"Look, I don't know what she said, but—"

"She said you guys were there working on a *Zanella* lead, and that she was so happy you weren't *fired* anymore?"

*Dammit.*

This was so much worse than he thought. He had to remedy this and fast.

After a silent, expectant beat, Cole finally said, "It was just a misunderstanding. Luna must've misspoken."

Rose crossed her arms, and her eyebrows fell into a scowl. "What do you mean?"

Cole sighed and scratched the back of his neck, contemplating his next move. He'd been caught. He should just come clean.

Instead, he said, "It was nothing."

"Cole!" Rose demanded.

He blew out a breath and slumped his shoulders in defeat. "Okay, fine. Yes, I was technically fired, but it wasn't a big deal. I was late the morning of River's . . . *death* anniversary, and Nate got frustrated—you know how heated he can get. I was out for a few days, but then after a new Z lead fell into my lap, he told me to come back to work."

Rose scoffed. "Un-be-lievable."

He shook his head. How was this happening? "Rosie, come on."

"Don't 'Rosie' me right now. I can't believe you, Cole." A lethal combination of hurt and anger washed over her face. "I thought you were doing better, but you haven't changed at all."

"No, listen to me, you don't understand," Cole said, grabbing her hand. "This is different. Zanella sent me an invitation to participate in these acts—"

"An invitation?" Rose yanked her arm away. "Do you hear yourself right now?"

She stood up and grabbed her purse.

*Oh, no.* This was not going well. Cole scrambled to find the right words.

"Please, just listen to me for a minute. I know how this looks, but I'm telling you this is different—"

"Just stop!" She shot him a cold look, anger boiling beneath her skin. "I should've known better when you came to tell me you had a new lead the other day. Even after everything that's happened . . ."

She was now at the foot of the stairs, and Cole stumbled after her. "Wait, Rosie, please. I'm doing this *for us*. I had to get my job back, and this was the only way."

Emmett had spotted them coming down the stairs and was now beelining for Rose.

"I really thought you had changed." Rose threw her hair in a bun and slipped on her shoes.

"I *have!*" Cole pleaded, a look of desperation in his eyes. "You think I just jumped into this without taking everything into consideration? I lost *everything* because of that man. Trust me when I say this was the last thing I planned on doing, but I had to do something when Nate fired me, or I risked losing you, too. And I just couldn't let that happen. You're all I have left, Rose." He was breathing heavily now, his chest rising and falling like a stormy tide.

Rose stared at him and rubbed her temples. "I just need some space, Cole. Some time to think this over."

She stormed out the front door, slamming it in his face.

"Fuck!" he screamed.

Emmett whimpered and nuzzled his snout against Cole's hand, trying to comfort him. He screamed again and slid to the floor, falling into his dog's embrace. He took deep breaths and tried to steady his nerves, but his brain was too wired. The neurotransmitters shot off over and over, sending a new wave of shock through his body each time.

# NOW



*MONDAY, OCTOBER 14, 2024*

THE NEXT MORNING, COLE quietly made his way into Luna's office with a to-go container from the local diner. "Here," he said, "now we're even."

"Oooooo!" Luna squealed. "One hot breakfast for one hot meltdown. I like it."

Cole's cheeks flushed with embarrassment. He still couldn't believe what had happened. He'd been angry with Luna at first for telling Rose, but once he'd had enough time to calm down and think rationally, he knew he was the one who owed her an apology.

He cleared his throat. "I'm sorry about Saturday night."

Luna peeked up through her fanned-out lashes. "It's okay."

Cole nodded, wanting to say more but not knowing how. Eventually, he settled on, "Do you know if the woman is okay? The waitress."

Luna nodded and inhaled a bite of food. "She's fine. Was a little shaken up at first, but I told her . . . about, you know . . ."

She gave him a knowing look while shoving more pancakes into her mouth.

Cole nodded. "Thanks."

"No prob." She took a sip of her coffee, and an awkward silence fell between them. "Hey, I'm sorry about telling Rose about everything."

His chest spasmed at her words, but Cole waved his hand. "Nothing to be sorry for. I should've told her about it sooner."

For a moment, he wondered if the conversation was over, but then Luna asked, "So, have you told Nate yet? About the cave?"

"I called him yesterday after the hangover wore off."

"Oh, yeah?" Luna inhaled her last bite, leaving a drop of syrup on her chin.

Cole smiled as he surveyed the smudge and took in her black-framed, cat-shaped glasses. That, paired with her red leather jacket, reminded him of a superhero's alter ego. Weird, but she pulled it off.

*Focus.*

He cleared his throat and thought back to the task at hand. "He said he was going to talk to the editorial staff this morning about whether they want me to livestream it from our social pages, or if we should broadcast the event on TV."

"I feel like a social livestream would be more discreet."

"That's what I said, but ratings have been down at the station."

Luna twisted in her seat. "Yeah, but this is your story. Don't let them take this from you."

"I would still be doing the write-ups for print and online."

"Yeah, but Z chose *you*, Cole. Not Jason or Lydia."

He glanced at her before looking at the floor. "Yeah, I guess . . ."

She stood up, brushing crumbs off her pants in the process. "Come on. Let's talk to Nate. We need to livestream this bish."

He cocked an eyebrow as a lightness filled the air. "Do you ever cuss?"

"Not really, no."

He shook his head and smirked. "All right, let's go talk to him then, bish."

"Don't call me that."

An hour later, Cole and Luna emerged victorious from Nate's office. He had agreed to send Greyson with Cole and Luna Friday night, and he would set them up on a multistreaming app to broadcast to all their social channels. Then, he'd hand the phone off to Cole, and Luna would photograph the event, per usual. Cole wasn't thrilled about the idea of spending the night with Greyson, but if it meant completing the task so he could meet Z, he'd do it.

When Cole returned to his desk, he pulled out his phone to look up more details on the haunted house, but he was surprised to see a text from Rose.

**Rose:** *Why didn't you tell me, Cole?*

He scoffed, irritation lining his thoughts.

**Cole:** *Why do you think? I knew you'd react like this, and I didn't want to risk losing you.*

A pause, and then the typing bubbles reappeared on the screen.

**Rose:** *I just want you to be well. And be honest with me.*

**Cole:** *And I'm trying, Rose. I really am. I'm doing everything you've asked. I don't know what else to do.*

**Rose:** *You could start by telling me the truth.*

Cole's nostrils flared. Had he not just told her why he made the decision to omit this one small, miserable detail of his life? He started to type out a somewhat angry response, but after rereading it three times, he changed his mind and clicked the phone shut.

He loved Rose so much, but this was starting to get exhausting. For the first time, he wondered if their relationship was worth saving.

# NOW



*Friday, October 18, 2024*

Eager for a distraction from his personal life, Cole buried himself in work for the next four days. He needed to prep for the last task, and writing had always cleared his head. When five o'clock finally rolled around Friday evening, he felt both relieved and energetic.

He shot off a quick text to Sol confirming their plans and smirked when the singer sent back a series of moon, camping, and thumbs-up emojis. Cole grabbed his things and headed home to feed Emmett before switching out his work clothes for comfier ones, including his signature ball cap his grandpa had gifted him.

At seven on the dot, Cole pulled into the parking lot at Scare Minerals Scream Park. He had two hours until Z's stunt, and one until he met Luna, Sol, and Greyson. He supposed he could have waited until the others arrived, but he was too anxious. What else was he going to do—sit in his house and wait?

He opened his car door and stepped onto the pavement, a chill crawling up his spine as a breeze rolled by. Pausing, he pulled up the weather app on his phone and cursed when he saw the temperature was supposed to drop into the forties that night. It was mid-October, so he should've expected this, but Mother Nature had a bad habit of doing the unexpected in the Midwest.

Clicking his tongue, Cole rummaged through the backseat of his Jeep and breathed a sigh of relief when he found an old leather jacket his parents had gifted him a few Christmases ago. He shrugged it on and then turned to face the scream park once again.

Scare Minerals was a haunted attraction carved out of an abandoned cave, and it drew thousands of people every season. It had a reputation for being one of the scarier haunted houses and had even been featured in a few national blogs and magazines.

Cole hadn't been since River was fourteen when she begged him and Rose to let her go alone with a group of friends. They didn't feel comfortable letting her go without them, so they agreed to drive her there and hang out by the vendor tents while she went through the haunted hollow.

Now, staring at the entrance three years later, he felt a familiar pang in his chest as he worked to harden his emotions. He didn't have time for that tonight.

"How many tickets will you need tonight, sir?" the attendant asked as Cole approached.

"Just one." He pulled out his wallet and paid the woman before stepping out of the way to put on his wristband.

Once inside the park, he surveyed his surroundings, trying to re-familiarize himself with everything. The grand cave entrance itself stood at the heart of it all, its solid peaks and valleys remaining unchanged, but the rest of the park had certainly undergone a revamp. Cole wandered farther in, pulling his notepad out and taking notes as he went.

*Face painting*

*Balloon artists*

*Gift shop (new)*

*Revamped outdoor bar*

*DJ*

*Food trucks*

He jotted everything down and then tucked his pencil behind his ear. He still had a little time before the others would arrive, so after a minute of mulling it over, he decided to venture through the cave to get a better lay of the land before the real event started.

*Better to get it over with now.*

He looked at his phone, double-checking the time, and then walked back to the front and hopped in line.

*"Dad, you're embarrassing me!"*

*"What? You don't want your friends to know your old man can still scare the pants off of you?"*

Cole's chest tightened, the memory hitting him out of nowhere.

*River covered her face and groaned. "Stop! Mom, do something about him."*

*Rose giggled and tugged at Cole's arm. "Come on, hun. She'll hate us forever if we don't go away."*

Silence rang through his ears as he struggled to breathe.

*He stuck his tongue out at his daughter and then winked before turning away. "I suppose you're right. Come on, baby. River Bug, we'll be browsing the vendor tents if you need us."*

*Eyes widening, River said, "Yeah, I know. You've told me like, a hundred times, Dad. Bye!"*

"Sir? Next in line, please."

Cole heard the person murmuring, but he couldn't open his mouth to respond.

*He watched as his not-so-little girl entered the cave, and he squeezed his wife. "We're so lucky we get to raise her."*

"Sir? Are you okay?"

Cole felt a hand on his arm, and he jerked, his vision coming back to present day.

"Y—yes," he stammered. "Sorry."

"You're holding up the line, sir. Are you going in?"

Cole shook his head. "No. Thanks." He ducked out of line and tore into the bathrooms, scaring a little boy in the process. "Sorry, 'scuse me," was all he could manage before he vomited in the first stall.

He wiped off his mouth with toilet paper and then fell to the floor, clutching his chest.

*Breathe, dammit.*

His panting grew quicker as he neared hyperventilation territory. What was the grounding exercise the therapist had taught him? He tried to think as he gasped for air.

*Facts. Name facts.*

"My name is Cole."

He wrapped his arms around his knees and rocked back and forth.

"I'm in a bathroom."

*Inhale. Exhale.*

"I'm wearing a hat."

*Again.*

"I'm sitting on the floor."

*Last one.*

"I puked."

He took slow, steadying breaths as his pulse stabilized, and he suddenly wished he'd brought Emmett.

After another few deep breaths, Cole stood and flushed the contents of his stomach down the toilet. He shuddered as a chill wrapped down his spine, and then he exited the stall, embarrassment and shame written across his face.

How many people had seen him this time? And he hadn't even been drinking.

He approached the sinks and turned on the water, waiting for it to turn hot. Once it was near boiling temperatures, he splashed some on his face and let the burn soothe his pain.

This was not how he'd anticipated the night going.

After he'd collected himself enough to face the crowd again, he stepped out of the bathroom and pulled out his phone. It was a quarter to eight by now, which meant Luna would be here soon. Cole took a deep breath and contemplated his next move. He didn't know if he could do this.

*"Oof!"* A woman bumped into him, knocking his stance and almost causing him to fall. He caught his balance in the knick of time but couldn't say the same for his phone, which landed in a puddle.

"Oh, I'm so sorry!"

Cole reached for his phone and extracted it from the muddy drainage.

*Great. Just fucking great.*

He looked up to see who the woman responsible was, but she'd already run off, Cole realized, in pursuit of a child. He hung his head in defeat as he realized he couldn't even be mad.

Because he had been there before.

He understood.

Groaning, he used his sleeve to dry off the device as best he could and then stuffed it back in his pocket. He'd deal with it later.

Making an executive decision, he trudged off toward the food truck to find Luna.

# NOW



"HOLY PINEAPPLES, THIS IS so good," Luna said between bites.

It hadn't taken Cole long to find her. She was already seated at a picnic table with a tray of food when he arrived, a familiar face positioned across from her.

"Leave it to Americans to stuff a taco in a bag and call it a meal," Sol said. "Bloody brilliant."

Luna rolled her eyes. "Seriously. This is the best walking taco I've ever had. Cole, you have to get one. It goes great with the chili."

He shook his head, his stomach still rumbling from earlier. "I'm not hungry."

"Fine, suit yourself." Luna shrugged and continued to stuff her face.

"Is Greyson here?" Cole asked, changing the subject.

Luna swiped her face. "I haven't seen him."

"Who's Greyson?"

Cole turned to the rock star. "A coworker. Our social manager, actually. He's supposed to meet us here to help livestream the event." He paused, remembering his phone, and then turned his head toward Luna. "Actually, we may need to use your phone. Somebody bumped into me earlier, and I dropped mine in a puddle of mud."

"Oh, shiz," she said. "That sucks."

"No kidding."

"Yeah, sure, you can use mine. Just don't go through my nudies." Cole's mouth fell open as warmth flushed his cheeks, and Sol choked on his water. "Hah! I'm kidding," Luna said. "You two should've seen your faces."

She stood to go empty her tray, and Cole worked to compose his face.

"I like that one," Sol said. "She's got spunk."

Cole side-eyed him and opened his mouth to respond but was interrupted.

"Luna says you broke your phone, Grandpa."

*Greyson.*

"Someone bumped into me," was all Cole offered.

Sol looked at him with wide eyes. "Cole, you're not a grandpa, are you?"

Luna cut in before Cole could respond. "No, Greyson here just has an infatuation with older men."

"Do not," Greyson snapped.

"Do too," Luna mouthed.

Cole rubbed his eyes. "Can we just get started? Z said the event was at nine."

Greyson rolled his eyes and turned to Luna. "Here, give me your phone. I need to give you access to our Facebook account. Once you're live, I can go in from the app on my phone and multistream it to the other platforms. Then, you'll be good to go."

"What happens if the connection gets interrupted?" Cole asked. He didn't have a chance to check the signal in the cave.

"I'll stay with you guys, so if you have any technical difficulties, just hand the phone to me, and I'll fix it. But I see Instagram stories from this place all the time. I think the connection will be fine."

Cole nodded and then tuned them out as Sol proceeded to ask Greyson about his taste in men. He needed a clear head for this task, and his heart was still beating out of rhythm from the panic attack. And then another thought occurred to him: what if he had another episode *on camera*?

His eyes grew wide at the thought.

*Luna.*

He needed her help.

"Hey," he said, grabbing her wrist as they made their way back toward the cave. "If something happens to me, while . . . while we're in there, I need you to take the phone."

She looked at him with a question written on her face. "What do you mean?"

He hesitated, struggling to find the words. "Earlier, I, um." He cleared his throat, his eyes roving over the haunted decorations. This was the last thing he wanted to talk about. "I used to bring my daughter here when she was younger."

She brushed her hair out of her face. "Oh. Yes, yes, of course. Just throw it my way. I'll handle it."

Cole breathed a sigh of relief, grateful for her help. "Thank you."

"No problem." She smiled softly and then continued walking.

*Okay*, Cole thought, *you can do this.*

He followed after her and the others, eager to find out what Zanella had in store for them.

"THIS SHIT BETTER BE good." Sol took off his star-shaped sunglasses and squinted into the cave.

They were standing at the foot of the entrance with another group of attendees, many of whom looked like college-aged kids.

"It's Zanella," Luna said. "It's always good." She handed her phone to Cole. "Here, Greyson has it all set up. All you have to do is tap this button to start."

Since nobody knew what Z's plan was, they had decided to go live before entering the cave and spin it as a Halloween feature. Cole would take the audience through a virtual tour of Scare Minerals from start to finish, and if they happened to capture a live performance piece from America's greatest underground artist, then that was an added bonus.

"I hate being on camera," Cole said.

Luna blew a loose hair out of her face. "Yeah, well, tough nubs."

He rolled his eyes at her and then lifted the phone and tapped "Go Live."

*Help your ole man out tonight, Riv.*

"Good evening, Suttonville. This is Cole Sloane reporting live from Scare Minerals Scream Park. I'm here with a few colleagues of mine, and we're going to take you inside the depths of Ohio's most popular haunted attraction tonight."

He rambled on for a few more minutes, waiting for viewers to hop on. Once the audience was built up enough, Greyson gave Cole a nod, indicating he was now multistreaming across all of their social channels. Cole answered a few questions from the comments, and then their group attendant announced it was time to begin.

"Here we go, folks," Cole said. "Who's ready to be scared?"

He smiled at the camera as a plethora of comments and reactions streamed in. Cole waved one final time and then flipped the screen on the camera so the audience could see what was happening.

"Ladies and gentlemen," the tour guide yelled, "we are about to embark on an adventure through one of Ohio's oldest caves, where legend has it that runaway inmates from the local psychiatric hospital would seek asylum."

"Oooooo, this sounds fun." Luna squeezed Cole's arm.

"Here, their spirits dwell in a state of unrest, and it is up to you to come out of this alive. Because let me tell ya, these monsters are angry, and they're ready for a new form of medicine."

Cole's gut twisted as a sinister feeling snaked its way into the atmosphere. He shuddered and checked the WiFi connection.

"I must warn you," the attendant said as he gestured toward the black shadow of an entrance, "that once you cross this line, there's no going back. If any of you are too afraid, now's your chance to turn around."

A chorus of screams erupted from inside the narrow path, and a little girl at the back of the line cried, "I changed my mind, Mommy!"

Others laughed, but Cole's heart ached at the sound; he tuned them out as the child's screams wailed all the way out.

"Anyone else?" The attendant cast his eyes over the group. "Okay, then. Well, may I welcome you to *Fright Night*!"

Cole jumped as Michael Myers' theme song blasted through the speakers. It was now pitch black—with the exception of a red light that lined the walking path. Then, Cole heard the employees rolling out the signature stone that blocked the exit. Immediately, he sensed someone new behind him, and he braced himself for whatever monsters lurked inside.

APPROXIMATELY TWENTY SCREAMS LATER, Cole's anxiety was seeping through his pores. The cave was set up like a maze, and the tour guide had already escorted them through three scenes with no sign of Zanella. Cole wanted to ask Luna and the others if they'd noticed anything peculiar—other than the screaming, bloodied actors, but he couldn't risk discussing it while he was still live on the internet.

They were coming up on a new scene now, which Cole had determined to be a hospital room.

*I can't see!*

*Is that an evil nurse?*

*These ppl r crazy*

*Mental health is wealth y'all #bet*

*I wanna go!*

Viewers continued to flood the comment section, but Cole ignored them. His senses were on high alert as they got closer to the actors.

"Is that a pregnant person?" Luna whispered in Cole's ear.

His eyes widened at the thought. He didn't remember this from years past. Surely that wasn't a real pregnant woman, right?

*"My body, my choice! My body, my choice!"* The actress chanted the words on repeat as she rocked back and forth on a makeshift delivery table.

*"My body, my choice! My body, my choice!"*

Cole glanced at Luna, and although it was dark, they managed to make eye contact.

"Z," Luna mouthed.

Cole nodded and nudged his way to the front of the crowd, double-checking the video's connection as he went.

"Time for your procedure, Mary!" An unhinged doctor popped out of the dark, and the audience screamed.

*"My body, my choice! My body, my choice!"*

"Or maybe we should take a volunteer from the audience!" The doctor-actor inched toward the crowd with a collection of bloody surgical tools. "Who wants to help me?"

An evil laugh erupted from him, and then the pregnant woman jumped up from the table and attempted to tackle him.

*"Help me!"* she bellowed, which elicited a few laughs, as well as screams.

"Come on!" the tour guide yelled. "We better get out of here before they capture us."

Cole's shoulders slumped as he realized this wasn't Zanella—just a weird twist on an old scary movie. He turned to follow the group down the tunnel to the next performance, but that's when the power went out.

Screams erupted through the cave, and a teenage boy in their group said, "Show us something really scary this time!"

The attendant paused and glanced around.

*What's happening??*

*OMG this place looks sick*

*It's not even that scary.*

*I can't see anything ughhhhh*

Cole shone the light from his phone around the group as viewer comments continued to roll in. He couldn't see much, but the device did provide enough light for Cole to see the look of pure panic on the attendant's face.

This was not part of the program.

A large boom sounded deeper within the cave, and adrenaline rushed through Cole's body. He looked back at Sol, who was also livestreaming this for his Instagram followers, and they nodded at each other before racing down the path.

"Hey! Where are you going?"

Cole ignored the employee and kept moving with Sol, Luna, and Greyson hot on his tail. He could hear more sounds as they wound through the maze of black tunnels.

"I hope you blokes are ready for a wild ride," Sol said to his camera.

At last, Cole rounded another corner and stopped dead in his tracks.

"I think we found it," he said with a hoarse rasp.

"Is that—" Luna started.

"Oh, shit," Sol said.

"What the cinnamon toast fuck is this?" Greyson blurted.

A circular display of large glass tubes sat in the middle of a clear opening. Cole squinted and held the phone up, trying to see what was inside of them. It looked like . . .

*No*, he thought. *It couldn't be.*

But it could.

He edged closer and confirmed the glass cylinders were test tubes, each showcasing a fetus in utero. They were backlit with pink and blue lighting to represent gender, and as he took another step forward, he noted they were all varying gestations.

*Oh, fuck.*

"Luna," he said as he thrust the phone toward her.

She grabbed it from him and walked closer to inspect the display while Cole clutched his stomach in the corner.

Just when he thought Zanella couldn't take it any further, he does some shit like this.

Cole was both disgusted and fascinated by the man.

He wiped the back of his mouth for the second time that night and then straightened. He took a deep breath and turned back to face the display. "Here." He held out a hand as he walked back to Luna. "I'm good now. Thanks."

She opened her mouth to respond, but the same familiar siren from the previous events started beeping overhead.

*ARE THOSE BABIES*

*What the fuck*

*Somebody stop this!*

*Best haunted house ever!*

Cole turned the camera back to forward-facing and yelled, "I don't think this is part of the act! Hang tight, guys."

A burst of screams sounded from above Cole's head, and he turned the camera around quickly to catch whatever it was.

"Holy mother!" Luna yelled.

Cole cringed as a group of deranged doctors, nurses, and—presum-ably—mothers dropped from the ceiling. They must've each been attached to individual wires from what Cole could tell, because everyone fell at a different rate.

"That was my *baby!*"

"They said the shot was safe!"

"It was all in the name of science!"

"The government took my baby!"

"I wanted the payout!"

*Holy shit, Z.*

"He really went there," Luna said, her camera in hand and eyes wide.

One by one, the actors screamed their antics into the air as they continued to drop to the ground. Once they'd landed on the cave's dirt floors, Cole watched as they slowly crawled onto the same platform as the fetuses. Some hugged the test tubes while others rolled into the center and cried.

"What the hell?"

Cole's head snapped backward at the sound of a new voice.

An employee, he figured. He glanced around now and realized others in the cave had wandered over and discovered the art.

"Who authorized this?" the man shouted.

*"My body, my choice! My body, my choice!"*

Cole's heart sank to his stomach as he saw the pregnant woman from earlier barrel through with a fire torch in hand. Up close, she looked to be in her late teens or early twenties.

The same age Rose was when they had River.

Cole's chest knotted as the woman waddled onto the stage, followed by the doctor who'd been in the scene with her.

*"My body, my choice! My body, my choice!"* Her voice echoed through the cavern walls.

And then Siri's imitation voice projected over the speakers.

*"Vaccination is recommended for all people aged six months and older. This includes people who are pregnant, breastfeeding, trying to get pregnant now, or those who might become pregnant in the future."*

"Oh, fucking tits," Sol said from somewhere behind Cole. "Vaccines and reproductive rights all wrapped up in one. The bloke has a death wish."

*"It was my body and my choice,"* the pregnant woman yelled. *"And now, my baby is dead!"*

Bile crept up Cole's throat again.

"Lu—"

She grabbed the phone from him, before he could even finish.

And then the pregnant woman winked at everyone before lifting her shirt and allowing the doctor to slice her belly open. Gasps hit the air as an infant rolled out of her stomach and dropped to the ground, hanging only by the umbilical cord.

It did not cry.

# NOW



Cole lost count of how many times he threw up that night. After the man started extracting the baby, Cole ran for the exit, his lungs desperate for fresh air.

"Here." Luna handed him a bottle of water some odd hours later.

*It must be after midnight*, Cole thought.

"Thanks." He accepted the drink and gulped it down.

"Greyson said the video is already going viral. You did good, Cole. We got it."

His body stiffened as he thought about the horrors he'd just witnessed. "I can't stop . . . picturing it."

"I know," Luna said. "Me neither."

Cole rubbed his face and pulled his phone out of his pocket.

*Fuck.*

He forgot about dropping it.

"We can get it fixed in the morning. I know a guy," Luna said, shoving her hands in her jacket pockets.

Cole looked at her and cocked an eyebrow. "You know a guy?"

"Mhm," she said, shaking her head. "My uncle owns one of those computer/cell phone stores. He can fix it for you."

"Oh. Okay, yeah, thanks."

"No sweat," she said, sitting down on the sidewalk beside him.

Cole glanced at her as she stretched out her legs and yawned. She had been so wonderful to him throughout all this, and he hadn't even stopped to consider the emotional toll it'd taken on her. "Hey, Luna," he started.

"Yeah?"

The words caught in his throat. He hated that his mental illness and grief affected the people in his life, especially her. They'd grown close lately, and he'd realized she carried such a lightness in her heart. Cole didn't want his darkness to dampen that.

"Thank you. For everything."

She smiled at him and tucked a strand of blonde hair behind her ear. "I lost my little sister when she was just a baby. I know it's not the same as a child, but . . . I think about her all the time."

Her words hit him like a ton of bricks.

"I—I'm so sorry, Luna. I had no idea."

She waved her hand. "How could you have? I never talk about her."

Cole let her words sink in. Did she want to talk about her now?

"What . . . happened to her?"

"She had a heart defect," Luna said simply. "The doctors tried everything, but in the end, there was nothing they could do. She passed in my mother's arms at three months old. It's actually why I've decided to never have kids. It's possible I'm a carrier for the disease, and I just . . . I can't imagine going through that experience as a parent. It was hard enough as a sibling."

Cole looked at her, and for the first time, he saw sadness etched in her face. He didn't think about what he did next, just acted on impulse.

His arms wrapped around her in a warm embrace, and although he felt her stiffen at first, her body quickly relaxed as she sank into him.

Maybe they were friends after all.

THE NEXT MORNING, COLE took Emmett with him to meet Luna at her uncle's repair shop, which was in a quaint town just outside city limits. He normally enjoyed the area's quiet nature, but today was their annual fall festival.

And Cole *hated* fall festivals.

He had fully intended on ditching as soon as he could, but after learning it would take at least an hour to repair his phone, Luna had insisted they partake in the festivities. He'd agreed to oblige her, but now, as he strolled the overcrowded streets with the same, run-of-the-mill craft vendors and tacky food trucks, he felt instant regret.

"They're just so . . . basic," he said as Luna scarfed down a funnel cake.

"And so what if they are?"

"I don't know . . ." He pondered her question before responding, "I guess I just don't get the appeal. They're overrated."

Luna feigned a gasp. "Cole Sloane, you are hereby banished from the Motley County Fall Fest until further notice."

He cocked an eyebrow and shook his head before reaching down to adjust Emmett's harness. A simple collar would not do for the oversized teddy bear with all the food here.

"Here, buddy." Luna tore off a piece of her fried dough. "You can have another treat."

Cole didn't tell her he was supposed to be on a diet. The vet had recommended he lose weight to help relieve pressure on his joints, but the dog just loved food so much it seemed too harsh a reality to restrict him from all human foods.

"So, have you talked to Nate?" Luna asked as she scratched Emmett's ears.

Cole shook his head. "Nope. Phone's broken, remember?"

"Oh, derp," she replied with a giggle. "My bad."

Cole shrugged and continued walking. "You said the video went viral, though, so I'm not worried about it. I'll do my write-up Monday morning, and he can worry about working it in."

Luna stopped at a nearby tent, eyeing a macramé plant holder. "I sent him my photos this morning just to get it out of the way. Last night was . . ."

"Brutal," Cole finished for her.

"Yeah."

They resumed somewhat comfortable silence for the next few minutes as Luna shopped and Cole recollected his thoughts. He knew he needed to start working through the next piece of the puzzle to determine the new password for Zanella's website, but he was drained from the previous night's events. After the stillborn child had rolled out of its mother's womb, the makeshift doctor cut the umbilical cord and stuffed the baby into an empty test tube beside the others. Cole had watched in horror as the other actors simply rolled away into the depths of the cave, leaving the macabre display as the only evidence of their presence.

Shuddering, he turned back around to see where Luna had gone, but just then, a blue reflection caught his eye. He paused and honed in on the item, waiting for his vision to clear. Upon further inspection, he realized he was staring at an Alexandrite ring. His heart ached as River's birthstone glared back at him.

"That's pretty," Luna said, catching Cole's attention.

He cleared his throat. "Yeah."

That was all he could manage.

Luna picked up the ring and tried it on. "Well, it's too little for me, but I'm sure someone else will find it lovely." She waved to the woman behind the register and proceeded to the next booth.

Cole looked at her then and realized she was shivering.

"Are you cold?"

"Oh, I'm fine."

Cole analyzed the goosebumps on her arms. "Here," he said, shrugging off his jacket, "take this."

"Oh, no, no, I'm fine." She tried to reject the garment but ultimately failed in the end. "Well, thanks. I appreciate that."

"No problem," Cole said with a soft smile.

"Ope, somebody's FaceTiming me I think?" Luna said more as a question. She pulled her phone out and laughed when she saw the name. "Solstice Blackwood, how very noble of you to FaceTime a fan."

Now it was Cole's turn to nudge his shoulder next to hers for a change. "What's up, Sol?"

"Mate, have you seen the text?" He blurted the words as beads of sweat rolled down his forehead.

"No?"

"Ah, bloody hell." He bent over and grabbed his knees. Had he been running? "He wants—us—to go back to the brewery."

Cole glanced at Luna, who returned his questioning gaze.

"What did the text say?" she asked.

"Your final instructions lie with the fox. Don't let it sneak up on brew."

"Wait—" Cole started.

"Holy crap," Luna interrupted with a laugh. "Did that psycho just make a pun?"

"Right?" Sol looked at the screen again and offered a shit-eating grin. "It's a bit wild, innit? Z has a sense of humor after all."

Cole's eyes widened as reality set in. "We have to go back."

"No, duh," Luna said.

"That's what I've been trying to tell you," Sol said with an exaggerated breath. "I got the text during me morning run."

Cole noted the time on Luna's phone. "It's one in the afternoon."

"Yeah, time for me morning run, just like I said," Sol repeated without so much as a pause.

Luna snorted, and Cole rolled his eyes.

"I'm going to freshen up a bit and then head there," Sol said.

"All right," Cole said, "I just need to grab my phone. Want us to meet you there?"

"Does the Pope drink on Sunday, mate?"

"I don't think he does."

Sol groaned. "Ahh! Come on, Coley, you know what I meant. Yes! I will see you blokes there in an hour."

# NOW



*Saturday, October 19, 2024*

Approximately six high-pitched squeals and an uncategorized number of questions later, Cole and Luna rolled into the parking lot at Forest Fox Brewing Co., yet again. Cole was nervous to go, mostly because he was worried the staff would recognize him from last weekend's episode, but also because the final piece of the puzzle was about to lock into place. Only twelve days stood between him and this elusive Halloween art gala, and Cole could hardly stand it. He was ready to meet Zanella and find closure in this chapter of his life.

"I don't know if they allow dogs," Luna said, throwing her hair up in a messy topknot and shrugging on a tattered flannel.

Cole shrugged in response. "I have paperwork for him as an ESA pet. It'll be fine."

Luna's eyes widened. "Oh." Then a beat later, "You never told me that before."

Cole shrugged again. "I didn't think it was relevant. I don't always need him."

She continued to stare at him and then looked down at Emmett. "Well," she finally said, clearing her throat, "looks like you're having a big adventure today."

Emmett panted and wagged his tail at her before jutting off behind Cole's footsteps. Once inside, they saw Sol wave a hand from one of the round hightops near the bar, a drink already in hand.

Sol's eyes widened as he noticed Emmett. "What the devil is that thing?"

"My dog," Cole said flatly.

"He looks like a horse!" He made an exaggerated face and scooted away from Emmett.

"Wait," Luna said with a laugh. "Are you scared? Of this big teddy bear?" She looked at Cole. "This is rich. We're gonna have so much fun with this. Come here, Em!" She motioned for the dog to come closer to her, and Sol screamed.

Cole smirked. "He's harmless, I can assure you. Now," he said, shifting gears, "the text said our final instructions would be here. Last time, it was the name of a cocktail. So, maybe there's something else on the menu that will give us a clue."

Sol shook his head, taking a sip of his beer. "Ahh, that's so vague. I'm willing to bet the bastard left instructions with a person or written out somewhere like the bathroom!"

"I can check the women's restroom," Luna said.

"Okay." Cole nodded. "Great. Sol, you check the men's. I'll talk to the waitress when she comes back and see if she knows anything."

Sol and Luna nodded and then headed off toward the bathrooms. Cole focused his energy back on the task at hand, his body buzzing with adrenaline and his thoughts seemingly having moved on from the horrors of last night.

Emmett whined, and Cole leaned down to scratch his ears, but that's when he realized the dog wasn't whining at him. Instead, his pet was pulling him toward the connected warehouse where they brewed beer.

Cole rolled his eyes. "Emmett, we can't go back there. Emmett, sit."

When the dog didn't obey, Cole tugged at his harness with extra force. "We can't go back there, bud. Come on, sit. Sit!"

Emmett whimpered again, desperation seeping from his jowls.

Cole was about to flag down the waitress to ask about Zanella—and order a snack for Emmett—when the mastiff took off without Cole's permission, dragging his human with him.

"Dammit, Emmett!" Cole tried to regain control over his pet, but the dog was too strong. At two hundred pounds, Emmett could do whatever he wanted when he put his mind to it.

"Em, come here!" Cole hissed as he tried—and failed—once again to pull the dog's harness. "Emmett, what are you—"

Cole's voice cut off as he tumbled through the staff-only door and saw what Emmett had been pulling him toward.

"What the fuck?" His jaw dropped open as his face twisted in both horror and amusement.

Emmett whined in response.

*See, Dad.*

Cole stood in the midst of the brewery's warehouse. A few employees lurked up ahead, but none had seemed to notice him or Emmett, or the large swarm they'd encountered—literally.

With shaking hands, Cole took out his phone to take a picture and then called Luna.

"Why are you calling me?"

"Warehouse. Through the double doors. Now."

He hung up and then slid the device back into his pocket, still bewildered by the sight. In front of him, rows of tall, see-through brewing kettles filled the room, but the one that caught Cole's attention was the honey-colored batch to the left of the entrance.

"Oh." Cole heard the voice before he saw it. Luna had walked through the doors, Sol trailing close behind.

"Are those . . . fucking *bumblebees*, mate?" Sol shook his head and scrunched his face, a coat of fear stretched across his skin. "Oh, dear. No, no, no. I don't like bees. Uh uh—I do *not* like bees."

Luna cocked an eyebrow at him and then turned to Cole, who had moved closer to inspect the kettle. The pot buzzed in disarray as a colony of bees flew every which way, fighting to escape.

Cole's eyes darted to the top and scanned the makeshift lid that had trapped them before letting his gaze fall to the bottom. There, a broken beehive lay smashed in the center, and a piece of honeycomb floated in the beer.

"Someone must have just done this," Luna said. "There's no way those bees would still be alive otherwise." She crouched down to get a better view of the hive, and her face melted. "Such a shame. Bees are misunderstood creatures." She stood on her tiptoes, glancing around. "How have the employees not noticed this?"

"Don't know," Cole muttered half-heartedly. He was busy punching in password options into Zanella's website. This had to be it, right?

*Bee*

*bee*

*Bees*

*bees*

*Bumblebees*

*bumblebees*

After several failed attempts, though, he started to question it. "Sol, any luck?"

The singer shook his head, dark curls shaking all around him. "No, noth—OUCH!"

Cole and Luna both snapped their heads to him.

*Oh, no,* Cole thought.

"*Did I mention I hate bees?*" Sol yelled as he doubled over in pain, clutching his wrist as a bee flew off him. "Oi, I've been hit! I don't think I can go on, loves." His voice hit a high-pitched note at the tail end of his words, and Cole rolled his eyes.

*Always so dramatic.*

"You'll be fine," Luna deadpanned, shushing his wails as she grabbed Sol's phone to start typing in passwords herself. "Cole, what have you already tried?"

He rambled off the quick list of variations. Luna nodded, twisting her lips to the side. Cole watched her think as the expressions played vividly on her face. Finally, she said, "Hold on, what's the name of this beer?"

Understanding sliced through Cole's core. He gazed back at the kettle, inspecting it for a name plaque. After a minute, he said, "I don't know. I don't see one written anywhere."

Another exaggerated cry broke out from Sol. "Oh my God, I think I know."

Cole and Luna looked at each other and then at him, an obvious question written in their unified expression. "How? What is it?"

"Ughhhh, because I bloody-well *drank it*!" he hissed. "I drank bee juice. I drank *bees*." His voice cracked again on the last word, and he flailed his body forward to a sitting position.

"Sol," Luna said, snapping her fingers in his face. "Hey, focus. What was the name of your beer?"

He mumbled another slew of complaints before finally groaning, "Well I don't know how to pronounce it, so I'm going to butcher it."

"Sol!" Cole interjected this time.

"Der Keim lager," he sputtered.

Cole's fingers moved with a vengeance. It took a few tries until he spelled it correctly, but after the third attempt, the same *Access Granted* note greeted him like an eerily warm hug.

"Ahhhh!" Luna silently screamed. "You got it!!"

Cole's face glowed with pride and excitement as a grin spread across his face. Solving a lead was like getting high from your favorite cannabis strain—only better. This was a natural euphoric experience that took root deep within his veins and blossomed wildly throughout his soul.

It was a feeling Cole never wanted to lose.

Yet, it was the same one that cost him everything.

*Breathe*, he told himself.

Still in a trance, he didn't object when Luna and Sol both hovered over his shoulders while one of them hit play on the new video. Together, the trio watched as a digital invitation unfolded on screen, narrated by the familiar electronic female voice.

"Congratulations! You are cordially invited to Zanella's final act: THE GALA. Please arrive at 6 p.m., Thursday, October 31st, at the Forest Fox Brewing Co. warehouse. Attire is open to interpretation, but costumes are encouraged. Prepare for a night of living art, life, and death."

Cole looked up from the screen and felt a wave of heaviness wash over him.

*Life and death.*

"Death!" Sol said. "That's it. The bloke's finally lost his marbles."

*Life and death.*

"I—I don't know about this, you guys. Maybe we should inform the police." Luna dragged her teeth over her bottom lip, a sudden uncertainty in her voice.

*Life and death.*

"No," Cole finally said and then glanced at the two. "We do not intervene. Our mission is to capture the story—always."

"Cole," Luna pleaded, "people could die."

"Which is why we have to go. This is *the* story, Luna. The one Zanella's been waiting to tell." They couldn't risk stepping in and changing this moment in history. Absolutely not. This was Pulitzer-level shit for crying out loud. "We have to do this," he pleaded. "*I* have to do this."

And he did. Not only for his career and marriage but for River. Cole had to meet Zanella and solve this story, even if it was the last thing he did.

Luna shook her head and looked at Sol, who glanced nervously between the two of them and then said, "Well, no sense in fighting about it like me mum and dad. We've got just over a week to get our costumes ready, and no offense, but I can guarantee neither of you have the proper attire for this. Come on, I'll call my stylist." He looked at Emmett, hesitancy flooding his features. "The horse has to stay outside, though. Sorry, mate."

# NOW



Nearly an hour later, the group arrived at Sol's temporary home—a mansion-sized remote cabin on the outskirts of Rhododendron Lake. Cole had protested at first, reiterating the invitation's "open to interpretation" line, but his groans were quickly muddled once Luna was on board.

"I thought you didn't want us to go," he said to her as they followed Sol into his living room and waited for his seamstress, Belinda, to arrive.

"I didn't, still don't actually, but who would say no to a custom Solstice Blackwood masquerade costume?"

"I would," Cole deadpanned.

She rolled her eyes. "Honestly, Cole, your lack of enthusiasm is exhausting sometimes."

He let the comment slide, his eyes wandering to explore the cabin. It was more modern than he'd expected upon first glance. A wrought-iron chandelier hung from the ceiling, and the windows and walls were trimmed with black edges. Cole couldn't remember the last time he'd been inside a cabin now that he thought about it.

"How'd you find this place?" he asked Sol.

"One of my buddies told me about it." He flung himself over the back of the couch and landed on a heap of pillows. "Part of the Remote Renegade circle."

Cole was almost nervous to hear the answer but asked anyway. "What the hell is that?"

"It's a list of remote locations me and a few other celebrities share with each other—for when we need to escape."

"Like for writing?" Luna asked, joining in the conversation.

Sol shrugged. "Writing, hiding from the press, and what have you."

Cole racked his brain, trying to remember any famous people making sudden appearances in the area; he couldn't think of any. "Why've we never heard of it before?"

"Well, that would sort of spoil the fun, eh?" He winked at Cole before continuing. "And speaking of, I better not see this in one of your articles! Wrenner Scott and his crew would have my head."

"You know Wrenner Scott?!" Luna all but squealed.

"Ha!" Sol threw his head back in laughter. "Do I know Wrenner, Wrenner, chicken dinner? 'Course I do! Who do you think I got me blow problem from?"

Cole tuned out their banter and stepped outside to check on Emmett, who was lying lazily in the afternoon sun. "Hey, bud."

He walked over and sat down beside the dog. The smell of fresh pine needles and haunted rain floated into his nostrils, and a familiar memory tugged at his brain.

*"Daddy! Daddy! Can we swim in the lake, pleeeaaase? Mommy said to ask you."*

*"Oh, she did?" Cole smiled at his daughter, a twinkle of delight in his eyes.*

*"Yeah! Can we? Can we? Please!"*

*"Okay," he said, rising from his spot where he'd been reading. "But you know who lives there, right? THE LAKE MONSTER!" He chased after her, and River screamed with glee.*

The sound of River's faded laugh echoed in his head, and Cole's heart ached. He finally remembered why this place felt so familiar, yet displaced. He and Rose had taken River to a lake house once when she was a kid, maybe seven or eight—Cole couldn't remember exactly. It was supposed to be a week-long vacation before school started, but a storm hit late on the second day and completely knocked the power out.

The ache continued to throb in his chest, and he pulled out his phone, acting on impulse.

**Cole:** *Do you remember when we tried to take Riv to that lake house? The one in Kentucky?*

He wasn't sure if she'd answer, so when he saw the three little dots appear at the bottom left-hand side of the screen, his heart thumped a beat quicker.

**Rose:** *The one where the power went out and we went home early? I still can't believe they wouldn't give us our money back.*

**Cole:** *I still think we should've just stayed.*

**Rose:** *With no A/C? And a seven-year-old?*

Cole smiled. He knew she was still pissed, but never enough to deny him a conversation about their lost little girl.

**Cole:** *Yeah, I guess you're right.*

A few minutes passed before she texted back.

**Rose:** *What made you think of that?*

**Cole:** *I'm at a cabin with Solstice Blackwood.*

**Rose:** *WHAT?!*

This time he laughed—audibly—and responded with a photo of him and Emmett.

**Cole:** *He's inside with my coworker. Long story—can I tell you in person?*

He didn't realize until this moment how much he needed to see his wife. They had been doing so good up until their fight, and something gnawed inside Cole's chest as he thought about their separation reaching an end date soon. He chewed on his bottom lip and then sent a second message, desperate to make things right.

**Cole:** *Please, Rosie. I don't wanna wait until therapy. I want to explain.*

He held in a breath as he watched the three little dots reappear.

**Rose:** *Only if you agree to let me meet the rock star you're suddenly BFFs with.*

"Oh, thank God," he mumbled to himself, which warranted a curious eyebrow raise from Emmett.

He glanced back at the cabin, considering her request. It wasn't ideal, and it may be awkward, but . . . it was better than nothing.

**Cole:** *Okay. Deal. You free tonight?*

**Rose:** *I'm having people over for a bonfire. Bring him. And your coworker if you want. Jenny's going to flip when I tell her.*

Cole looked up at Emmett as her words sunk in.

*Your coworker.*

How had he not considered Luna in this equation? The skin on the back of his neck prickled.

It's not that he didn't want her to go, but he imagined things would be awkward, especially after what transpired last weekend. Plus, it somehow felt . . . inappropriate? They were just friends, but he still felt uncomfortable about the interaction for reasons he couldn't quite comprehend.

He groaned and shook his head; he was being stupid. He couldn't not invite her. That would be rude. He looked at Emmett, who gave him a solemn expression, and then typed out a quick response before he could change his mind.

**Cole:** *Sounds good. Text me the time.*

"It'll be fine," he said aloud to Emmett, if not only to reassure himself.

The dog blinked.

*If you say so.*

# NOW

*Saturday, October 19, 2024*

The sun was now setting at the lake, and Cole, Luna, and Sol were packing up to head to Rose's parents' house. They'd all met with Belinda, who carefully curated a unique look for each of them to wear at The Gala. Cole was less than thrilled about his selection, but he was too nervous to argue.

In a matter of mere hours, he was going to tell his wife about solving Zanella's last clue and pray she'd forgive him for not telling her about getting fired. Their trial separation was nearing the end, and well, even though things had been rocky, he hadn't allowed himself to think about the outcome if tonight didn't go well.

Now, not only did he have this important feat to tackle, but Sol and Luna were tagging along—the latter, a colleague-turned-friend that he should probably put some boundaries in place with.

Luna was attractive; he couldn't deny it. But that's all it was—a fleeting attraction he'd inappropriately misplaced whilst pining for Rose. She was who Cole really wanted to be with. She was his wife. And Luna was just a friend. That's all there was to it.

"Are you sure he won't bite?" Sol asked as he stared at Emmett in the back of Cole's Jeep.

Cole rolled his eyes. "You can take your own vehicle, you know."

"Yeah, but then I'd get lonely."

Luna laughed. "Well, then I guess you'll have to risk sitting next to big, bad, scary Emmett!"

The dog barked, and Sol screamed.

AFTER WHAT FELT LIKE a miserably long car ride, Cole pulled into his wife's parents' house. He turned off the ignition and took a deep breath.

"Hey," Luna said, placing a hand on his shoulder. "It'll be okay."

Cole looked at her and couldn't mask the confusion and vulnerability in his gaze.

"Rose would be silly not to take you back." She offered a soft smile and then hopped out of the vehicle, leaving Cole dumbstruck.

"She's a keeper, that one," Sol said as he made his exit.

"Which one," Cole mumbled under his breath.

Shaking off his jitters, he helped Emmett out of his seat before heading around to the back entrance, Sol and Luna in tow. He could already see smoke billowing in the wind, which meant the bonfire had started. Swallowing down the last of his nerves, Cole slowly opened the gate and led the way in.

It had been more than two years since he'd seen Bob and Margee's backyard. He and Rose had brought River over for a Labor Day barbecue, and Bob had accidentally set his grill on fire. Cole smirked, remembering how they'd ordered pizzas instead.

"Oh my *gawd*, you weren't kidding!" The shrill, high-pitched voice of his wife's best friend broke his trance-like state. "It's really Solstice Blackwood!"

Cole watched as Sol feigned a shocked reaction and then kissed Jenny's hand. "At your service, my love."

"Ahhhhhh! Rose! Where are you?"

Cole's gaze snapped up as he, too, wondered where his wife was. He took in his surroundings, surveying the crowd. Off to the left, he spotted a few women he recognized from Rose's book club chattering over too-full glasses of wine, and to the right was a group of men and women he couldn't place. Maybe relatives, or perhaps people from church.

He started to wonder if Rose was inside, but then a flash of copper-red hair caught his eye. There, next to the fire, was the mother of his child. His chest ached as the feelings of longing came flooding back.

Fuck, how he missed her.

She caught his eye and waved before setting off through the crowd. Cole felt his face flush as he watched her hair dance in the firelight before walking toward him.

"Hey, Cole." Her words melted over him like warm butter.

"Hey, Rosie."

"Ahem." Sol cleared his throat, and Cole thought about how he clearly must not be used to *not* having the spotlight on him.

"Rose, meet Solstice Blackwood."

She blushed as Sol reached out to kiss her hand, the same way he had Jenny's. "It's so nice to meet you. I loved your last album."

"Ahh, that old thing?" Sol waved his hand in dismissal. "That rubbish was for the record label. Just wait 'til you hear the shit they don't want me selling."

Rose giggled and then turned to Luna. "It's nice to see you again, Luna."

"Likewise," Luna said. "Although this time it's under better circumstances."

*Ouch.*

Cole felt her words punch him in the gut.

"Yes, well." Rose looked at Cole and cocked an eyebrow. "Don't speak too soon. There's enough booze at this party to start an explosion."

"Ha ha," Cole said, the awkward tension radiating through the air.

*A drink does sound good, though . . .*

He shook off the thought and focused his attention back to the two women in front of him. "I thought you said you were just having a few people over."

"Well, that was the plan, but once this one"—she jabbed her thumb at Jenny—"blabbed about Solstice coming, everyone wanted to come."

"Well, I can't say I blame 'em," Sol said to a blushing Jenny. "How about you and I get a drink, darlin', and then I'll play you one of those little numbers I mentioned earlier."

Cole rolled his eyes as Jenny, a thirty-something-year-old woman, fangirled over the eyelined musician.

"Do you mind if I grab a bite to eat?" Luna asked Rose.

"Of course not. Go, help yourself, please."

"Thanks!" She winked at Cole and then skipped off to the buffet, leaving him and Rose alone at last.

"So, you just have a habit of befriending rock stars these days?"

"Uh, something like that." Cole shoved his hands in his pockets in an effort to stave off his anxiety. He needed to talk to her now that the anger had dissipated between them. "Do you think we could go somewhere more private?"

Rose made eye contact with him for a beat too long before responding. "Okay. Let's go inside."

Cole felt his shoulders relax at her acceptance, and then he followed her inside. "Are your parents here?"

"No." She shook her head as she led him toward the front of the house and into the sunroom. "They're on a cruise. Won't be home until Monday."

Cole laughed. "Mom and Dad are away, and Rose throws a party. Sounds just like old times."

She gave him a smirk. "I guess some things never change, huh?"

Cole smiled to himself and fiddled with the hood strings on his pullover. He felt a weird mixture of relief, comfort, and anxiety thrum through his veins. This is the moment he'd been waiting for. Tonight, he'd tell her about Zanella's final invitation to The Gala, beg for her forgiveness, and hopefully have her back home in his arms and in their bed tonight.

"Rose—"

"Cole—"

They both paused and shared an awkward laugh between them. "Sorry," she said. "You go first."

Cole nodded, and before he knew it, he had spewed out a chaotic string of sentences, rehashing the details of the firing, The Gala invitation, his poorly thought-out decision to hide it from her, the events since—all of it. When he finished updating her, she breathed a mere, "Wow," and clutched her chest.

"I know," Cole responded. "I'm so, so sorry I lied to you, Rose. I just didn't know what else to do."

She looked up at him through soft lashes. "So, are you going to go? To this gala?"

He stared at her, unsure of how to respond. He had to if he wanted to keep his job, never mind the fact this was something he desperately wanted to do, but the way she was looking at him . . .

"Not if you don't want me to."

Rose held his gaze. "You'd really throw it all away, after all that, for me?"

He answered without hesitation. "Of course I would, Rosie. You're my everything." He would be devastated, yes, but he knew at that moment the heartache of losing his wife would be far greater than that of losing the story.

Tears brimmed her eyes. "Oh, Cole. But what if it's dangerous?"

He shook his head. "No, it won't be dangerous for me or the other story-tellers. He needs us there, to capture whatever it is he's been working on." Of course, Cole couldn't say the same for the participants, but he didn't voice that concern. "And once this is all said and done," he continued, "I'll have a stable career again, babe. The stories I write about this . . . they could open Pulitzer Prize doors. I mean, my career will be set for life. I'll likely have multiple offers streaming in, so we could even move if you want."

"Yes, but success is fleeting, Cole. And what happens when this is all over? When Zanella's revealed himself?"

"What do you mean? I'll just . . . move on to the next story." But even as he said it, he felt an odd sense of discomfort settle over him.

He'd been focused on Zanella for so long he really hadn't thought about what life looked like post-Z.

"I don't know." Rose turned around and walked toward the wall of windows lining the street. "I mean, I'm happy you're feeling better for right now, but . . ." She turned back to face him. "Is it enough?"

Cole wrinkled his brow. "What do you mean?"

"I mean," she started, "am I enough for you? Can I be enough for you this time once Zanella is gone?" Her lip quivered on the last word, and for a moment, they stood in the quiet, letting the unspoken words rest between them.

Finally, Cole cleared his throat and looked at her with earnest eyes. "Of course. Of course you're enough for me, Rosie. You always have been. Even when I didn't know how to show it."

She opened her mouth to respond, but a sob escaped instead. Cole moved to her and wrapped his arms around her, not caring about the awkwardness between them.

"Shh—shh, it's okay." He brushed his hand over her hair and tucked her head under his chin. "It's okay, baby."

"No, I—I'm so sorry." She pushed off him and turned away. "I shouldn't have—"

"Hey," Cole said, stepping back around her. "It's okay, Rosie. I promise, things are going to be better this time."

She looked down at the dated shag carpet in her parent's house. "No, Cole, there's . . . something I need to tell you."

"What is it?" He looked at her quizzically. "You can tell me, Rose. Anything. I promise, we'll work through it."

She broke out in another round of sobs. "I—don't—think—you—understand."

Concern brushed at the edge of Cole's thoughts. "Rose, what is it?" He ran through his mind, trying to think of anything that would have upset her this badly. "Is it your parents? Are you worried about what they'll think? I can talk to them—no, *we* can talk to them together."

Rose shook her head. "No, it's not that."

"Then, what is it?" He put his finger on her chin and gently lifted it to meet his gaze. "What's wrong, Rosie?"

She sniffled one last time and then said the words that would break Cole's heart forever.

# THEN



*FRIDAY, NOVEMBER 17, 2006*

"CLASS DISMISSED! ENJOY YOUR Thanksgiving break, but don't forget to work on your Watergate evaluation papers. I really want you to dig deep and think about the ethical dilemmas Bernstein and Woodward faced and what you would have done if given the same opportunity. They're due first thing Monday morning when you get back!" Cole's professor took off his glasses and grinned at everyone. "Well, go on, get out of here! I've got a week's worth of food to help my wife cook."

The class erupted in a chorus of hoots and hollers as they filed out of the room and into the university's student center. Cole dug his hands in his pocket and pulled out his Razr flip phone to call Rose. He'd been trying to see her all week, but she'd been dodging his calls, leaving a sickening feeling in his gut.

When the line ended and her electronic voicemail picked up yet again, he snapped the phone shut and groaned. Something was off, but he couldn't tell what.

"Hey."

A hand slapped on Cole's shoulder, and he jumped.

"Shit." His roommate, Harley, laughed. "I didn't mean to scare you."

Cole relaxed his shoulders but didn't erase the scowl from his face. "It's fine."

Harley slung his backpack onto one of the nearby sofas and sank into it. "What's got you so high-strung?"

Sighing, Cole stuffed his phone back in his pocket. "I still can't get ahold of Rose."

"Oh, shit." Harley tugged at his sloppy black hair, an awkward expression smudged on his face. "Sorry, man."

"Yeah," Cole said, sitting in a chair catty-cornered from him. "I just wish I knew what was up."

Everything had been great between them since the homecoming game—so good, in fact, Cole had been considering buying a ring. Graduation was nearing, and he had a gut feeling about securing a future with her.

"Maybe she's just stressed about classes," Harley said as he stuffed more chips in his mouth, his hand tattoos on full display. "Didn't you say she gets anxiety sometimes?"

Cole looked at his roommate and chewed his bottom lip, mulling over the question. Rose *did* have a tendency to get overwhelmed near the end of each semester.

"Yeah, actually," he said slowly while nodding. "That would make a lot of sense, especially with finals right around the corner."

Harley dusted his fingers off on his already-stained jeans. "See. I'm sure everything's fine. You should just talk to her."

Cole agreed and silently chided himself for thinking the worst. His roommate may have been odd, but he was thankful for his help today.

"Rosie, it's me!" Cole stood outside her door, eager to see his girl.

After talking to Harley, he'd decided to march over to her dorm room so they could figure this out together. If they were going to get married, Cole had to learn how to be there for her, even on her worst days.

"Babe! You in there?" he asked, knocking louder this time.

At first, he received no response, but then he heard something shuffle behind the door. "I can hear you, you know."

His pulse started to quicken as he wondered again if this had nothing to do with school and everything to do with him.

*Or someone else.*

The sound of a lock clicking grabbed his attention, and he let out a sigh of relief when she opened the door and no one else came out. "Rosie," he breathed, smiling at her and walking in. "I've missed you." He wrapped his arms around her, but after a beat too long, he realized she wasn't reciprocating. He pushed back and looked down at his girlfriend, immediately detecting the dark circles under her eyes. "Rosie? What's going on, babe?"

She met his gaze and burst into tears, burying her head in his chest.

"Hey, hey, shh-shh. It's okay," Cole soothed as he ran his hands up and down her arms. "It's okay, babe. If this is about school, I know the end of the semester is always tough for you, but we're almost done. In the spring, we'll both walk across the stage and never have to worry about another exam or project again." He paused to kiss the top of her head. "It's going to be okay, babe, I promise."

She pushed off of him and opened her mouth to speak, but instead, something strange happened. Rose's eyes widened, and Cole watched as she cupped a hand over her mouth and ran to the bathroom before puking.

# NOW

## SATURDAY, OCTOBER 19, 2024

*I'M PREGNANT.*

Cole tore through the house in a fit of rage and pain.

*I'm pregnant.*

The air inside his lungs twisted, making it hard for him to breathe.

*I'm pregnant.*

He had to leave—immediately. Where the hell was Sol and Luna?

*I'm pregnant.*

He stopped just outside the house and staggered against the wall, allowing the brick to shoulder his fall. Rose's words blared repeatedly in his brain, so loud that he couldn't hear his own thoughts. He hadn't slept with her in more than six months, which meant there was no way the baby could be his.

"Fuck!"

He grabbed at his chest as a mixture of a sob and an attempt to breathe got caught.

*I'm pregnant.*

How had things gone so horribly fucking wrong?

"Cole?" a gentle voice interrupted.

He knew who it was and didn't want her to see him this way, but he couldn't help himself. The woman he loved, the woman he'd made and lost a child with, was carrying *another man's baby*, and something inside of Cole's heart snapped.

"I need to leave," was all he could manage.

"Okay," Luna said. She offered him her hand and pulled him to stand. "Come on, let's go."

"Sol—" he started, "I don't want him to—"

"Don't worry about him. He can call an Uber or go home with Jenny, for that matter."

Cole nodded and followed Luna to his Jeep.

*I'm pregnant.*

How had he been so fucking stupid? To think all this time she was being abstinent, loyal to their vows, when they didn't even live in the same fucking house. And now she was going to have a—

He let out another cry and staggered to the ground.

"Cole, it's okay. Come on, let's just get in the Jeep." Luna tugged on his elbow, but he wasn't moving.

How could she have done this to him?

To River?

His breaths became frantic now as the panic attack set in.

"Cole? Cole!"

He looked up at Luna and registered the alarm on her face, but he couldn't do anything about it. His heart was torn into a million fucking pieces, and breathing, standing, walking, doing anything but drowning in self-pity seemed entirely out of the question.

A familiar, comforting warmth nudged its way into Cole's side, and he wrapped his arms around the dog in a sigh of relief.

*Emmett.*

He laid on the dog and cried, allowing his fur to soak up his tears.

"Cole, sweetie, let's get in your car if you don't want anyone to notice."

He heard Luna's voice again, and though it sounded miles away, he winced at the thought of others coming to his aide.

"Okay," he finally said minutes later through muffled tears and dog hair.

He stood up and wiped his eyes, following Luna and Emmett away from the worst fucking place on earth.

"NO!" Cole jolted awake, his body slick with sweat.

*No, no.*

Bloodied images flashed through his mind, and he hugged his legs.

*Not again. Not again.*

He felt the tears fall as he rocked back and forth.

"Hey, hey, it's okay." Luna's arms wrapped around him. "Shh-shh—shh. It's okay."

Cole laid his head against her chest and cried. "She was my baby girl."

"I know, Cole. I'm so sorry." She cradled him and ran her hand up and down his back.

He burst out into full-fledged sobs, unable to hold it back any longer.

"She—was—my—daughter, and—I—couldn't—help—her!"

His body shook violently, the thoughts and guilt consuming him.

"I'm here," Luna cooed. "It's okay."

Cole buried his head into her chest as the familiar ocean of grief washed over him yet again.

He couldn't save his child.

He'd tried and failed.

She was dead because of him.

*It should've been me, not her.*

And now, he couldn't save his marriage.

He sobbed until his throat burned, the ache intensifying with each cry. Looking back, he couldn't remember how long he laid like that, buried in Luna's arms and crying like a baby. It must've been hours, though, he noted later, because when she finally left, the sun was starting to rise. He felt like a fool for letting himself break in front of her, but he couldn't help it. Grief was a master manipulator, always toying with you and taking over when you least expected it. Just when you think you're getting better—*poof*—it sneaks up on you and grabs a chokehold over your body, threatening to squeeze the life out of you.

What a fucking treat.

Cole spent the next morning lazily drifting in and out of sleep, only waking to let Emmett outside to potty. His body was so physically exhausted from the crying, and his mental energy was completely shot. He was depleted on all levels and didn't know if that would ever change.

He'd lost his daughter.

And now he'd lost his wife.

Cole groaned as he remembered his interaction with Rose last night, and he sunk into the couch. He slept the rest of the day.

# NOW

*Friday, October 25, 2024*

Sunday soon fell into Monday, and then Monday into Tuesday, and by Wednesday, Cole's boss was texting him asking when he'd be back. Cole had told him he needed time off, but the news doesn't stop. There was work to be done, stories to be told, and a gala to prepare for. At least, that's what Nate had said in his texts.

Cole knew he was on thin ice, but he also knew Nate needed him. No one else at the station had been invited to Zanella's event, so if he wanted this exclusive, he had to be patient with Cole.

And so Cole took Thursday off, too. Finally, by Friday morning, he managed to return to work, but only by the grace of Zoloft and the promise of the impending weekend.

"Cole!" He heard Nate before he saw him.

Cole turned around in his seat, as ready as he'd ever be to face his boss. "Good morning, sir."

"My office, now."

Cole slumped his shoulders and sighed. He really didn't think Nate would fire him with the event so close, but maybe he'd overestimated his value at the company. Maybe he'd talked to Luna and convinced her to write the article.

*Could she even write?* Cole didn't know.

174

He pushed his way back into Nate's office, mentally preparing for the worst, but instead, he was met by a team of coworkers.

"We need to debrief about this gala," Nate said, nodding for Cole to take a seat.

He obeyed and then looked around at the people in the room. Luna, Greyson, Mary from HR, and Sal from legal were all in attendance.

"Oh," was all Cole said.

"Luna told us about the verbiage on the invitation, and we need to take a few precautions before you go."

Luna winked at Cole, who said nothing.

"Now, if this really is a matter of life and death—and who knows with this guy, it may very well be—we need you to understand we don't expect you to take that risk, Cole. Your safety and well-being are our top priority here at *The Suttonville Chronicles*."

Cole looked at his boss, finally realizing what was happening. "You need me to sign a waiver."

Nate blanched, if only for a second, and then said, "Yes."

Cole blew out a breath. "Sure. Fine. Give it here." He waited as Sal slid over a document.

Cole's eyes glazed over the words, and he signed it as soon as a pen was in hand. "There."

Nate clapped his hands in praise while Mary notarized the document. "All right, then. Mary, Sal, thank you for your time."

They nodded—Mary's a bit curtly—and exited the room, leaving Cole with just Nate, Luna, and Greyson.

"All right," Nate started. "Now that's out of the way, it's time to strategize."

Cole rolled his eyes and quickly tuned out, nodding when he needed to but adding no other contribution to the conversation. Instead, his mind was elsewhere.

*Rose.*

The mental image of her in her parent's sunroom replayed again and again in his mind. He knew he needed to stop but couldn't. It was purely a form of self-torture Cole couldn't resist.

*I'm pregnant.*

Somewhere around the second or third day of wallowing at home, Cole had moved past the pain enough to think of one, fixating question: who was the father? This knowledge evaded him, and he was angry about it. So, so angry. Yet, there was nothing he could do but sit and wonder.

He'd thought about going back to Rose's house and asking, but what good would that do? Then he'd just have another depressing thought looping in his brain.

"Cole?"

"Hmm?" He snapped his attention back to the group, realizing a beat too late he'd missed a question.

"What do you think about me attending with you?" The question came from Luna.

"Sure."

"You don't think Zanella will be upset about someone coming uninvited?"

Oh. He hadn't thought about that. "On second thought, maybe you should sit this one out. I don't think it's a plus-one affair."

A look flashed across Luna's face at that response, but Cole couldn't tell if it was hurt or something else. "I'll try to take some pics," he reassured her.

She nodded but didn't meet his eyes.

"I still think we need some kind of safety measure in place," Greyson said.

Nate looked at him. "What do you suggest?"

"Here." He pulled out his phone and opened an image. "Bluetooth earbuds. Small enough that Z shouldn't see, and we can have inside access the entire time." He paused and looked at Cole. "In case . . . you know, things go south."

Cole nodded in response. "Sure. Whatever you guys want."

His mind drifted again into the abyss of nothingness. He only knew the meeting ended once everyone started scooting in their chairs.

"Hey, Cole," Luna called as he made his way out. "Can we talk?"

His heart sank at her question. If he was being honest, this was another reason why he'd avoided coming in: he didn't want to see Luna. He was too embarrassed. "Sorry, kinda busy. Can it wait?"

"Oh, um, yeah. Sure."

"Great, thanks." He scurried away from her and headed toward the coffee pot in the breakroom before going to his desk where he planned to hide all day.

The rest of the morning passed by quickly as Cole buried himself in work. He had several follow-up articles to write and an endless supply of emails to respond to. When he finally looked at the clock, he gawked, shocked to see it was nearly two in the afternoon. He hadn't eaten much this week, but now, his stomach growled. He supposed he could take a break to grab a late lunch.

When he pulled out his phone, though, his chest tightened. There, blaring on the screen, was a text from Rose. His pulse quickened as his thumb hovered over the unopened message. Did he want to talk to her? To know what she had to say? His first impulse was to delete it, but then curiosity got the better of him, and he swiped it open.

**Rose:** *Can we talk?*

It wasn't lost on Cole that she was the second woman to ask him this today. He sighed and debated on what to send back.

**Cole:** *Why?*

**Rose:** *Because we need to.*

He grimaced.

**Cole:** *I guess . . .*

**Rose:** *Can you come over now? I'm off today.*

He looked back to his desk and considered her question. He still had work to catch up on, but it was Friday. Most of it could probably wait until Monday.

**Cole:** *Ok*

With that, he shut his laptop, grabbed his keys, and headed to Nate's office. He was going to tell him he was heading out for interviews, but his door was locked, which meant he'd already left for the weekend.

Even better.

# NOW



*Friday, October 25, 2024*

"You look like shit," Rose's dad said, staring at Cole in the doorway.

"Thanks, Bob. Nice to see you, too." He was so not in the mood for this. "Is Rose here?"

He grunted in response and then turned away. "Rose! Company."

Cole rolled his eyes and let himself in, closing the door behind him. He should've asked her to meet somewhere else. Rookie mistake.

"Thanks, Dad. Hey, Cole." She sauntered down the stairs in a pair of sweatpants and a sweatshirt.

Her hair was up, and her face looked pale yet flushed. She was still incredibly beautiful, but Cole stiffened as he realized why she looked like this, a memory of their pregnancy resurfacing.

"You have morning sickness." It was a statement, not a question.

Rose flinched as she walked closer, if only for a second, and then cleared her throat. "Yes."

He nodded and locked his jaw, looking away.

"Um, come on. Let's go in here." She led him once again to the sunroom—the one that now haunted Cole's memory.

He followed her in, reluctant at first but eventually caving. He'd come this far—might as well get it over with and see what she had to say so he can leave.

Once seated, Rose looked at him and opened her mouth to speak but hesitated.

"Go on," he said. "Spit it out."

He watched as her eyes widened in response. He was usually so gentle with her, but not today.

"So, um, I know this is obviously a lot to take in, but, um, in light of everything, I figured we should talk about next steps." She lifted her eyes, meeting his gaze.

Cole's response was unmoving, despite the pain her words yielded in his chest. "Fine."

She stared at him waiting for more, but when it was clear he wasn't going to speak, she nodded and pulled out a manila envelope. "So, I had my attorney draw up the divorce paperwork. I—I think it's time, Cole."

And just when he thought he had nothing else to lose, he felt the rug ripped out from underneath him. He felt like a fucking idiot—of course she wanted to talk about divorce. She was carrying another man's baby, for Christ's sake.

He shook his head and actually laughed. "How long after we split did you wait to fuck someone else?"

Her already-pale face whitened more. "I—Cole—"

"Or was it while we were still together?" He shook his head and stood up. "Were you fucking another man while you were still sleeping in our bed?"

"Cole, of course not!"

"Oh, because that would be a sin, huh? But screwing around once we separated was fine? I don't know, Rose, I don't think your almighty God would like that very much." He started pacing around the room.

"Cole, please."

He could hear the pain in her voice and was glad for it. His soul was on fire. Until now, he'd felt nothing but numbing pain. Now, however, he felt an inconceivable amount of rage.

"Don't fucking say my name like you care." She was crying now, but Cole continued. "Who is it, Rose? Who's the father of your *new* baby?" His voice had lifted to shouting volumes by now, but he didn't care. "Who is it, Rose?"

She covered her face with her hands. "I—I don't—wanna—say," she said through whimpers.

"You don't wanna say?" Cole saw nothing but red now. "You don't wanna fucking say? Maybe you should have thought of that before you spread your legs while we were still married!"

"Hey!" a voice cut in.

Cole turned, expecting to see her father, but instead was greeted by his brother, David. "What the fuck are you doing here?"

He stared at him, confusion evident in his gaze.

"You can't speak to her like that. I think you should go."

"I'm sorry, what?" Why the hell was his little brother here, in Rose's parent's house? What the fuck was happening?

Unless . . .

"No." He shook his head as realization dawned on him. "No, no. That doesn't make any sense."

"Cole—" Rose tried again.

But he wasn't listening to her. His mind was operating at a million miles a minute. All those times they'd hung out together, all the times they'd seen his brother, all the times he'd *cried* to his fucking brother about Rose.

"How long?" he asked her. "How long have you been *fucking my brother*?"

Her whole body flinched at his words. Cole stared at her waiting, but it was David who spoke. "I kissed her once right before River passed, but we didn't sleep together until about a year ago."

Every blood cell in Cole's body exploded as his heart flamed with rage, burning him from the inside out. "Are you fucking kidding me right now?"

Rose looked at him and closed her eyes, her voice soft. "I'm so sorry."

Cole blinked rapidly, staring at the two of them in astonishment and at a total loss for words. His wife cheated on him with his brother, and now they were going to have a baby.

A fucking baby.

Was this real?

At last, he said the only thing he could think of at that moment: "Imagine what River would think if she was here."

And with that, he hailed his fist back and slammed it into his brother, feeling no remorse as the blood rushed out.

# NOW



STILL REELING FROM THE news and the adrenaline of hitting David, Cole slammed his foot on the gas pedal. How could she fucking do this to him? To River? They were all going to be one big fucking happy family now. Cole laughed in hysteria as he merged onto the interstate and immediately swerved into the fast last.

He didn't know where he was going—and didn't care for that matter. All he could feel was the absolute guttural pain of betrayal. The sight of David in Rose's childhood home played in his brain on repeat as the intrusive thoughts flooded in.

*Your brother screwed your wife.*

*Your wife screwed your brother.*

*They probably fucked in your bed while you were busy crying.*

*That's why she left you.*

*That's why she cheated on you.*

He let out a raspy scream from deep in his throat, trying to shake the words before they took root.

This wasn't his fucking fault. It was theirs. He would not feel shame for their actions.

*No, you'll just die alone . . . like River almost did.*

An explosion of grief sizzled inside his chest, licking its way up his sternum like wildfire. He tried to focus on the road, not caring when the speedometer climbed past eighty, then ninety, but the torment was too much. Cars honked at him as he trailed too closely and then cut them off, but he didn't care. Reckless endangerment seemed like a cakewalk compared to the shit ripping in his chest.

He floored the engine again, daring the needle to hit one hundred.

Along the road, he spotted a sign for a strip club, and his manic state twisted back to laughter. "Hah! I guess I can go there now, right?" he said to no one but himself. "I'll just tell the bouncers, 'It's cool. Wife cheated on me with my brother. Got any ones?'" He passed another billboard and cackled again when he saw a beer ad. "Or hey, what about the liquor store?" Tears streamed down his face, staining his upturned lips and bright white teeth. "No one left to care about whether I'm drinking too much!" He wiped his face and passed another car. "Hey, God! You got what you wanted! This is my punishment I guess for skipping all those sermons. Thou shall go to church, or your spouse will cheat on you with your brother and get her pregnant and start a new fucking family! That's one of the Ten Commandments, right?"

*Make it stop. Make the pain fucking stop*, he silently begged.

Suddenly, a blue light flashed in the background, and a familiar siren sounded in Cole's ears.

But once again, he didn't care.

Nothing in his life mattered anymore.

Instead of pulling over, he cut across three lanes of traffic, deciding a high-speed car chase could be fun. At the sight of the cop following him off the exit ramp, Cole felt a new surge of adrenaline. "Hah! Can't catch me now, coppers! Too busy having my heart ripped out!"

He zoomed through three red lights and then turned down a back alley, zig-zagging his way through the town.

Sirens blared in the background, and Cole knew they were close. Heart thumping, he scanned the area for a hiding spot and all but squealed when he saw a lifted boom barrier at the lower level of a nearby parking garage. He slammed his foot to the pedal one last time, barely making it inside the building before it lowered. He swerved past the oncoming car and circled his way to the top, burying himself in the middle of several other parked cars, now hidden in plain sight.

"Hah!" He let out a sigh of relief as he heard the echo of sirens soften, and he sank down in his chair. What a fucking rush.

Several minutes went by before the sounds completely disappeared, but Cole didn't think it wise to chance leaving just yet. They were likely still patrolling, looking for him. He tapped his fingers on the steering wheel, contemplating his two options: wait it out in his car or walk around, which prompted a new thought:

*Where am I?*

In the midst of the chaos, he hadn't paid attention to the name of the exit. He looked around but didn't see any noticeable landmarks. He huffed and pulled out his phone, fingers trembling. According to the map, the street below him was lined with small shops and restaurants. Cole moaned at the idea of having to see people right now, but he also didn't want to sit and wait. His anxiety couldn't handle it.

Hands still shaking, he zoomed in on the map and looked again, clicking on individual businesses until he found one called Ted's Bar.

"Perfect."

He wiped his face with his sleeve, pulled out a ball cap from the back seat, and slipped out of the Jeep, ready to drink his sorrows away.

ONCE INSIDE THE ESTABLISHMENT, Cole seated himself at the bar and ordered a shot. "Keep 'em coming," he said to the bartender, who nodded and obliged.

Cole looked around, surveying the joint. It wasn't pristine by any means, which was exactly what he wanted. The sketchier, the better. He didn't want to be bothered by people today.

He only had room for one solace in his life right now, and the bartender, Mario, understood this.

Approximately six shots and one hour later, Cole felt a fraction less of the pain. He'd also learned Mario was working to help pay for college, and Cole thought that was just fucking swell.

"Good for you, Marioooo! Go to college, get an education—" Burp. "Do all the things my daughter never got to do."

Mario looked at him and raised an eyebrow. "Your daughter?"

Cole nodded matter-of-factly. "Yep. She didn't get to do those things—none of 'em." His voice fell, and he lowered his drink as a memory surfaced. "She wanted to be a writer." He hiccuped and pointed at his empty glass for a refill.

His new friend raised an eyebrow but didn't object. "Why didn't she go to college?"

"Because she's dead." Mario's face paled, but Cole didn't miss a beat between completing his sentence and tipping his head back to down his shot. He savored the burn as it slid down his throat in comfort. "I gotta piss."

He wobbled off his stool in pursuit of the bathroom, and his thoughts began to swirl with memories of his River Bug—some of her as a baby, others as a teen. She was such a beautiful child with light and love in her eyes. She would have changed the world; Cole was sure of it.

He shook his head and washed his hands, ready to stagger his way back to the bar.

"Ope, sorry," he said after bumping into someone.

"You all right, bud?" The stranger sized him up.

"Dandy. Doing *swell*, thanks." Cole pushed past him, determined to find his way back to his seat. "Ah!" A sudden gleam caught his eye, and Cole shielded his face. "What the hell—"

His words broke off as he turned to the source of light and saw a man cutting into a half-cooked burger. The knife had hit the sun's reflection, and Cole winced at the shiny metal blade as it dripped with blood.

*No.*

*River.*

He tripped over a rug, jarring his reality.

The man with the knife stared at him, asking if he was okay.

"I have to go," he sputtered before scrambling to his feet.

"Hey, man," Mario's voice cut in. "You okay?"

"Here."

Cole threw a wad of cash at him and rushed out the door without looking back. He ran down the sidewalk and stopped when he felt like he'd put a safe distance between himself and the ghosts of his past. He bent over gasping, watching as his breath mixed with the cool air on each exhale.

After several sobering moments passed, he stood up and unrolled his shoulders, willing his body to relax.

And then he spotted the liquor store.

# NOW



What happened next was a series of events that could only be described as Cole's unequivocal notion to move on autopilot. Without thinking, his body launched forward, carried him through the twenty-four-hour convenience store, and pushed him back to his car. Once he was on the freeway again, his foot pushed down on the gas pedal, leading him to the only spot where he could truly process his trauma: River's gravesite.

He pulled into the gravel parking lot at the cemetery and cut the engine, ready to numb the pain. Taking a deep breath, he grabbed the brown paper bag that concealed the bottle of Evan Williams and set off for his daughter's grave. Fallen leaves crunched under his feet as he walked in the darkness, reminding him of how River's face would light up during this time of year.

Some people loved Christmas, but his daughter was a sucker for Halloween.

He laced his way through the other graves, careful not to step on any, and then stopped when he came to her name.

*River Adeline Sloane*

*6/8/07 – 10/3/22*

*Beloved daughter*

He sighed heavily and dropped his shoulders. "Hey, baby. It's Daddy."

He took a swig from his bottle and let the amber liquid settle on his tongue before he swallowed. Then, he took another.

And another.

And sat down.

"It's been a while since I've been to see you." He flexed his jaw and thought about the circumstances that brought him here now. "I wish I could say this visit came with truer intentions."

He paused and took another swig.

"To be honest, honey, I'm kind of in a bad spot right now. Your mom—" A mix between a laugh and a yelp escaped his lips as tears lined his eyes. "Your mom, she, uh, she did a bad thing. And I know I'm not supposed to speak badly of her to you, but you're the only person I want to talk to right now, River Bug."

A cricket chirped somewhere in the background as Cole pulled his knees into his chest and wrapped his arms around his legs. "I suppose I should just tell you what happened, seeing as you may already know anyway. I don't know how it works up there."

*Swig.*

"She cheated on us, Riv. With your uncle David. And now"—he ran his tongue along the inside of his mouth, the anger seething beneath his skin—"they're going to have a baby."

A heaviness settled over him as the words clung to the air. He always thought the day River died would be the worst day of his life, but this? Crying over his dead daughter's grave about her mother and uncle's sexcapades and a brand-spankin'-new baby came in at a close second.

He wiped the mix of tears and snot that coated his face and raised the amber bottle of liquid once more, thankful for its numbing effects.

A new thought occurred to him then, and he nearly spit out his drink.

This child would be his niece or nephew.

His flesh and blood.

*River's sibling.*

He broke into a new fit of laughter at the thought, hysteria once again taking over as his cackles quickly turned into sobs.

"You have a new baby sibling on the way, River. I suppose that means we should be celebrating, huh?"

Celebrating a new life while his daughter was lying six feet under.

Seemed appropriate.

He cackle-cried again, only pausing for another drink.

"I don't know where we go from here, hun."

Another negative thought began to swirl in his mind, but his phone vibrated in his pocket, stopping it from taking root.

*Luna: Hey, just checking in. You left in a rush today. How are you doing?*

"Hah! How am I doing?" Cole snorted, the rage inside his chest rattling, like a locked cage.

*Just fucking swell.*

"Daddy's friend is checking in on him, Riv. At least I have one woman left in my life I can trust. I think you'd really like her, actually. She eats like you did." He paused and looked back at his phone, another idea popping into his head. "Actually, I think you two should meet."

He snapped a photo of River's headstone and texted it to Luna, along with his location.

*Cole: Doing great. Wanna hang at the cemetery?*

"I think I'll use that as my new pickup line."

Forty-five minutes later, Cole's eyes glazed over, and he smiled as he watched his favorite blonde strut toward him in the sea of death. "Luuuu, you made it!"

Luna slowed once she reached the gravesite. "Hi, Cole."

He squinted up at her, and a warm and fuzzy feeling bloomed in his chest. Her champagne-colored hair was braided into short pigtails, and she was bundled in an oversized sweatshirt and blanket-sized scarf. *Pretty as ever,* Cole thought.

He placed his hands on the ground and pushed himself up, stumbling in the process. "Lu, allow me to introduce you to my lovely daughter, River Sloane."

Luna moved to help Cole stand upright. "Geez, Cole, you reek. How much have you had to drink?"

*Good question.*

"Dunno."

"Here." Luna sighed and pushed him back to the ground. "Sit. I had a feeling you'd been drinking, so I brought some food to help sober you up."

A grin broke out on Cole's face. "See, River, I told you she loved food. Probably even more than you did!"

Luna cast a glance between Cole and the gravestone before sitting down and pulling out her takeout bags. "River was a fellow foodie, huh?" She unwrapped a cheeseburger and handed it to Cole.

He took it without hesitation. "Yup," he said through a large bite. "Ate everything in sight but never gained a pound, same as you. You both have the fastest metabolisms I've ever seen."

Luna gave a half-smile. "Us girls know what we like, right, River?"

Cole looked at her now, and Luna winked. He smiled and went back to eating his greasy food.

"So," Luna started, looking at the ground. "Are you ready to talk about whatever's going on?"

The question hit Cole like a loaded bullet. Technically, he didn't think he'd ever be ready to share this news, but if there was one person who deserved an answer, it was Luna.

He finished his sandwich, wiped his hands off with a napkin, and then launched into the full story. Maybe it was the fact he'd already ripped the Band-Aid off by telling River, or the near-gone bottle of booze beside him, but his chest didn't ache quite as much when he recounted the events from last weekend and earlier in the day.

When he was finished telling her about how Rose and his brother now had a baby in common, Luna simply looked at him, empathy washing over her face.

"Cole," she finally said under a low breath. "I am so sorry. That's . . . awful."

Cole nodded. "Yeah."

The silent air settled between them, the eeriness of their surroundings no match for the darkness that clouded Cole's heart.

"You even offered to give up The Gala for her," Luna said after a minute.

Cole laughed at that. "Yup. My life is just one big fucking joke." He tipped his bottle of whiskey back and slugged the last of it, another thought occurring to him. "I may as well not even go to The Gala."

Luna's head whipped to him. "What do you mean?"

"I mean—" Cole tried standing again, this time more successful. "What the hell is the point? Kid's gone, wife's gone. Who do I have left to impress? To make a living for?"

Luna scrambled to stand. "Um, how about yourself?"

Another laugh from Cole. "I don't give a shit about myself. Why would I? No one else does. Certainly not Rose or David."

He started to saunter off into the graveyard, but Luna caught his hand.

"*I* care about you, Cole."

She brought her eyes to his, and when she did, Cole shuddered. He took a step toward her, and Luna took in a breath, their hands still clasped.

"You do . . . don't you?" She'd been there through all of his worst moments over the past few weeks, and none of it had scared her away. "You've been right here all along."

She stuttered, "A-as a friend, of course."

"Right," Cole said, taking another step toward her and closing the space between them. "As a friend."

Her breath caught in the wind on an exhale, and something inside Cole snapped. Heat rushed through his body, despite the near-freezing temperature, and he felt her hand tremble in response.

She would be so easy to get lost in right now—to make the pain go away. They were closer than they'd ever been, and Cole could feel the wisps of her soft hair tickling his chin. His gaze fell to her mouth, and the air felt tight. He'd been working so hard to resist this temptation, but why? So his wife could leave him for his brother and start over with a new family? Their marriage had died the same day River did, and Cole knew it.

He only wished he'd accepted it sooner.

Slowly, Cole brushed a loose strand of hair behind her ear. He let his hand linger for a moment before cupping her face. He traced her lips with his thumb and met her eyes one last time before leaning in so close that his nose nestled in beside hers.

He felt the heat of her breath as their mouths hovered, neither of them moving. And then, just as Cole was about to brush his lips against hers, she whispered, "Don't."

He let out a quiet groan and leaned his forehead against hers. "Why?"

"Because." She paused, clearing her throat as the tension hung in the air. "You're still in love with her. And you've been drinking. You will regret this tomorrow."

"Luna," he whispered. "I don't think I would ever regret you."

He felt her body tense at his words. She chewed her bottom lip for a moment, and just when Cole thought she was going to kiss him, she said, "Not like this. Not at your daughter's . . . gravesite."

The rejection stung all the way to his core. He dropped his hand and stepped back, scrubbing his face with his hands and flipping his hat back around. "I'm sorry," he said. "I shouldn't have done that."

Luna rubbed the side of her face where Cole's hand had just been. "It's okay."

"No, no, it's not. We're coworkers. I'm sorry—it won't happen again. Let's just go." He brushed past her and started stalking back to his Jeep.

"Cole, wait." Luna rushed after him. "Cole, we should talk about this."

Another shred of embarrassment seared through him. "Nothing to talk about," he said over his shoulder. "Like I said, it won't happen again. Sorry you drove all the way out here tonight. I'll just see you at the office Monday." He stepped over another grave, almost to the parking lot now.

"Cole, stop, at least let me drive you home."

He heard her voice behind him, but he didn't stop. "Nah, I'm good now. That pretty much sobered me up, thanks." He threw a hand up in the air as he unlocked his car door and then hopped inside, slamming the door and drowning out Luna's words.

*"Cole Sloane!"*

Her cries were muffled as he threw the gear in reverse. He'd been so stupid. Luna was the one person in his corner right now, and he just fucked it all up. Of course she wouldn't be interested in him. He was way older than her and still married—not to mention the dead kid thing. *Yeah, Cole, you're a real catch. It's a wonder women aren't throwing themselves at you.*

He slammed his hand on the steering wheel again and again, screaming as he turned out of the cemetery and onto the main road.

His life was fucking miserable, and he hated himself for the decisions he'd made.

*"Stupid—fucking—piece—of—trash!"*

He screamed again as the dam inside his chest broke. He'd been trying to glue the pieces of himself back together again for so long, but it was useless.

Cursing as he missed his exit, he slammed on his brakes and did a U-turn. No one was supposed to be on this road late at night, so when his vehicle swiveled around and met the onslaught of bright, white lights, he was too startled to think.

He simply drove, first as a reflex and then without remorse as he braced for impact, all while one unyielding thought crept into his brain:

*Maybe I'm meant to be alone.*

# THEN



*MONDAY, OCTOBER 3, 2022*

"WHAT IS HAPPENING?" COLE screamed. "Save her! Save her *now!*"

"Sir, we need you and your wife to step outside while the doctors work."

Cole glared at the nurse, wondering why someone with a huge facial scar was working in the trauma unit. "Like hell we are. River! River!"

"Oh my God, River! Cole, what's happening to her?" Teardrops shone on Rose's face as she looked at her husband.

Cole pushed past the nurse who was trying to usher them out, and he grabbed his daughter's hand. "It's okay, sweetie. Daddy's here. Stay with us, Riv! The doctors are going to fix you."

"Sir, please, if you and your wife don't step out, we'll have to call security."

His eyes snapped to Rose, who looked petrified. She sniffed and motioned for Cole to let the medical team do their job. "Come on, honey. River, we'll just be right outside."

He looked down at his daughter one last time and wished like hell he could see her eyes staring back at him. He kissed her forehead and said, "I love you."

Then, he dropped her hand and followed his wife out of the room. Together, they huddled by the window watching, but one of the medical assistants closed the curtains, and that's when Rose lost it.

Cole wrapped his arms around her and held her while she cried. He felt her shoulders shake, and he tried to comfort her the best he could, but the truth was, he was scared out of his damn mind. He'd seen the movies—he knew what was happening wasn't good. Stomach acid tickled the back of his throat as he pictured the blank expression on River's face when her eyes had rolled back in her head.

"That's my child. Somebody help her!" Rose's cries echoed through the hospital corridor.

"Shh—shh—shh." Cole rubbed a hand down her back and cradled her head. "It's going to be okay. The doctors are here now, and they're going to make sure she's okay." But even as he said the words, it felt like a lie. Suddenly, Cole had the urge to run back into the room, to hold her one last time in case it was his last chance.

"I—don't—even understand—what happened." Rose's snot drenched Cole's shirt. "How—did—this—happen—Cole?"

"I don't know," he choked, tears now clouding his vision, too. His mind reeled as he tried to make sense of the last few hours.

*The knife.*

"Rose." He pulled his wife back now to look at her. "What did the police—"

His voice was cut off as the doctor walked back out to them, a grim expression on his face.

*No.*

"I'm so sorry," he said.

*No.*

"We did everything we could, but her blood loss was too substantial."

Cole lost his balance and staggered to the ground.

*No, no, no.*

Somewhere in the background, he heard his wife scream.

But that didn't matter anymore.

Nothing mattered.

Because *she didn't make it.*

River was dead.

His child, his one and only daughter, was gone.

Cole retched on the hospital floor.

# NOW



*Friday, October 25, 2024*

"Sir, are you okay?"

What happened next was a series of fragmented blurs.

"We've got a white male, mid-thirties, coming in with a head wound and lacerations across his chest."

*Where am I?*

"Sir, can you tell me your name?"

Cole's pupils dilated as someone shone a light on them. A throbbing pain pinched under his skull, and he screamed.

"Somebody page Dr. Williams!"

"Sir, can you tell us what happened?"

*Headlights.*

Cole remembered headlights. And a crash. And then the pain. He groaned as his body wailed in agony, all while medical personnel buzzed around him, asking questions he couldn't answer. His head swam with shattered memories as he tried to piece them together.

"We need to get a head CT," a new voice said.

Cole winced as someone touched the wound on his head.

*Headlights. There were headlights.*

A visual of a red car popped into his brain, and Cole flinched as the memory of the collision crashed through him. He opened his mouth to speak, but nothing came out. He groaned and tried again.

"Ca—"

"What's that, sir?"

He grunted and tried again.

"Ca—caaaaar." His voice felt foreign in his body. "Car. Car!"

"Yes, honey, you were in a car accident."

He shook his head. "Red."

He locked eyes with the nurse, willing her to understand.

"Yes," she said after a moment, "you crashed into a red car. It was a woman. She's here, too."

Panic raced through his body. Cole never meant to hurt anybody else, not in a million years—much less a woman. He needed to know she was okay.

He opened his mouth to speak again, but someone hushed him by placing an oxygen mask over his face.

*Christ.*

Who had he hit? Was she okay? How old was she? His mind raced with questions, needing to know more than anything what he'd done. She was someone's *daughter*, for crying out loud.

He felt a surge of energy as he knocked the mask off his face and blurted, "Is she okay?"

That got everyone's attention. They all stopped and looked at one another before a burly man said, "She's being treated now. We don't know the extent of her injuries yet, but let's just focus on you for now, Mr.—" He pulled Cole's wallet out of his pants pocket and read the name on his license. "Sloane."

Frustration burned his insides. He tried to sit up then, determined to go find out if the other person was okay, but his body groaned beneath him.

*Fuck!*

He felt hands pushing him back down as his vision blurred. Suddenly, he felt extremely hot and, once again, found himself battling to stay awake.

THE NEXT FEW HOURS passed by in a blur. Cole skated the borderline of consciousness as the nurses and doctors worked quickly to tend to his wounds. When he finally came to, the clock on the wall suggested it was just after three in the morning.

Suddenly, a flash of blonde hair and bright red blood fielded his vision.

*The woman.*

He needed to know if the woman was okay. Now heavily medicated, he sat up, ignoring the increasing pain in his head. He slowly inched his way off the bed and staggered to a standing position. A new wave of discomfort racked through his body, but he didn't care. He grabbed the IV pole that hovered beside his bed, and he set off for the front desk.

"Sir!"

He'd made it approximately one-and-a-half steps outside his room before a nurse came rushing to his side.

"Sir, you need to lie down."

"The woman," he croaked. "I need to see her."

The nurse was a middle-aged brunette, and judging by her face, she was not happy with Cole right now. "You need to focus on your own recovery, sir."

She tried to usher him back into the room, but Cole grunted and waved her off. If this woman wouldn't help him, he'd find someone who would.

He made it ten steps before he passed out.

WHEN HE CAME TO again, it was daylight outside. He blinked at the rapid intensity of the sun and pushed his call light for the nurse. Thankfully, this time, it was someone else.

"The woman I hit—is she okay?" The man had barely made it into the room before Cole blurted out the words.

"Oh, honey, has no one told you yet?" he said with a sympathetic look. "She died last night."

Cole felt the world shift beneath him. "What—"

"I'm just kidding, but that's what you get for drunk-driving head-on into a lane of oncoming traffic, endangering yourself and everyone around you."

A rush of air escaped Cole's lips. "So, she's alive?"

The nurse rolled his eyes. "Yes, baby, she's alive. But I won't lie to you, she's not looking so good."

Not looking so good? "What does that mean?" He locked eyes with the man, desperation written all over his face.

"You know what," the nurse said, "why don't I take you to see for yourself? She's been asking to see you, too."

Cole's heart thumped outside of his chest. "Yes, please." It was all he wanted—to see this person and know she was okay. And to apologize for his recklessness. He'd been so selfish.

It took longer than he'd like to admit, but finally, after half a dozen curse words exploded from Cole's mouth, he was settled into a wheelchair.

"Thank you—"

"Jerome," the nurse offered.

"Jerome," Cole repeated. "Thank you, Jerome."

"Mhmmmmm."

With that, he rolled Cole forward and pushed them onto an elevator. They waited for the light to ding on the fourth floor, and then Cole's heart thumped as Jerome pushed him into the unit.

His anxiety continued to rise as they rolled closer to the woman's room. He was consumed with guilt, but he had to do this. He had to see what he'd done to her.

"You ready, baby?" Jerome asked as he rolled to a stop outside a door.

Cole nodded in response and took a deep breath.

"Okay, then. Knock, knock." He opened the door and slowly pushed into the room. "You have a visitor, Miss Luna."

# NOW



*No.*

Cole felt a new sense of dread awaken at the sound of her name.

*It couldn't be.*

His eyes widened, and Jerome pushed him closer.

"Luna," he breathed.

"Hey, Cole." Her lips turned upward as Cole's eyes raked over her tattered body. "The pudding here is great. Have you tried any?"

*The pudding here is great?*

He was speechless for a moment. He had anticipated the worst when the nurse rolled him in, but other than some swelling and bruising, Luna looked relatively unscathed.

"You're . . . eating?" he finally said. "And sitting up, watching TV."

Cole turned back around to look at Jerome, his mind racing. "You said she didn't look good."

"Hey!" Luna interjected. "I take offense to that."

"He deserved a little scare after the trouble he put you through, Luna."

"Telling me she was dead wasn't enough?"

Luna's eyes widened, and Jerome threw his hands up in mock innocence. "Next time you decide to off yourself, try a less destructive method."

"Jerome!" Luna said through a mouthful of pudding. "You promised not to say anything."

"I'm just saying. His problems are his own, baby. He didn't need to be dragging you into them."

Cole's heart softened as he listened to their banter.

*She's okay.*

"You're okay."

"A little banged up, but yes, I'm okay."

She paused, putting the spoon down. "Jerome, could you get me some more water, please."

The nurse gave her a skeptical look and side-eyed Cole. "Sure, honey, but I'll just be right down the hall."

"Thanks." She turned to Cole, and the pair waited for Jerome to leave.

Once the door was shut, Cole opened his mouth, but no words seemed significant enough to express the vat of emotions he felt. He'd *hit* Luna. All because he'd wanted to be reckless with his own life. Guilt stirred inside of him, causing his nausea to return. He'd been so selfish.

"Luna, I'm so so—"

"Don't," she said, interrupting him. "I'm still trying to decide which emotion I'm feeling more right now—angry at you for what happened, or relief that you're okay."

Cole stared into her aquamarine eyes, fully taking in her face for the first time since entering the room. He admired the freckles that scattered across her nose and fanned out on her cheeks. He noted the white scarring that fell just on the tip of her upper lip and found himself wondering what happened.

And then he looked at the bruising that swelled on her forehead, and he felt the ache in his chest throb again.

He couldn't believe he'd done this to her.

A single tear slipped down his cheek, but he didn't bother to brush it away. "Luna," he rasped, trying again, "I am so, so sorry."

She stared back at him, twisting her lips to the side as she contemplated his words. Cole didn't expect her forgiveness, but he needed her to know he had never in a million years meant to hurt her.

"What were you thinking?" she finally asked.

"I don't—" he cut off as his voice faltered. "I don't know."

"You almost killed us both, Cole."

"I know." He blinked back more tears and struggled to maintain his composure. Looking down at the floor, he wrestled with his hands, mulling over the next part. "I think . . . I think that I wanted to die, Luna."

And that's when his emotional dam finally broke for good. There were no scary dreams or drunken hysterics to set it off this time. Just Cole and his deeply wounded self, lying bare for the world to see. He was completely broken in every way.

"Cole." Luna leaned forward in her hospital bed and placed a soft hand on his shoulder. "Hey, look at me." She paused and waited for him to meet her gaze. "I want you to listen to me right now and listen good. Because I'm only going to say this once."

Cole nodded, although he wasn't sure he was ready to hear what she had to say.

"I'm still mad as heck at you," she began, "but I need you to know something." She took a deep breath and then spilled her sentiment on an exhale. "You are cherished, wonderful, and *worthy* to be here and be loved by God. Because he has never stopped loving you, even if you stopped loving him."

Cole sobbed at her words and noticed that she, too, was crying. "You are important—so, so important—and your life matters, okay?"

He shook his head, soaking in her words. He wanted to believe her, truly he did, but the voice inside his head was shouting: "It should've been me, not her."

"Cole, listen to me." Luna took his head in her hands, and his eyes widened as he realized he must have said the words aloud. "It shouldn't have been anyone. That wasn't God's plan for your daughter. What happened to River was terrible—a terrible, awful tragedy, but it wasn't your fault, and she wouldn't want you living your life like this, blaming yourself for it."

Silence rang in his ears as he took in the gravity of her words.

*Could she be right?*

"It just . . . hurts . . . so fucking bad, Luna." He searched her face. "I miss her every moment of every day. She was my little girl. And now this thing with Rose and my fucking *brother*."

Luna nodded with a calm, gentle nature. "I know, Cole. I'm so sorry you lost her, and that they betrayed you." And with that, she scooted to the edge of her bed and leaned into Cole, holding him while he cried.

"I am so sorry. I never meant to hurt anyone, especially not you."

"I know. It's okay."

Together, they sat like that for what felt like ages to Cole. With each passing breath, the tightness in his chest eased, if ever so slightly. Hours ago, he'd almost ended his life and endangered others in the process. He'd almost let his daughter's death be in vain and drank himself into a coma.

But not anymore.

Because enough was enough.

He was ready to change.

To do better—*be* better.

He was ready to live.

For River.

And for himself, starting with completing his mission.

He wiped his nose and pulled away from Luna, admiring the beauty in her words and the friendship she still offered. "Would you be my date for The Gala?"

Her eyes widened as a smile stretched across her face. "Ohmygosh, I almost forgot to tell you! Look at this text I got last night."

**Unknown:** *You deserve a night out after that. Please consider this your official (belated) invitation to The Gala. I have a surprise for you. — Z*

"Oh, fuck." Cole looked back at her. "What could it possibly be?"

Luna wiggled her brows. "I don't know, but I intend to find out."

# THEN

*Friday, September 30, 2022*

"Dad, you promised you'd be home this weekend!" River stared at her father across from the kitchen island.

"I know. I'm sorry, honey," Cole said. "But I've got a huge lead on a Zanella story Nate wants me to cover. I have to fly to Chicago tonight." He looked at his daughter with an apologetic smile. "I promise we'll do something next weekend."

"That's what you always say." She threw her backpack over her shoulder and grabbed a muffin before storming out the door, leaving for school.

"River," Cole yelled, the sound of the screen door slamming her only response.

Dammit.

"She has a right to be mad, Cole. I don't blame her." Rose entered the kitchen, having heard the fight from her home office.

"I know, I know." He brushed his hands over his face. "I feel awful, but I have to go."

Rose walked past him and grabbed the coffee pot, topping off her mug. "Can't you just tell Nate no? He has to understand you have a family and a life outside of work."

"I don't know." Cole shook his head. "If I don't go, he'll just send somebody else. The rookies are already eager enough . . ."

"Are you saying you'd rather disappoint your daughter than let another reporter cover your story?"

He looked at her and felt the metaphorical knife twisting in his gut. He hesitated and rubbed the back of his neck. "Fine. You're right. I'll talk to Nate when I get to the office."

Rose leaned in and kissed him on the cheek. "Thank you, baby. River will be so happy. She's performing at the coffee shop's poetry slam tonight. I'll let her know you're coming."

"Great," Cole said with a smile that didn't quite reach his eyes.

# NOW



*WEDNESDAY, OCTOBER 30, 2024*

WEDNESDAY MORNING, COLE ARRIVED at work an hour early. He and Luna were both released from the hospital Sunday night, on the condition they both take it easy for the next few days. And because faith was on his side, no one from the medical team had tested his blood alcohol level, meaning he'd avoided a nasty DUI charge.

He would've accepted the punishment, no questions asked, if Luna had decided to press charges or pursue further legal action, but of course, she didn't.

Because she's Luna.

Instead, all she'd asked was for Cole's insurance to cover her medical expenses and vehicular damages—plus a car rental.

Now, he shifted his own temporary Chevy Cruze into park and shut off the engine, eager to start the day with a fresh outlook. The Gala was tomorrow night, and that, combined with the unusual amount of coffee these people drank, meant the newsroom would be buzzing with excitement.

"Howdy, partner!" Luna yelled from across the lot as she slowly climbed out of her F-150, a smile plastered across her face.

Cole had tried to talk her into something smaller, especially since she'd never driven a truck before, but she'd insisted on it "just for funsies."

"Luna." Cole jogged over to her. "Here, let me help you."

"Ah," she said, waving him off. "I'm fine."

Cole wished she'd stayed home another day, just to be safe. "You really should be resting."

"And you really shouldn't be telling me what to do." She raised an eyebrow at him and then turned to walk inside the building. "I know Nate's going to have us in meetings all day. And I need to get caught up on some edits before tomorrow."

Cole wanted to protest more—to argue she wasn't up to it, but instead, he said, "Okay. Can I at least get you some coffee?"

"That, I will take."

He opened the door for her and placed his hand on the small of her back as she walked past him and inside.

"Cream and sugar?"

"Is the Pope Catholic?"

Cole let out a half-hearted smile and looked at her as a mixture of emotions washed over him. Here this woman stood after he'd almost cost Luna her life—and not to mention the embarrassingly drunken kiss he'd attempted, and still, she wasn't mad at him.

"Hey, Luna?" he said as she started to walk away.

"Yeah?"

"Thanks, for everything. I . . . I really appreciate you."

She smiled back at him and nodded. "Anytime." They held each other's gaze for a moment, and Cole thought about saying more, but just then she said, "Espresso Patronum!"

It took Cole a moment to register her words, and then he cracked a smile. "I'm sorry, what?"

"You heard what I said. Caffeine now, please!" she yelled over her shoulder and then bounced off to her desk.

It was going to be a good day, Cole decided.

THE REST OF THE morning was a whirlwind. Cole was required to do another debrief with HR, and Nate called a meeting with the editorial team to discuss their coverage strategy for tomorrow night. Last was social, and Cole was both excited and mentally drained by lunch.

"Hey, I'm going to run out and grab a sandwich. You want anything?" He had stopped by Luna's desk to check on her for the umpteenth time, but this time with a legitimate excuse.

"Nah, I'm good."

He raised an eyebrow. "What? You're turning down food?" This was concerning.

"Don't get your panties in a wad. I already DoorDashed wings. They should be here any minute."

"Oh," Cole started to say, "well, let me know, and I'll go—"

"*Sloane!*" Cole's voice dropped as he heard the roar of Nate's through the office.

Luna looked at him and whispered, "What'd you do?"

"I don't know." Cole's heart stammered as he tried to remember if he'd done anything problematic as of late. "Can't think of anything." Unless . . .

*Oh no.*

Did he text Nate Saturday night, too? He only remembered drunk-texting Luna.

He turned around and watched as his boss stormed over, his face beet red.

"Sloane! Did you see this?!" Other employees were staring now, curiosity piquing their interest.

Cole shook his head. "What?" Now he was more confused.

"This!" Nate shoved his phone in his hand, and Cole saw a news headline from their neighboring TV studio that read: *Breaking: Local Brewery on Fire.*

Alarm bells rang in Cole's head, like a bad omen.

"What the hell?" He scrolled down the page and clicked on the live update feed, where his colleague, Josh, was doing a standup outside of Forest Fox Brewing Co.

*No.*

"I just got off the phone with Henry down at the station," Mila chimed in from behind. "He said they have two confirmed fatalities at this point, but they aren't releasing any names."

Cole looked at Luna and threw the phone to her before digging out his own. He pulled up Zanella's website and found it locked with a new home screen that read:

*Our final event has been relocated. Come find it if you dare.*

"Dammit!" Cole yelled. After all this time, so close to the event, the chase is still on. Zanella was still playing games.

"What does the website say?" Nate demanded.

"He's changing the location." Cole turned his phone around so they could see. "He wants us to find it."

Luna's mouth dropped open. "How the heck are we supposed to do that? The event is tomorrow."

"I don't know," Cole said. He felt like throwing his phone on the ground and screaming. "Call Sol. See if he knows anything."

"On it," Luna said.

*Two fatalities.*

The words rang in Cole's ears. The Gala hadn't even started, and already, two people had died. Maybe more, for all he knew. And now, he had to go around chasing for more fucking clues if he wanted to learn of the new secret location.

This fucking man.

Cole felt his body pulse with adrenaline.

"Where could the new location be?" Nate's body language was filled with rage.

"I don't know!" Cole snapped. "I just need a minute to think."

*If I were Zanella . . .*

Cole's mind raced as he racked his brain for answers. Why set the building on fire? Why move the location a day before? Why harm innocent people?

"Z doesn't do anything without thought," he murmured to himself. Everything had meaning, purpose, intention.

"Sol didn't answer." Cole heard Luna say from somewhere behind him.

*Exorcisms. Shootings. Vaccines.*

He ran through a mental list of the previous events.

*What's the common theme?*

Nate barked out another disgruntled order, but Cole ignored him.

*Think. Think. Think.*

"Luna, what were the previous passwords?"

"Uhhhh, 'babies' was the first one." She paused, trying to remember. "And the second was a cocktail name, something like—"

"Momma's Milk," Cole finished for her.

"Yes!"

"And the third one. It was a beer, right? What was it?"

"Hold on," she said, spinning around in her chair and pulling up the brewery's online menu. Anxiety spiraling, Cole waited as she scrolled down to the seasonal options, pausing when she found it. "Der Keim."

He mulled over the words, but only for a moment. "What does that mean?"

Luna pulled up another tab and tapped it into the search bar. "Let's see . . . looks like it's the German phrase for 'sprout.' " She frowned and kept scrolling while he leaned over her shoulder.

And then Cole's eyes landed on the third definition listed.

"Oh," Luna squeaked, indicating she'd seen it, too.

"What is it?" Nate's voice was urgent.

"Embryo," Cole answered.

His boss twisted his face in confusion. "What the hell? Sloane, what is going on?"

He wasn't sure yet, but the answer was on the tip of his tongue, just waiting for his brain to slide the last clue into place.

"They were in honey," Luna said, her voice softer than normal.

And that's when it clicked.

Cole's eyes snapped to her, and he felt the world shift beneath him.

"Come on," he said, moving to steady himself. "I'll drive. You text Sol—let him know what's going on."

"Can somebody tell me what the fuck is going on?" Nate shouted after the two of them.

"I'll text you if I'm right," was all Cole said as he barreled out the front door and waited for Luna to join him.

# NOW



*WEDNESDAY, OCTOBER 30, 2024*

TWENTY MINUTES LATER, COLE'S car swiveled into the parking lot of Honey Creek Fertility Clinic. Aside from a maternity ward, it was the absolute last place Cole wanted to be after the bombshell from his family, but he didn't have a choice.

He had to push those thoughts aside for now.

"I can't believe I didn't piece it together sooner," he said to Luna, slamming his door shut.

"Yeah, that mother trucker had this planned from the start."

Cole grimaced at her revelation and shuddered at the thought of the brewery on fire. Z's tactics were getting worse, building and building into an impending crescendo, and Cole had a sinking feeling he'd discover what that was at The Gala.

"Still nothing from Sol?" Cole asked as he threw the front door of the clinic open, desperate to find out where the new location was.

Luna followed quickly behind him. "No. He's probably sleeping, ugh, or drunk already."

Once inside, the pair did a full three-sixty, and then it was Luna's turn to shudder.

Cole raised an eyebrow. "You okay?"

"Yeah," she said. "I just . . ." She blinked a few times as she struggled to find the words. "It's nothing."

Cole looked at her with a puzzled expression, but as soon as he opened his mouth to respond, a woman walked in and sat down behind the front desk.

"Hello, how can I help you?" She smiled at them both, the wrinkles rearranging on her face.

"Uh, hi," Cole cleared his throat. "I'm Cole Sloane from *The Chronicles*. I'm here covering a story regarding Graham Zanella. Has he been here?"

He watched as the color drained from the woman's face.

"Oh," she said. "You're here for him."

Cole and Luna exchanged a look.

"Yes, has he been here? Or maybe left something, like a note?"

The woman eyed them both cautiously, and Cole noticed a bead of sweat form on her forehead. "I guess I knew this day was always coming." She stood up and gestured for them to follow. "Come on. I'll escort you back."

Adrenaline shot through Cole's veins, and he and Luna followed the woman through the door and back to an exam room.

"Stay here," she ordered.

The door clicked shut, the sound ricocheting off the walls. Cole's brain reeled as he tried to conjure his disordered thoughts into something coherent. He didn't have a chance to think long, though, because less than a minute later, a light knock sounded at the door.

"Hello," a woman said, stepping inside, "I'm Dr. Rodriguez. I understand you're here regarding Mr. Zanella?"

"Yes," Cole sputtered. "We think he may have left a message or a note for us."

The doctor held up her hand. "HIPAA prevents me from telling you everything, but Mr. Zanella is one of our largest clients—or, at least, he used to be. Ever since . . . the incident, we had to put out a restraining order against him."

"What? Restraining order?" Cole and Luna said in unison.

"Yes." Dr. Rodriguez nodded and continued. "After his last donation, things got a little out of hand." She shifted on her feet, clearly uncomfortable. "Usually, when a client deposits a sample, we have them leave it in the room, and we collect it when they leave. We'd never had an issue before with Mr. Zanella, so our nurse didn't think anything of it when he walked the sample to her this time instead of leaving it. But, then—" her voice broke, and Cole felt his eyelid twitch. "But then he drank the specimen and spewed it all over my nurse's face."

Luna gasped, her hand flying to her mouth.

"He said he wanted her to participate in an art performance. Something about showing the world how careless we are when it comes to the preservation of life. I think." Dr. Rodriguez paused and looked away before settling her gaze back on the two of them. "I believe he said he wanted to do an exhibition of women dripping in semen, posing as if they'd just finished intercourse."

"Oh, dear God," the words slipped from Cole's mouth before he could stop them.

"Yes. Yes, it was quite traumatizing for our employee. I had to call the authorities and file a report. It was a whole ordeal last month."

Luna sat down, her face white as a ghost.

"Did he happen to say where this exhibit or performance would take place?" Cole asked.

Dr. Rodriguez shook her head. "No, but he kept talking about a man named Achilles Pugh."

Cole took another metaphorical hit of Zanella's drug, the high of the chase rising with each passing moment.

"The Pugh Library," Luna said, her voice a whisper. "At the university's south campus."

Cole's eyes widened. "You mean at Springhill?"

Seeing her nod, he pulled out his phone and refreshed Z's website. His fingers moved faster than his brain could as he typed "pughlibrary" into the passcode box.

*Access granted.*

"Bingo," he mumbled before looking up. "Come on, let's go."

He grabbed Luna's hand, helping her stand, and then spun to the doctor for a quick "thank you" before rushing out the door. Together, they hightailed it to his loaner car. Once inside, Cole fumbled with his phone, pulled up the now formulaic video, and clicked play.

"Hello," the Siri-generated voice said, "and congratulations. You've now passed the final test by locating our true destination for the event."

Cole winced at the confirmation that this was all premeditated.

"For those who don't know, Achilles Pugh published *The Philanthropist*, which was an abolitionist newspaper in the 1800s. Slave owners in the area were outraged by the publication, so they attacked his establishment, causing him to relocate his business elsewhere. In honor of his determination to persevere against all odds, we thought, what better way than to play an attack on our own establishment to see how our participants would react?"

"Cheese and rice," Luna breathed.

"So, to those watching this, congratulations. Truly. You've proven your worth, and we are reminded again of why we chose you."

Cole felt a pang of pride in his chest and watched as the video continued. The masked man from the previous clips walked onto a stage and paused before pulling a black curtain to the ground, unveiling the completed mural he'd been painting. Cole had expected something gory or problematic, but instead, his eyes traced a haunting illustration of the Pugh Library with the words "Happy Death Day, Pugh" written on it.

"Tomorrow," the voice continued, "we celebrate the anniversary of Pugh's death from the comfort of his namesake."

"Esqueeze me, what?" Luna chimed in.

"He died on Halloween," Cole said.

"Oh."

"But his death will not be the only thing we celebrate. No, tomorrow we will celebrate, explore, and mourn the very essence of life itself." The screen went black, but the electronic voice continued with one final message. "Now that you are aware, we invite you to enter . . . but only if you dare."

"Holy shiz," Luna said.

Cole's pulse quickened.

*The essence of life itself.*

"The man knows how to raise the stakes—I'll give him that," Luna said.

Cole squeezed his eyes shut, trying to think. Z's performances always had some tie or connection to a deeper meaning in life, but this felt bigger than the ghosts of Zanella's past. This, Cole feared, would be the moment where the artist finally crossed the line—the one he'd been toeing for so many years, just barely skirting by the fingertips of authority.

This? This would be different.

Cole felt it in his bones.

Luna's phone started ringing then, and she nearly dropped it trying to pry it from her back pocket. "Sol, where have you been?"

Cole laid his head on the steering wheel, exhausted from the rush of it all, and listened while Luna recounted the news.

# NOW

*THURSDAY, OCTOBER 31, 2024*

"YOU FEELING GOOD ABOUT today, bud?" Cole patted Emmett's head the following morning as he waited for his coffee to brew. The dog only blinked in response, of course, but Cole felt it was an affirmation of sorts. "Figured as much."

He had debated on bringing Emmett with him to The Gala, but he couldn't fathom subjecting the dog to whatever horrors awaited him. Luna had argued he'd be a valuable asset, but the truth was, Emmett was scared of his own shadow. He was wonderful at comforting Cole and being there for him, but when it came to thunder or loud noises? Forget it. Even tiny dogs startled him. The idea that mastiffs are scary is quite the misconception—they're giant, loving teddy bears that want to lay in your lap.

And eat food, in Emmett's case.

He bent over to scratch behind the dog's ears and buried his face in Emmett's double-coated fur. "Always such a good boy."

Hearing his coffee pot beep, Cole stood back up and poured a large cup of hot, black liquid into a thermos. It was going to be a long day, and he'd need all the fuel he could get. The invitation said to arrive at six o'clock, but Cole had a feeling it'd be many hours before the evening was finished.

He took a long sip of his beverage, savoring the bitter flavors before capping it with a lid. His plan was to go to work, business as usual, and then leave early to get ready at Sol's. The library where they were heading had been closed for over a decade, which Cole learned after a little research, so he was hopeful they could slip in unnoticed, even with the ludacris outfits. It was Halloween, after all, so if anything, their costumes would help them blend in, right?

Right.

With a deep breath, he took in the familiar surroundings of his home and wondered, for the first time, what River was doing in Heaven.

"Sloane! Meeting in five. Don't be late." Nate's voice barked from across the newsroom.

"Copy that." Cole offered a quick thumbs up without taking his eyes off the computer screen.

He'd been in the zone all day interviewing employees from Forest Fox Brewing Co., and now he was attempting to bust out an article before the meeting.

How else was he supposed to stay distracted as the day dragged on?

He jammed his fingers against the keys before closing the document and emailing it to his editor. "There," he said to no one other than himself.

He rolled away from his desk and stood up, the energy in the office buzzing. Everyone knew about the event, despite HR's suggestions to keep it on the down low. It was too big of a story to put a lid on—especially in a place like this.

"All right, listen up!" Nate shouted over the chatter as everyone huddled together in the editorial room. "It's t-minus three hours until history is made at Graham Zanella's first-ever gala." He paused and smiled, basking in the sound of reporters whooping and hollering. "And if this goes well? It could mean big things for us."

Another round of applause erupted from the crowd, and Cole felt a surge of pride pulse in his blood.

"Cole will be our lead reporter on the case." There was a pause for a few "hell yeahs" and back claps. "Luna will be the photog, and Greyson will be on standby outside for social coverage. Now," he started, looking around the room, "with that said, this will be an all-hands-on-deck kind of night. Jada will be leading the team here, all of whom have been briefed on the severity of a timely publication. The events of tonight will likely lead into tomorrow, meaning you should all be prepared to rock and roll after the morning meeting. We'll need to pick up where the night crew left off, and as I said, everyone will need to pull their weight."

"Um, sir?" Cole turned his head to see where the voice came from and creased his eyebrow when he saw the latest intern. "Um, you said Cole would be the lead reporter. Does that mean you're sending someone else? As a Springhill student, I could offer a unique spin—"

A large smile spread across Nate's face as he held up a hand, stopping the boy. "I like your fire, kid, but this one's for the big dogs." A few chuckles sounded from the others in the room. "Cole's been covering Zanella since he vandalized the Statue of Liberty, what? Five years ago? Who knew the adventure we were about to embark on when I sent you to cover that story, huh?"

"An adventure it's been, sir," Cole said.

Nate nodded. "All right, everyone. Class dismissed. Get back to your day jobs, and don't let me down tonight!"

The crowd dispersed at their leader's final words, and Cole took it as his cue to leave.

"You ready?" he asked Luna on their way back to their desks.

"Yep, just gotta grab my stuff. Meet you there?"

Cole cocked an eyebrow. "You sure I can't drive you?"

"Nah, I'm good." She wrestled her jacket on and picked up a hot pink backpack. "I need to run a quick errand, so I'll just see you at the cabin."

Cole arched an eyebrow. "And by running an errand, I assume you mean picking up food?"

"That is precisely what I mean, Cole. It's going to be a very long night, and you know I get cranky when I don't eat."

Cole chuckled. "Fine, see you there. Be careful."

"Meh, I don't know. There's this crazed drunk guy that keeps trying to run me off the road, so, like, no promises, you know?"

He stopped dead in his tracks. "Luna—"

"I'm kidding!" She cracked a smile and winked before skipping off to her vehicle, leaving Cole frazzled, embarrassed, and thankful.

# NOW

*Thursday, October 31, 2024*

Cole breathed in the chilly autumn air as he faced the university's withered library. It was a quarter to six now, and his nerves were shot. While he and Luna had gotten ready at Solstice's cabin, Zanella had sent another text with instructions to create a special knock on the front door when they arrived. And now that he was here, Cole's bones itched beneath his custom-tailored Clark Kent suit.

"We need a code word in case things go south," Luna said as she tucked a listening device inside her right ear.

She was dressed in an ivory lace gown that had newspapers jutting out at her hip bones to form the skirt, paired with a hot red leather jacket that read *FAKE NEWS*.

"Why not just say help?" Greyson pushed a button on another Bluetooth device and handed it to Sol.

"Because," the rock star argued from behind his feathery jungle mask, "that would be too obvious, wouldn't it?"

"Yeah!" Luna said. "We need something fun and casual that rolls off the tongue and doesn't give us away. Something like 'chocolate bananas' or 'deep-fried steak.'"

"Luna, in what world do you think those phrases just *roll off the tongue*?" Greyson's southern twang spilled out as his sass level rose.

"I don't know," Sol cut in. "I kinda think those are too generic. Maybe 'deep-fried chocolate bananas' would be better."

He shot Luna a knowing look, and she giggled, Greyson's eye now twitching.

"Lighten up, Grey," she said, "We're just teasing. If we need help, we'll definitely, maybe, not say those words. Right, Cole?"

The sound of his name stirred Cole from his inner monologue, and he nodded, words escaping him. All he could think about was how the man who'd consumed so many years of his life was just inside that building. This obsession with interviewing Zanella had eaten away at him for so long, and now, after all this time, Z was just . . . there. Sitting inside, waiting for them to knock.

Cole couldn't wrap his mind around it.

"Hey." Luna's soft voice interrupted his thoughts again. "You okay?"

Cole cleared his throat and nodded. "Mhm."

"Cole . . ." She placed a hand on his elbow, as if willing him to look at her. "You can do this, you know. River would want you to. It's going to be okay."

He took a deep breath and nodded as a gust of wind whirled by, settling deep under his skin.

*This is it.*

The moment they'd all been waiting for.

He cast a glance to the side, scanning for students and professors alike. "I don't see anyone," he said. "I think we should head inside."

Sol and Luna nodded in agreement, and Greyson wished them luck before retreating to his car. "Remember," he said, looking back over his shoulder, "just say 'HELP' if you need me to call 911."

He popped the "p" on the code word and rolled his eyes when Luna offered a coy shrug.

"Let's get this show on the road, boys and girls!" Solstice slapped a hand on the back of either journalist and eased them forward as they set off to whatever predetermined fate awaited them.

They approached the steps to the Pugh Library and paused at the bottom of the landing to admire its entrance. It was a grand building, complete with white pillars and a sun-bathed, faded red brick exterior. Strands of green ivy laced the way down the building's cracks and crevices, and crumbled pieces of stone gave way to the ancient architecture.

Cole thought it was stunning.

"Wow," Luna breathed, all jokes seemingly lost on her. "This is it." She looked at Cole and squeezed his hand. "You ready?"

He took a deep breath, and for a brief moment, he wondered: *Will I ever be?*

"I can't handle the suspense. Let's go," Sol blurted, running past them and barreling up the long staircase to the front door.

Once there, he let out a melodic whistle and then proceeded to pound his fists against the large, wooden door to the opening beat of "In the Air Tonight" by Phil Collins.

At the sound of the last drum, a voice from inside sang, "I can feel it coming in the air tonight."

"Hold on!" Sol belted with a shit-eating grin on his face and then laughed. "All right, motherfuckers! This is Solstice Blackwood here for Graham Zanella. Let us in!"

Cole felt a swell of anxiety in his chest and watched trepidatiously as the door creaked open.

# NOW



*Thursday, October 31, 2024*

Cole stepped inside the library.

"Hello," a voice growled as they shut the door.

Cole squinted at the man who'd greeted them, but it was too dark to make out his features. They were enclosed in what he assumed was the building's antechamber, and black curtains were draped over all the windows, the only light coming from a five-prong candelabra.

"We're here for—"

"Zanella," the man rasped. "Yes. Congratulations on making it to the final event. Not many of you did."

The ashes in Cole's veins smoldered, anticipation rising with every breath.

"Before you enter, though," the voice continued, "we need to discuss a few things. In order to preserve the authenticity of tonight's artistic performances, we will be sealing the doors once all guests have arrived. If at any point you would like to leave, someone from our team will escort you to the holding room where you can wait until the final act is complete. We will also need to collect your phones."

"Wait," Luna said. "So, you're *locking* us in? And taking our phones?"

"We will unlock the doors once the night is complete, and you may leave then. Of course, this is an at-will event, so if you do not wish to abide by the rules, you are welcome to leave now."

Silence filled the air as the group contemplated his words. Alarm bells were going off in every direction of Cole's brain, and yet—

"Fine. I'm fine with that."

"Cole," Luna said, a warning in her voice. "We would be *locked* in with no way to call for help."

He couldn't see her very well in the dim lighting, but he imagined she was biting her bottom lip, the way she always did when she was worried.

"I'm not turning around, Luna. You and Sol are welcome to if you don't feel safe, but I'm staying." His soul was on fire now, ready to see this through.

"This is all bloody mad, mate," Sol said, pausing for a beat. "But I would expect nothing less from Zanella."

The shadowy man nodded, then turned his attention back to Luna. "So, what'll it be, miss? You in or out?"

Cole placed a hand on her shoulder. "It's okay if you want to back out. I completely understand."

Nanoseconds ticked by as the gentlemen waited for her answer. Cole gave her a gentle squeeze, reassuring her he meant what he said when she blurted, "Okay. I'm in. But for the record, I do not like this."

Cole's lips turned upward, gratitude swelling inside of him. He wanted nothing more than for his friend to be safe, but he'd be lying if he said he wasn't happy about her decision.

"All right, then." The man's voice was harsh yet excited. "Then may I welcome you to The Gala." He twisted a handle from somewhere behind him and then flung the large door open, revealing a world of chaotic bliss.

"Holy . . . shit," Cole breathed.

"You can say that again," Luna mumbled.

# NOW



*Thursday, October 31, 2024*

Cole floated through the entryway on a cloud of journalistic ecstasy, his brain short-circuiting from all there was to see. He took his glasses off and blinked rapidly before wiping his eyes and then replacing the nonprescription lens.

*This is . . .*

"Spectacular," he whispered under his breath.

Cole stepped forward, inching farther into the room and took in his immediate surroundings. In the lobby area, women and men alike floated atop varying-sized tables, each wearing their own eccentric costume. The woman closest to Cole was dressed in a black-and-gray flapper outfit, her body adorned with jewels and sequins, and asymmetrical lines. He watched as she danced in slow motion, pausing between each pose.

And the *books*—Cole had always gone to the library on the main campus, and it was nothing like this one. The Pugh Library had aisles upon aisles of bookcases, all filled to the brim with some overflowing. It even *smelled* like books in here—not in the new-age way fresh releases did, but in the old, withered, dusty way.

Cole loved it.

Luna's camera flashed beside him, awakening his senses and reminding him to take notes. He scrambled for his notebook, thankful he'd brought one as a backup.

"Oh, there we go," Sol said from behind him. "The man's got a bar. I'm in, lads!"

Cole turned to see where the singer was headed. There, in the front left corner of the building, was a dimly lit bar. It spanned the length of the check-in counter and was covered with floating antique mirror frames. Cole squinted and realized the bottom row had hands positioned in the centers, each with a drink. He watched as Sol grabbed a champagne flute from one of the outstretched arms and then grinned as the hand quickly retracted and returned a moment later with a fresh beverage.

"It's bloody wicked!" Sol called over the music.

Dumbstruck, Cole moved his attention to the middle of the room, where a grand staircase fell front and center. It was draped in divine autumnal hues, and creamy flowers cascaded down the stairs. At the top of the landing, Cole saw a fountain, which he could only assume was filled with more champagne. He watched as a woman in red held her cup beneath the liquid falls and then brought it to her lips.

Snapping his gaze back to the main floor, he surveyed the other guests at the party. Each was dressed to the nines in an outlandish, upscale costume—much like his own. He counted roughly a dozen and jotted that down, making a note to look into their backgrounds. He also noticed there were several mimes at this event, and they appeared to be part of the service team. Cole watched as one walked toward him with a tray of appetizers.

"No, thank you," he said as the mime gestured to the food.

He responded by making a sad face and then patting his belly and smiling.

"I'm really not hungry, but thank you."

The man feigned sadness again but then jumped for joy when Luna grabbed a handful of treats off the plate.

"Thanks so much!" she said in between bites.

The mime bowed and then set off in pursuit of another guest.

Speaking of other guests—

"Where's Sol?" Cole looked around for the sequin-studded top hat but didn't see it.

"Dunno," Luna said through a muffled bite of crab cake. "Probably getting another drink."

Cole nodded and was about to say something else, but then a flame caught his attention out of the corner of his eye. He swiveled around to see what it was and laughed as he watched a series of acrobatic women drop from the ceiling. They were all positioned inside a hoop, with black chiffon fabrics laced around them. Each held a single candlestick, and applause erupted from the audience below as the actors made their landing. Cole scribbled more notes as they each took a bow and then proceeded to drift through the crowd.

"This place is like The Great Gatsby and the circus but on crack," Luna said, a hand gripping Cole's arm. "Wait, you don't think they actually have crack, do you? Ohmygosh, I never considered drugs. I'm not into that, Cole."

He chuckled and leaned down to whisper in her ear. "You're safe with me, Luna." He pulled back and added in a normal voice, "And no, I seriously doubt there's crack cocaine at this event."

She smiled at him, a faint hue of red smudging her cheeks. "Come on, let's find Sol."

He let his eyes fall as she moved away, and he drew his attention to the right side of the library's opening, his jaw dropping when he realized what he saw.

"Tattoos! Get your tattoos here!" a man in a vintage clown suit yelled from the inside of a black-and-white striped carnival-like tent.

Cole moved toward the exhibit, once again mesmerized by Z's creativity. Patrons buzzed in and out, much like the firefly lights that danced around the fabric's edges. It was the most haunting, alluring thing Cole had ever seen.

"Ohmygosh, I *love* tattoos!" Luna squealed and pulled Cole's arm inside. "Come on!"

"Like real tattoos?" Sol's voice made Cole jump.

"Obviously," Luna said. "Where've you been?"

"Checking out the back. There's some twisted live portraits lining the walls, full-on Harry Potter shit, I kid you not."

Cole made a mental note to check it out later.

"Hello! Hello!" the mock clown said as they moved closer. "Welcome to Graham Zanella's gala! Enjoy a commemorative tattoo to mark the occasion for all eternity!"

Hesitant, Cole walked past the clown and peered down at the man in the tattoo seat. He was getting something inked on his inner left wrist, but Cole couldn't make out what it was from this angle.

"They're drama masks," the tattoo artist said, not looking up from her work.

Cole turned his head and saw what she meant. The ink resembled the traditional theater icon, which represented both life's comedies and tragedies. He watched as the artist switched out her needles and added a drop of red to the tragedy side.

It looked like a tear.

"All right," the woman said as she drizzled witch hazel on his wrist and then ran a clean paper towel over it. Cole remembered the sandpaper feeling well from his own tattoos. "You're all set."

The man smiled and winked at her. "Thanks, Blythe." He stood to leave but not without first inspecting the work in the mirror. "Sick!"

"Who's next?" Blythe asked.

"Ooooo, me!" Luna chimed and then slid into the seat.

"Wait," Cole said. "You're really going to get one?"

"Of course. Aren't you?"

Never in his wildest dreams did he expect this tonight, but then again, that's how Z operated.

"Everyone gets the same symbol in honor of tonight's event," Blythe said, interrupting their conversation, "albeit the red ink. Are you a Thalia or Melpomene?"

Luna looked at her with a confused expression. "Esqueeze me, what?"

The tattoo artist smirked. "Thalia is the name of the comedy mask, and Melpomene represents the tragedy side. I can either put a red teardrop on Melpomene or a red heart on Thalia. Dealer's choice."

"Oh, well, in that case, red heart, one hundred percent," Luna said with more than a dash of confidence.

"Where do you want it?"

Luna pursed her lips, deep in thought. After a moment, she said, "The back of my neck."

Blythe gave her a curious look. "You know that's going to hurt, right? Like worse than somewhere else."

"I can handle it."

Cole waited while Luna got inked, a gleam in his eye at the absurdity of the moment. He started to pull out his phone but then remembered they'd confiscated it, which led to another thought: *Greyson.*

"You're up, baby," Blythe said, looking at him.

They still had the earbuds in, but he didn't know if they'd work without their phones. He cataloged the thought for later and sat in Blythe's chair.

After a few debates with Luna about why he wasn't going to get his tattoo on the back of his neck to match hers, he landed on a discreet placement on his inner ankle. He took a deep breath and exhaled, shuddering when the needle met his skin. It had been almost a decade since he'd gotten a tattoo.

When Blythe was finished, she asked Cole if he wanted a red teardrop or heart. He looked at her with an earnest expression. "I—"

His words were cut off by a sudden change in the music. What was once an iconic techno beat was now replaced with a soft yet blaring, beeping noise. The chatter among the audience fell to a hush, and the lights dimmed. Cole watched as the acrobats from earlier moved up the stairs, lining it on either side with their light.

And then the same electronic voice that'd haunted Cole's dreams for the past month blared over the speakers.

"Hello, and welcome to Graham Zanella's first-ever gala. We are delighted to have you here tonight. It has truly been an honor to serve this mission with you," the Siri-like voice said. "Together, we have raised the stakes for Americans everywhere and made them question the very essence of their core beliefs."

Cole's heart raced in his chest as he looked around for Zanella.

"Tonight, we are embarking on the final chapter of this journey, and it is your mission to complete this series through your method of documentation. Capture and share it with the world so as to stop them from being so oblivious to the atrocities in our country today. After all, that is the true purpose of art, isn't it?"

*Thump. Thump. Thump.*

Where the hell was Z?

"Now that everyone is here, we invite you to take a step farther inside our gala and join us at the top of the stairs for a night you won't forget." A brief pause, and then: "You may now enter, but only if you dare."

# NOW

*Thursday, October 31, 2024*

Sol adjusted his hat and wiped a bead of sweat from beneath his mask. "Come on, mates. Let's see what the bastard's got in store for us."

Cole took a deep breath and followed him and the other participants up the grand staircase, guided by the light of the candlesticks. An ominous sound returned to the speakers, furthering the dark ambiance in the room.

*Talk about a way to spend Halloween night.*

Reaching the landing, Cole did a quick scan of the room, but it was still too dark to see beyond the glowing fountain. He didn't have to wait long, though, because as soon as the last person reached the top of the stairs, the electronic female voice said, "Welcome to Act One of The Gala."

*Holy shit.*

Cole's body tingled at the realization that this was going to be a multi-layered event.

*Honestly, though, did you really expect anything less?* He silently chided himself and then refocused his attention on the exhibit.

Slowly, a bright white spotlight turned on in the middle of the room, and a drumbeat sounded in the background. Cole stepped forward, desperate for a closer look.

"Is that a—" Luna started.

"I think so," Cole answered before she could finish her words.

In the middle of the dome lighting, a man sat with a bag over his head. He was bound to a chair with ropes, and as Cole inched closer, he could make out the vague hint of muffled screams. He watched in both horror and amazement as the man's body writhed under the confinement of the straps.

He looked around at the other ten or twelve guests and noted their equal level of intrigue. Everyone had collectively stopped about twenty feet away from the man—close enough to see everything that was happening, or make their exit.

The sound of a prison alarm blared, making Cole jump. The noise came from above, and he sucked in until his lungs hurt as he watched a jumbo screen descend from the ceiling. It landed just above the man's head and hovered for a moment, silence filling the air. Then, it clicked on, and to Cole's surprise, a news clip began playing.

*"A local Texas politician has been indicted on more than thirty counts of sexual assault of a minor. Authorities arrested Attorney General Alex Nelson yesterday after a number of victims identified him in a police lineup."*

The video stopped there and quickly transitioned to another.

*"Sexual assault suspect Alex Nelson has been released on bail after someone paid the $125,000 fine late last night."*

Cole pulled out his notebook and started writing down the reporter's words before he forgot.

Another tape rolled.

*"A jury has found defendant Alex Nelson not guilty in today's federal trial. The court released him immediately after, where he was seen hugging his wife and children moments before protestors charged the courtroom."*

The screen clicked off, and the woman in red Cole had seen earlier appeared beside the masked man. She winked at the group and then grabbed the top of the cloth, pulling it off in one swift motion.

"Holy watermelons," Luna breathed. Everyone around Cole gasped in horror, and he felt Luna's claws dig into his arm before she added, "That *fucking* bastard."

More muffled cries erupted from the man, and Cole locked eyes with the politician. Attorney General Alex Nelson stared at him, eyes wide with terror and rage.

The woman dropped the mask on the floor and circled around him. "This man raped, murdered, and sold thousands of children in the Texas sex trafficking ring. He posed as an advocate for the cause and took advantage of the access points it granted him." She paused and looked at the audience. "Tonight, we have invited a handful of his victims to take justice into their own hands and seek revenge as they see fit."

"Oh, fuck," escaped from Cole's lips. This was so much worse than he thought.

"Please feel free to capture the moment in whatever medium you'd like."

She started to walk away, but then a man dressed in a wolf costume blurted, "You can't be serious."

"We are completely serious, I can assure you," she deadpanned.

"Mad," Sol said, shaking his head. "I told you this man was fucking mad."

What was happening? Zanella had never resorted to murder. He had inflicted injuries, sure, but this? Z was about to commit a serious crime. Cole couldn't just stand by and watch.

It was his job to cover whatever happened here tonight without intervention, but sitting on the sidelines while a man was killed wasn't what he signed up for.

*What if it had been River?*

The words pounded into his skull like a jackhammer, and he squeezed his eyes shut, trying to expunge the thought. The man had been proven innocent by a court of law—case closed. And even if he did commit these crimes, Cole still couldn't stand by and watch a man die.

*Can't you?* the sinister voice in his head whispered. Cole grimaced and rubbed the back of his neck. He needed time, time to think.

"We have to call the authorities," the wolf man said over the crowd's murmurs.

"We can't," another woman added, this one in a midnight-colored unicorn ensemble. "They took our phones."

Cole's heart palpitated as he remembered the Bluetooth device in his ear. "Greyson?" he mumbled, placing a hand on his ear. "Greyson, are you there?"

Silence.

*Shit.*

He started panicking now as arguments flew from the crowd. If what this woman said was true, then Attorney General Alex Nelson was a predator, one who'd escaped thanks to the government's gatekeeping. Stories like this were why he went into journalism in the first place. He had a duty to protect the First Amendment and inform the public of the government's mishaps.

And there was only one way to determine if these accusations held any merit worth investigating . . .

A chorus of screams erupted from somewhere deep in the library, stalling his inner debate. Cole's body tensed as a warm series of red lights turned on and glowed around the chained man, the distant screams growing closer by the second.

And that's when the first victim struck.

*"You mother fucker!"* A teenage girl swung a wooden baseball bat, sending a blow to the head.

A stream of expletives traced through the audience, and chaos erupted. Cole watched as a few attendees attempted to run toward the exit, but they were all caught by muscular men in black.

*The holding room,* Cole thought.

He could go back there and—

*No.*

This was where he needed to be.

This was where the story was.

"Cole!" He snapped his attention back to the violent scene at play and saw Luna weaving her way to the front of the crowd, her camera at the ready.

*Holy shit.*

"We're really doing this?" he asked.

"The man's a pig," Luna spat. "Yes, we're doing this! Start writing, *now.*"

Shock rang through his system, but he obeyed, ripping his notebook out again and scribbling furiously.

*"You fucking pig!"*

*"This is for me! And this one's for my sister!"*

*"I trusted you!"*

Cole shrank in both guttural terror and wonder as he watched the young women, some still just girls, swing again and again. It was a bloodbath, to say the least—a complete and total *bloodbath* as they bludgeoned Nelson's wrecked body, again and again. The smell of iron hit the air, and Cole's stomach churned.

He wrote quickly, though, trying to document it all. This was madness, he knew that. Total madness. But he'd come here for a reason, right? And this atrocity was going to happen whether he reported it or not, so . . .

He continued writing and then flipped his notebook shut to help Luna.

"I can't get a good angle," she yelled over the noise. "It's too crowded. I need to get higher."

Cole reacted instantly, bending down onto his knees and patting his shoulders. "Here, hop on!"

Luna wrinkled her forehead for a moment before agreeing.

"Come on!"

"Okay, okay!" She rushed toward him, hiking up her dress as Cole helped her climb onto his shoulders.

Once he'd gotten his footing, he moved quickly, lacing their way through the crowd of survivors.

"This is good! Stay here," she yelled.

He paused, letting her get her shots, and another thought occurred to him: *Where was Z?*

His head snapped up, and he looked through the sea of red in the room. Blood and anger and batons and whips blurred his vision. He blinked, trying to clear his eyes as he searched through both the maze of traumatized individuals and scattered attendees, but his hunt was soon interrupted. The same prison siren from before sounded in his ears, and the movement in the room ceased—the sound of Nelson's cries drowned out by the siren.

And then he saw her.

A pregnant girl, who couldn't be any older than fifteen or sixteen, barreled through the crowd. The other survivors separated for her, welcoming the destruction in her path. She stood in front of Nelson and placed a hand on her belly. Cole suddenly felt weak at the idea of reliving another moment like the one from the cave.

"This is so my son never has to know the monster who created him."

She pulled out a Glock-17, cocked it, and shot him point-blank in the head.

# NOW



*Thursday, October 31, 2024*

Cheers erupted from the survivors while Cole's ears rang at the sound of the shot. He fought to stay upright, but when he saw the pregnant woman turn back around with splattered brain matter on her belly, he doubled over and puked, causing Luna to tumble off in the process.

"I'm sorry," he yelled as he wiped his mouth off with the back of his hand, his eyes catching on one of the other guests in the process.

*Others.*

How many had stayed?

Cole's eyes darted around the room. To his right, he spotted one group attendee cleaning off blood from a video camera while another inspected Nelson's remains, a sketch pad in hand. He tried scanning the rest of the crowd for familiar faces, but the smell of iron made his stomach curdle and his head sway.

He paused and took a deep breath before slowly rolling his shoulders up, all while one unrelenting thought snaked its way through him: *He wasn't the only one.*

"Are you okay?" Luna stood beside him, dusting off her leather jacket.

Cole started to nod, but one of the men in black appeared in his line of vision, handing him a bottle of water and a warm hand towel. Although confused, he and Luna graciously accepted the items before being ushered toward the back of the room. He glanced up and realized he was facing another set of stairs. He furrowed his brows and squinted, but he couldn't see beyond the fifth or sixth row.

"That was some fucking rock and roll shit," Sol said, appearing beside Cole, a warm washcloth and water bottle also in hand. "Twisted—hell, demented—but wicked." He wiped his face, a few drops of blood smearing off in its wake.

Before Cole could respond, the electronic female voice returned to the speakers. "Thank you to those who chose to stay and document this monumental moment in history. Your work today will help raise national attention for the sex trafficking issue in our country. With any luck, we hope this will save hundreds of innocent lives."

She paused, and Cole saw the acrobats climb the staircase, once again lighting their path.

"Now, we invite you to join us on the next level for Act Two." A brief pause, and then, "Don't worry. We understand this first event was traumatically painful to witness, so we have created a softer, yet no less powerful artistic scene for this portion of The Gala."

Luna nudged him, linking their arms. "Come on."

Cole shuddered, and together, they ascended higher into the living nightmare, Sol following right behind them.

It was pitch black again at the top of the landing, but Cole thought he detected the faintest sound of cries. He felt Luna squeeze his arm, meaning she must've heard it, too.

Then, slowly, the acrobats at the top set of the stairs walked farther into the room, using the light of their fire to reveal a door. The woman on the left turned the knob slowly and swung it wide before slipping in. Cole looked at the others in the group and realized they were all waiting for who would be the first to follow.

"Come on, then," Sol said after a beat. "We didn't make it through that catastrophe to just sit around like a bunch of animals."

Good point, Cole supposed. He took a deep breath and followed his friend into the mysterious glowing room. Sure, he was traumatized from the events downstairs, but the high of the chase was too good to back down now.

He still had to find Z.

Once inside, Cole blinked, and his eyes adjusted to the new lighting. It wasn't much, but it was enough brightness to make him squint after being trapped in the darkness. When his vision finally settled, his breath hitched at the sight.

There, on either side of the room, sat a row of hospital beds. No one was in them, but the sheets were ruffled, with various flowers scattered throughout.

"Hello," a new female voice said as they all entered. "Welcome to Act Two of the night."

Cole watched the woman approach, a knot tightening in his chest as he observed her pink scrubs.

"For the safety of everyone involved on this floor, we ask that you kindly refrain from touching anyone, and if you feel sick at all, please wear a mask." She paused and pulled out a box of hospital masks, as well as a bottle of hand sanitizer. "Please also use this to help minimize the risk of germs."

A few curious looks passed through the group, but everyone obliged, nonetheless. Cole squeezed a glob onto his own hands when the contents made their way to him, but he declined a mask.

"Please also try to refrain from screaming or making loud noises so as not to startle our youngest participants."

*Shit. Shit. Shit.*

"Thank you, and welcome," she said at last, "to the postpartum unit."

Gasps once again echoed through the group, and Cole felt like his feet had been knocked out from under him. Why did everything in this fucking event have to involve pregnancies and children? Anger rippled through him as he worked to shut out thoughts of Rose, River, David, and the new baby.

Luna's grip tightened around his bicep. "You can do this."

He nodded and took a deep breath, willing his nerves to settle.

The nurse—Cole presumed that's what she was—stepped away, and a series of multicolored lights turned on, revealing a live statue made of women and infants.

At first, Cole couldn't tell what he was looking at, but after loosening his arm from Luna's grip and taking a few steps back, the image clicked into place: they were forming a heart.

Not the cute, conventional shape you'd see on Valentine's Day, but an anatomical heart.

His eyes skirted over the participants, trying to make sense of how Zanella had pieced them together. From a distance, it looked like they were all floating—the moms cradling their newborn babies in midair while collectively positioned just so, forming the heart. Upon further inspection, though, Cole realized the women were sitting on varying-sized glass cylinders.

He started to scribble the details in the notebook but snapped his head up when a little one started crying. It was coming from the bottom, and once Cole spotted them, he watched as a young woman unbuttoned her crisp white shirt and offered a bare breast to her infant.

A serene feeling washed over Cole as he remembered watching his own daughter latch for the first time. It was so beautiful, and he remembered feeling a twinge of jealousy that he'd never be able to bond with River in that way.

*And now Rose is going to experience it all again with a new baby.*
*Your brother's baby.*

Cole's heart ached at the thought, and he cleared his throat, trying to keep the tears at bay.

"Bloody hell," Sol mumbled as he averted his gaze.

Cole ignored him and stepped closer. His eyes danced around to the other women, and near the left ventricle of the display, he noted a twin mom nursing both of her babies at once, a Boppy pillow positioned around her midsection.

*What if Rose and David have twins?*

Another stab of rage landed in his chest, which infuriated him even more, because he didn't have time to let his emotions take over tonight.

*Dammit. Keep it together, Cole.*

He took a deep breath, and this time when he opened his eyes, he noticed an added detail he hadn't seen before. "What are those flowers?"

Luna lowered her camera. "Where? On the beds? I think they were random. Looked like several different ones."

Cole shook his head. "No, look. They all have a flower tucked behind their ears."

"They're Forget-Me-Nots," Sol said, apparently ready to face the bare-breasted woman now.

Cole and Luna looked at each other, confusion evident in their gaze.

"Why—" Cole started but was interrupted by the familiar Siri-like voice from somewhere overhead.

*"Rainbow baby. Noun. Plural noun: rainbow babies. A baby born subsequent to a miscarriage, stillbirth, or the death of an infant from natural causes."* She recited the Google definition, and a somber mood engulfed the room.

Cole swallowed. "So, these . . ."

"Are all rainbow babies, yes," the nurse from earlier said. "Every woman here experienced a miscarriage or loss before conceiving again. The babies you see today"—she gestured a hand toward the infants—"are all miracles. The promise of a rainbow after a storm." A sad smile settled on her lips as she spoke the last words.

Cole's heart softened, and he looked back at the women, a sense of companionship twisting its way around his heart.

They, too, had experienced grief and loss.

They knew the pain of losing a child, and yet, here they were—living with the hope of a new day, absorbing the love of a new being.

A chill ran down his spine.

"We invite you to take a moment and capture the beauty and essence of these women's stories," the nurse continued. "Rainbow babies are the symbol of hope for so many parents when they're deep in their grief. Let the stories of these mothers and their children be the guiding light for those facing their fertility journey."

A new sensation tugged at Cole's heart as the voice faded out. He was so angry with Rose and David for what they'd done—and probably would be for all his years to come.

But, standing here and seeing these women and their babies . . . it reminded Cole of how precious life really was. He realized at that moment, this wasn't *the child's* fault. And he hoped when the time came, he wouldn't resent his niece or nephew for who they were.

He took a deep inhale and walked up to a woman who was sitting cross-legged with a baby sleeping in her arms. "Hello, ma'am. My name is Cole Sloane, reporter for *The Chronicles*. Would you mind if I asked you a few questions?"

She smiled at him and nodded.

# NOW



*Thursday, October 31, 2024*

Some odd minutes later, while Cole was in the midst of another interview, the siren went off again, signaling the end of the event. He snapped his head up, looking for Luna and Sol.

"Over here!" Luna waved from the left side of the room.

He set off toward her as the electronic voice once again sounded over the speakers. "For the safety of those on the unit, we now ask that you kindly make your way to the bottom of the next set of stairs in preparation for the final act."

The lights illuminating the participants began to dim, and Cole ushered past them with the rest of the group. The acrobats from earlier were already there, lining the stairs on either side, again by candlelight. He watched the flames dance in the darkness and felt his heart rate flicker.

The voice announcer had said *final act*, meaning this was it. All he had to do was walk up these stairs, and then, finally, he would come face to face with Graham Zanella.

He gulped and followed the light of the path, ready to conquer this monumental moment.

"Cole," Luna's voice floated to his ears. "Wait."

He stopped and turned around to face her. "Yeah?"

"I . . . I don't know. I have a bad feeling about this one."

Cole cocked his head, searching her eyes for words left unsaid. "Why—"

A scream pierced through the air. Cole swiveled back around on high alert.

"Let me in!" Another sobbing cry broke from above, and a swarm of what looked like bodyguards rushed by, urging Cole and the others to move.

"Move, please!"

"Outta the way!"

A hushed silence befell the artists and storytellers as they listened in unison. Was this part of the act? Or an interruption they hadn't planned for? Cole couldn't tell.

"Jonathan! Jonathan! This is your mother! Stop this madness—"

Her cries were muffled, Cole assumed by the men in black, but that didn't stop her from protesting. He listened as the woman thrashed and screamed, her voice growing further away with every breath. A man descended the staircase and placed his hand to his ear as he brushed by and mumbled "all clear" to someone through a walkie-talkie. Cole's eyes widened as he realized what must have happened, and he looked back at Luna, who was biting her lip.

"I think . . . I think maybe that was a sign we shouldn't go."

He stared at her as fear and urgency tore through his senses. Luna had been his sounding board through this whole fiasco, so if she was saying they shouldn't go, she was probably right, but—

"I have to," Cole said before he could finish the thought. Regardless of what was up there, regardless of why that woman was screaming, he had to do this. "I can't turn back now."

A look of concern washed over her face, but she didn't object. Instead, she simply nodded and took his hand. "Okay, but you owe me *big time* if something bananas happens."

He offered her a gentle squeeze before turning around and dragging her with him. At the top of the stairs, they were greeted once again with darkness, but this time, he felt a chill in the air. His spine tingled as the coldness stung against his skin, and Luna stuffed her hands in her jacket pockets.

"Why's it so bloody cold up here?" Sol trailed just behind them, vocal as always.

"Probably a fucking morgue at this rate," a woman near them said as she reached the landing.

If only he'd known the veracity of her statement, maybe Cole wouldn't have been so quick to dismiss it. "It's an old building in late October. The HVAC unit probably doesn't heat properly throughout."

The rest of the attendees joined them, and an unsettled stillness mocked the air. After a moment of silence, Sol said, "All right then. We're here, Z." He threw his arms out and shouted, "What's next?"

They all waited anxiously for a response or light to turn on making some grand reveal like on the other floors, but nothing happened. Instead, Cole heard the faint sound of footsteps from behind. Heart pounding like the sound of a newborn's sonogram, he turned around, hoping it was Z. Instead, though, he realized it was simply the women from the stairs walking up to join them. Disappointment laced through his body as one approached him and reached out her hand.

"Here," she said. "A candle to light your way—to help you celebrate the horrific beauty of life and death."

Cole felt a familiar discomfort settle in the pit of his stomach, but he couldn't put a name to it. Hesitantly, he accepted the candle and murmured a quiet "thanks."

She nodded and turned to leave but not before leaning in and whispering, "Enter if you dare, Cole."

A shiver rippled through his body as the heat of her breath brushed his skin. He swallowed and watched her disappear, her figure slipping into the darkness.

"This better not be some satanic ritual bullshit." Sol's presence drew Cole back to the moment at hand. "I tried that shit once in college, wasn't me cup of tea, no thanks."

Cole looked at him as the singer stuck his tongue out and pretended to drag it through the tip of the flame. He started to ask him what he was doing but then thought better of it.

Shifting his gaze back to Luna, who looked absolutely stunning in the glow of the candlelight, he nodded toward the black hole before them and said, "Let's go."

She met his gaze with a gleam in her eye. "Hold on." Moving swiftly, she lifted her camera and pressed a button, the shutter clicking faster than Cole could blink. "Okay," she said, peering up from behind the lens. "Now I'm ready."

A softness wedged itself onto Cole's lips, and he smiled. Then, he cupped his hand around the flame to protect it from any swift rushes of air and stepped forward.

At first, he saw nothing. The light from the flame was small, though, so he took small, calculated steps, advancing his way into the room.

After approximately twenty feet, he realized the area resembled an ordinary nineteenth-century library. Bookcases lined either side of the room, creating the narrow pathway he was on. He paused for a moment and watched as the others fanned out to explore, their tiny, distant flames disappearing behind the shelves. He resumed his path down the straight and narrow—like he so often did, but after another thirty or so steps, he concluded the room had been untouched.

*What the hell?*

"Where are you, Z?" He started to turn back around to see if his friends had experienced any better luck exploring the aisles of books, but a flash of something caught the corner of his eye.

*Bingo.*

He didn't stop to verify his suspicion before calling the others over. "Luna! Sol!" His reporter instincts were taking over, and he moved quickly.

A crash sounded behind him as Sol ran into a bookcase, but Cole ignored him.

"You're fine," Luna hissed. "Let's go."

His body coursing with energy, Cole internally screamed as he located the source of the light. "Back here! There's a door!"

The sound of hurried footsteps appeared behind him as his friends and the other remaining participants raced through the musty air to join him. Cole tried to wait a moment for them to catch up, but his anxiety got the better of him, and he moved to grab the door handle.

*This is it.*

Heart pounding, he swung it open and stepped inside the room. His eyes darted around every corner, searching for Zanella, but he didn't see anyone, at least not yet.

What he did see, though, was a grand, beautifully haunting room.

Portraits hung all across the walls, with ornate, iron sconces weaving between them, while black fabrics draped from the ceiling. Like the other exhibits, the room was dark, and the low lighting cast a dim, weathered glow on a variety of old Victorian pieces. Cole squinted and walked farther into the room, marveling at the wingback chairs and buttoned leather couches as he was transported to another time period, the smell of leather and books coating the air.

As a whole, the area should have felt large and isolated, but somehow, it didn't. Despite the vast size, dark corners, and cold temperatures, the room had an odd sense of coziness—like perhaps the architecture was built with the librarian's grandparents in mind.

Footsteps echoed behind Cole, disrupting his trance-like state. His friends greeted him, the rest of the group trailing close behind.

"Where are you at, fucker," Sol said under his breath, an electric buzz to his voice.

The response was almost immediate. "I'm right here, silly."

*No.*

A sweep of unease hit the air, and a chill raced up Cole's spine at the sound of a child's voice. He spun in a circle but still didn't see anyone.

And then the matches struck, and filtered light tore through the air.

"We're all right here, silly."

Cole's eyes landed on six individuals, each one holding a small flame as it licked at their fingertips. It was hard to make out their features, but he could instantly tell they were underage, some much younger than others.

"Can't you see us?"

Despite his inner voice screaming not to, Cole took a step forward.

And that's when he heard the voice, *his* voice.

*Zanella.*

# NOW



"Cole—I always knew you'd be the first."

A firepit glowed to life out of the corner of Cole's eye, revealing the outline of a man. He was seated on an oblong sofa with his back to them, but there was no mistaking the presence in his tone.

"Zanella," Cole breathed.

The man stood and turned slowly. Cole felt Luna's claws digging into his skin again as he held his breath, waiting for the full reveal.

"What an honor it is," he said, the front of his body now facing them, "to finally meet your acquaintance." A single spotlight turned on, and Graham Zanella lifted his head, at last locking eyes with Cole.

"It's really you," he breathed.

A smile cracked across Zanella's face, and Cole absorbed the pure magnetism that radiated off this man. He was tall, well over six feet, and had disheveled, coal-black hair that laid in waves atop his head. He was wearing a thin, black-feathered masquerade mask that swiped across his eyes, but even in the dim lighting, Cole could make out a piercing blue color staring back at him. His jawline was pronounced, and his cheekbones were high, mirroring the ideal image of societal beauty.

The outlier, though, was the red scar that ran down the left side of his face. It started just above his eyebrow and slashed through the puffiness of his cheek before landing at the top of his upper lip. It should have been terrifying, but somehow, it made him all the more alluring.

"Well, all right, then," Sol's voice cut in. "What's your costume supposed to be, mate? I'm not sure I get it."

Zanella threw his head back in laughter and clapped his hands. "Solstice. I'm so glad you made it." He paused and looked around the room, a mysterious twinkle in his eye, and then cleared his throat. "Once upon a midnight dreary, while I pondered—"

His voice trailed off, and then Luna spoke up, finishing the next line. "Weak and weary."

"By George, I think she's got it!" Z clapped his hands again and flashed Luna a dazzling smile.

Cole observed the interaction, trying to fit the pieces together. Zanella's ensemble was an unusual one, he'd give him that, but he hadn't expected anything less. The artist wore a black suit jacket, which was laced with small, white whimsical designs. Underneath, he sported a plain white T-shirt that had been splattered with what Cole could only assume were droplets of blood, and it was tucked into a high-waisted pair of black joggers. The most unique aspect, though, was his mask. Cole had originally thought he resembled a plague doctor, but upon closer inspection, he realized it was a raven.

"You're Edgar Allen Poe," he breathed in awe.

Z looked at him and winked. "Poe was an extraordinary man, was he not?"

So many questions steamrolled through Cole's head, but the one nagging thought he couldn't shake was the feeling that he'd seen him before.

*That scar. I know that scar.*

"Who are you?" Cole asked.

Z walked in a wide circle around the group, observing each one. "I am society's all-seeing artistic eye. The one who captures it all, even the hardest truths." He paused and walked over to the children. "I am, in other words, Big Brother's major pain in the ass," he said with a rueful smile.

The room was quiet, but after perhaps a beat too long, a laugh erupted from Sol. "You're a major pain in my ass, too, mate!" He chuckled so hard he snorted, and after a moment, Z joined him in laughter.

Cole felt the tension roll off his shoulders slightly, but not enough to let his guard down.

"What is the purpose of all this?" the woman in the unicorn dress asked, interrupting the hysteria-induced moment. "Why are we here, Zanella? Who are these children?"

Z shook his head and circled back to the fire, stoking the logs as they danced in the flames. "That's an excellent question, Deirdre."

One Cole also wanted to know the answer to—if only he could find his voice again.

"I have chosen all of you specifically for your remarkable and uncanny ability to capture the truth. Your portraits, for example," he said, nodding his head to her, "are brilliantly horrific. I hate them. And that's exactly what makes me love them."

She pursed her lips but didn't respond.

Running his fingers through his hair, Z continued. "Tonight, we are about to embark on perhaps the most catastrophic piece of living art ever to be known to mankind, and I have chosen you all to bear witness. I believe you are the ones who can tell these stories the best, and therefore, I am entrusting you with a part of my soul by breaking my own barriers and revealing myself before you tonight."

Hushed glances rolled through the group as the remaining participants eyed each other, all silently asking one question.

*What have you seen?*

Cole shuddered at the thought as he remembered all the worst stories he'd covered over the years—homicide, accidental drownings, domestic abuse. You name it, and Cole's probably reported on it. He had become desensitized to it.

Perhaps that was why he'd made it here.

Why they'd all made it here.

"And that leads me to my next point," Zanella said before offering a small, sad grin. "Ladies and gentlemen, I'd like to introduce you to tonight's final participants."

As he finished speaking, the children all blew out their matchsticks, and warm spotlights turned on, casting a glow on the small humans. Cole could see now they were sitting on stools, each one doing their own silent act of sorts, and a lump formed in his throat as his eyes landed on a young girl with a knife.

"Take a step up—they won't bite," Z joked, clearly not reading the room. "Everyone give a warm hello to Nadia, Jonathan, Elizabeth, Jaxson, Wolfgang, and Xander." He gestured to each of them as he spoke.

Cole's gaze stayed on Nadia, his breath hitching as she slid the knife into her stocking. Under the light, she looked like she was eleven or twelve years old. He watched as she braided her long, black hair into pigtails and hummed a song.

He knew he needed to speak, but words were evading him right now. He cleared his throat, working up the nerve to ask her why she was here, but then she opened her mouth and let out a blood-curdling scream before he had the chance.

*"Down the river, not across the stream!"*

His eyes snapped wide in terror as the child pulled the knife from her stocking and sliced it down her arm in one swift motion.

Her voice rang in his ears, but it didn't matter, because Cole wasn't there anymore. His body seized at the sight of blood, and the imagery of the knife flashed in his brain on repeat. He dropped to the floor, and a deafening silence invaded his ears.

# THEN



*Friday, September 30, 2022*

"What do you mean you're at the airport?" Rose said from the other line. "I thought you were talking to Nate and telling him you couldn't go."

Cole shifted his feet in the TSA line. "I know, honey. I'm sorry, I just . . . this is going to be a really big piece, and I don't want my own team member to scoop me."

"Are you kidding me right now, Cole?"

"I'm sorry. Please tell River I love her, and I'll be back Monday morning before she leaves for school. She can read me her poem then, or I can hear it next weekend."

Rose scoffed. "Absolutely not. I'm not being the bad guy for you. You're the one blowing off his daughter—you tell her."

She ended the call, and Cole swore under his breath. He felt bad enough already, but he really couldn't miss this opportunity. There would always be another poetry slam, but there wouldn't be another chance to be the first reporter to get an exclusive interview with Graham Zanella, America's most sought-after underground artist. He knew River would be upset, but he'd make it up to her later—maybe buy her a new album for her record player or take her to that improv comedy club she was always begging to go to.

He sighed and pulled out his phone to shoot her a quick text.

**Dad:** *I'm sorry I won't be there tonight, River Bug. But I love you so much and will see you Monday morning. Maybe we can go to a White Ember Improv comedy show next weekend? Be good for your mom, please.*

He saw three dots appear in the lower left-hand corner, insinuating she was typing, but after a while, the symbols disappeared, and a response never came. He sighed and slumped his shoulders as he boarded the plane and turned his phone on airplane mode. It was a short flight, so he promised himself he would check again as soon as they landed.

"Hello, passengers, this is your captain speaking." A gravelly voice sounded over the speakers. "I'm sorry to report we're running on a bit of a delay, but sit back and relax, and I'm sure we'll be in the air in no time."

*Figures.*

Cole groaned and rubbed his temples, wondering why Zanella made his job so damn difficult.

"Sir, would you like a complimentary beverage while you wait?"

He looked up at the sound of the flight attendant's bubbly voice and smiled. "You got liquor?"

She laughed in response. "I can do a mimosa, but that's the best I got."

Better than nothing, he supposed. "I'll take one, please. Thank you."

The rest of the flight remained uneventful, much like the entire weekend. On Monday morning, after Z artfully slipped through his fingers yet again, he woke up at the crack of dawn for his flight home and sent one last message before again boarding the plane.

**Dad:** *I'm sorry, River. You deserved my attention this weekend. I'll be home soon. Promise to make it up to you. Love you.*

When he landed and still hadn't heard from her, he called Rose.

She immediately ignored the call, though, and sent a quick "in a meeting" message back to him. Cole frowned.

**Cole:** *Is River with you? She still won't talk to me.*

**Rose:** *Maybe you should've thought of that before you left.*

A touch of anger boiled under his skin, but he let it go. She was right, after all.

An hour later, he pulled into his driveway, hopeful to see them both and make it up to his girls. He hopped out of his Jeep and heard Emmett barking loudly, the sound making him smile.

"Rose! River!" he called once as he walked through the side door. "I'm home! I missed you guys."

But the sounds of Emmett's barks drowned out his words. Cole paused in the doorway, an odd sensation prickling at the back of his neck. "Em?" he called, and the dog ran down the stairs, coming into view as he continued to howl.

Cole moved with a sense of urgency now. "Hey, what's wrong buddy?" He examined the dog's fur but saw nothing alarming. "What's going on, Em?"

Emmett barked again and shoved past Cole, heaving his large body back up the steps.

And that's when Cole knew something was very wrong.

"River? Rose!" The panic rose in his voice as he followed the dog up the stairs, and Cole all but halted from fear when he saw where his pet stopped.

*No.*

Emmett stood outside River's door, scratching his paw against the grain of the wood and crying for his human to understand. Cole bolted forward, his senses finally snapping into place. He shoved through River's doorway, but he was temporarily blinded as the glint of a blood-soaked knife hit the light.

*What the—*

"River!" Cole's expression widened in terror as he saw his daughter's blood-ied silhouette lying on the floor. "Oh my God, River." He ran to her and dropped to his knees. Her normally tan skin was now pale white, and dewdrops of sweat coated the baseline of her matted black hair. "River, baby? *River!*"

She slid her gaze to meet Cole's, but only for a moment before her eyes rolled back in her head.

"No, no, no. *Rose!*" He yelled for his wife before gently patting the side of his daughter's face.

"Hey, hey. Wake up, baby. Stay with me."

His eyes darted around the room, frantic with panic as he tried to piece together what had happened. There was the knife, but he also saw shards of glass strewn across the floor. His pulse quickened as his gaze followed the trail back to her shattered window.

*What the hell?*

"Dad?" a small voice croaked.

"River." He snapped his head back to her, heart thumping at the sound of her voice. "I'm right here, sweetie." He gazed into her icy blue eyes as she blinked at him, his chest cracking at the sight. "What happened? Please, you have to tell Daddy."

"I—" Her body began to twitch.

Fear shot through Cole's core. "Dammit, River, *stay with me.*" He patted his pockets, searching for his phone and cursing when he realized he didn't have it.

"Rose!" He ripped off his shirt, scanning River's body for the source of the wound and wincing when he found it.

*Fuck.*

If he could just stop the bleeding . . .

"Rose, call an ambulance *now!*"

"What's wrong?" He heard her voice—*finally*—from the hallway.

"We need a fucking ambulance." River's body was convulsing now, and Cole relied solely on the adrenaline pumping through his veins to keep him from falling apart.

*No, no, no,* he thought, *not my baby. Please, not my baby girl.*

"Oh my God!" Rose screamed as she appeared in the doorway.

Tears streamed down Cole's face as he tried—and failed—to clot the wound. No matter what he did, the gushing continued. He pulled her close to his chest and wrapped his arms around her before looking up from the thickening pool of blood to find Rose still standing in the doorway, frozen in fear.

"Rosie," he yelled, his cries scratching the back of his throat. "Snap out of it! She needs 911, now." His voice cracked on the last word as he pleaded with his wife to move, to do something.

But it was no use; Rose remained glued to the spot.

*Dammit.*

Desperate, he stood and heaved River's fifteen-year-old body into his arms. "It's going to be okay, sweetie." He pushed past his wife, who flinched when River's flailing arms hit her, and Cole flew down the stairs. "It's going to be okay," he repeated as his tears dripped onto her skin, mingling with the blood. "Daddy's here."

# NOW



### Thursday, October 31, 2024

"Cole! Hey, snap out of it, mate."

*"River!"*

"Cole, it's me, Luna. Hey!"

"River! What have you *done*?" Cole dropped to his knees, wailing in agony now. "Please, God, no!"

"Cole, you have to snap out of it."

Cold water stung Cole's face as Luna poured her water bottle over his head. He blinked rapidly, his eyes and mind trying to differentiate the past from the present.

"What the bloody hell?"

*Sol.*

"I had to shock his senses to ground him. It's a simple technique," Luna scolded. "Cole," she said again, snapping her fingers in front of his face. "Hey, look at me! You're here with me, Luna, and we're at The Gala, with Sol and the others."

He stared at her, and his eyes widened in horror as he realized what he'd just seen. "The girl," he rasped.

"Is right here!" Z's voice cut in, motioning to Nadia, who'd fallen off the stool and rolled into the floor. "The girl is right here and bleeding profusely, Cole."

Cole swiveled his head in the direction of Zanella's voice, and his heart palpitations reached new levels as the man came into view. "You have to help her! *We* have to help her!"

"I'm afraid I can't do that, Cole."

A wave of rage washed through him, alerting his senses. "And why the hell not? She just fucking slit her wrists—somebody call a damn ambulance before she loses too much blood!" He scrambled to stand, almost knocking Luna over in the process. "Nadia, hey!" He snapped his fingers at the girl as her eyes rolled back in her head, just like River's had done. "I'm here! It's going to be okay. I just need you to hold on a little longer. Luna, Sol, somebody get me a damn T-shirt or rag! We have to stop the bleeding *now* before it's too late."

"Cole—" Luna started, her voice straining.

"Don't worry, don't worry," Zanella interrupted. "I'll be the one to tell him."

Cole looked up from the bleeding child, the ghost of his pasts all but suffocating him. "What the fuck? Why is everyone just standing around?" He screamed as the anger rushed out of him, like a volcano finally erupting. "Nadia! *Nadia!* Stay with me. We're going to get you some help, okay?"

"She doesn't want to be saved, Cole." Z stood behind him as the others watched the scene unfold.

"Yeah, I get that she's fucking suicidal, Graham, but we can't just let her die! We need to stop the bleeding until the ambulance gets here, and then someone from psych can talk to her. Please!" The urgency rushed out of his voice, his eyes wild. "We have to save her. *I* have to save her." His voice cracked on the last line as he looked down at the child's face and saw a flashback of his own little girl's blood seeping into the floorboards. "Please," he begged, his tone softer now as his adrenaline crashed and the emotional scars he'd been carrying ripped open, wide for all to see.

"She came here tonight," Zanella said with a lighter approach, "to end her life with us. She wanted us here, you included, to capture it."

"That doesn't make any fucking sense." Cole pounded the palms of his hands against his eyes.

"It doesn't. It doesn't make any sense at all, but neither do the years of trauma and bullying she's endured." He took a step closer to Cole and Nadia, and crouched down. "I invited you here tonight, Cole, because her story deserved to be told. And I knew that you, better than anyone, would do it justice."

Cole shook his head again in protest. "I don't know what you're saying. We have to *help* her. Please! Somebody, help this poor child."

"She was going to do this whether we intervened or not. It was solely her choice, and I did not coerce her in any way. She, along with the others, have all chosen to end their lives here tonight and are willing to let us capture their stories so that we can help in the most powerful way we know how to." He stopped speaking and looked Cole dead in the eyes before adding, "By not letting their pain die in vain."

Cole blanched at his words. This was insane. "You're fucking nuts." He stood and ripped off his jacket and started unbuttoning his white-collared shirt. "If you won't help her, I will. Luna, Sol, can you guys help me? We need to tie her arm to help stop the blood, and dammit, we need our phones to call 911." He continued to ramble, not realizing no one in the room was moving to help him—not even his friends.

"Nadia, I need you to keep your eyes open and focus on breathing, okay? Can you do that for me?" He started to tie his shirt around her forearm in an effort to slow the bleeding when he felt her hand grip his. "Nadia?" He searched her eyes, desperate to save this poor girl.

"I—want—" Her voice cut off as she coughed, gasping for air.

"You want what, honey? Whatever it is, tell me what you need."

"I—want—to—die." Her words shook him to his core, and he didn't know what to say back.

"You don't know what you're saying," he finally managed. "Please, we can get you help. It'll be okay. Everything will get better, but we have to act fast."

She nodded and opened her mouth to speak for the last time.

"Help—sooner—next—time."

And with that last, dying breath, Nadia's head rolled to the side, her eyes staring wide but unmoving.

# NOW



Thursday, October 31, 2024

Every fiber in Cole's being broke.

*Help sooner.*

Is that what River had thought? When Cole found her lying there on the floor, had she been wishing her dad had tried sooner? Fought harder to see the warning signs before it was too late? Would he have known what to look for if he'd been more educated? Seen more stories about suicide in the media and society in general? Hell, had he known anything at all about suicide before his daughter took her own life?

His mind spun a million miles a minute as months' worth of therapy spilled out of his chest and leaked onto the floor.

"Have you started to reconsider my proposition?" Zanella asked.

Cole shook his head as the intrusive thoughts spiraled in his brain. "I—I don't know." A numbness took over his body as he tried to make sense of it all.

"I'll do it," a new voice said from the crowd.

Cole looked up, the comment a jarring reality to his manic state.

"Wonderful! Excellent decision, Alejandra." Zanella clasped his hands together again, apparently entertained by his own twisted house of horrors.

A woman with terracotta skin stepped out from the group and made her way to the front. She cast a glance at the other children, and when she spoke, a faint

Hispanic dialect laced her tone. "I will honor her life by drawing a depiction of this painful story, but I pray it is the only one I have to do tonight. Please choose wisely because, as you can see"—she gestured to Nadia's dead body—"this is a permanent, irreversible decision." And with that, Alejandra sat down, crossed her legs, and pulled out her sketchpad.

Cole looked at her, dumbfounded. Surely this wasn't the answer . . . was it?

"Cole." Luna's voice filtered through his thoughts. "It's okay. We don't have to do this. We can leave."

He looked down at Nadia's dead body, his own chest moving rapidly.

"Time is of the essence here, Cole." Zanella walked by him, a candle now in his hands as he bent down to inspect the woman's wound.

Silence filled the air as Alejandra drew and the remaining attendees watched, waiting to see what everyone else would do. Cole felt like his brain had short-circuited, and he was desperate to fix it.

To fix all of it.

To right the wrong he'd made all those years ago when he chose work over family.

When his daughter chose death over life.

But how could he fix this if he couldn't talk to her?

"She's already dead," he said finally.

Zanella's attention snapped to him. "What?"

Cole repeated himself and then added, "I can't interview a dead person."

A smile traced across Zanella's face as he took in the meaning of Cole's words. "Indeed, you can't."

"Luna." Cole's voice was hoarse now. "Can you take her picture?"

Her eyes grew wide at the request. She looked back around at Sol, who shrugged, and then took a gentle step toward Cole. "I don't know if we should."

"And why the hell not?" Cole snapped, waving his arms. "She's already fucking dead! How many more teenage girls must die before we wake up and realize we're the fucking problem?" He was yelling now, but he didn't care. Rage wrapped around his body, tuning out the numbness from before.

Luna didn't back down. "Cole, I think you're in shock. We need to take a minute."

"Nadia didn't have a minute," Cole rasped. "And neither did River." Tears lined his eyes now, and his voice broke at the mention of his daughter.

Luna closed her eyes and took a deep breath. Slowly, she peeled her lids open, locked eyes with her friend, and nodded.

Cole nodded back, sending her a silent thank you, and watched as she stepped up to the body.

"Nadia, sweet girl," Luna whispered under her breath. "You deserved so much more." She swiped a quick tear from her lash line and then proceeded to photograph the young, lifeless girl.

Cole turned away, his stomach in knots.

"Excellent," Zanella said before sweeping a hand at the other children. "Who's next?"

"I can't watch this anymore," someone said from the remaining few who Z had invited. It was a man with short, dark hair who appeared to be in his twenties.

"If you wish to leave, I won't stop you from joining the others in the detainment room until the event is complete, but I urge you to reconsider your statement, Zachariah. Imagine what this could do for your podcast—the people you could reach, the lives you could touch."

Zachariah scratched the back of his head as he stared at Nadia. "Man, this shit is too twisted. Even for you."

"That's the point, though, bloke." It was Sol who cut in this time. Everyone turned to look at him now, and he continued with a shrug. "Our ability to turn a blind eye to shit that's too *twisted* is the irony here." He cast a glance at Zanella. "Tell me if I'm wrong, mate?"

Z nodded, a twinkle of pride in his eyes.

"If we aren't willing to document this, to talk about it, then who will?" The rock star paused to take his hat off and throw his hair up into a haphazard man bun. "Could've warned a fucker, though, Z, before people just started offing themselves."

"That'd ruin the other semblance of symbolism," the artist retorted.

Sol let out a humorless chuckle and walked away, humming a new rift. "Wish I had my guitar."

Z focused his attention back on Zachariah. "So, what'll it be?"

The podcaster shifted back and forth on his feet but then ultimately shook his head no. "Nah, I'm out, man. Can't do it."

Zanella sighed but nodded in understanding, and one of his bodyguards appeared, escorting Zachariah out. "Anyone else?"

Cole watched as the scene played out. Sol continued to hum to himself, Luna and Alejandra continued their work capturing Nadia's corpse, and the remaining two attendees looked at each other with wild gazes in their eyes while Z held his breath.

"I can't—"

"I will—"

They both spoke at the same time, startled by the other's response. Then, Cole watched as the woman joined Zachariah to exit, and the man stepped forward and said, "I better not get arrested for this."

Zanella threw his head back in laughter. "That's the spirit, Marcus! Your videography is always divine. I can't wait to see what you create." He circled around the children, returning his attention to those who were still alive. "Now, who's next?"

Cole felt the bile creep up his throat.

A young boy with curly strawberry blond hair raised his hand.

"Jaxson." Zanella paused, a serene tone to his voice. "I knew it had to be you." Then, he did something new and used sign language to communicate with the boy.

"Is he Deaf?" Cole was past pleasantries at this point.

"Indeed."

His heart tugged at the response, but it didn't stop him. "I don't—I don't know sign language. Can he read lips?"

"I know ASL," Luna said, cutting in.

Cole's eyes shot to her now. "Can you interpret for me? Please." He gulped. "I'd like to talk to him."

She nodded and walked closer to the boy. Cole watched as she smiled at him and signed what he assumed was a welcome greeting.

Jaxson turned to look at Cole and waved, causing his heart to crack. It took him a moment to collect himself, but then he pulled up a stool—Nadia's blood-stained stool—and asked, "How old are you, Jaxson?"

Luna signed Cole's question, but he didn't answer at first. Instead, he played with a lighter he had in his hands, flicking it on and off, watching the flames dance. *"Nine."*

Cole shuddered when Luna repeated his answer.

*So young.*

He took a deep breath and tried to swallow the pain. "May I ask . . . why are you doing this, son? You have so much life to live. So much ahead of you." Cole knew it was a leading question—hell, he straight up offered his unsolicited opinion, but sometimes, rules were meant to be broken, and this was one of those times.

Jaxson looked back at Luna, sticking the tip of his finger in the flame as she spoke to him.

*"Because,"* he finally signed, lifting his eyes to Cole, *"she didn't want me."*

Cole waited for Luna to interpret. "What does that mean?" He held the boy's stare for a moment, not knowing it would soon be the new image that haunted his dreams. "Who didn't want you?"

Jaxson's eyes locked on Luna as she moved her fingers at lightning speed. A halting silence crashed over the room as everyone waited for his response.

This time, though, he spoke with a distinctive voice that rose from the back of his throat, all while staring at Luna. "You."

And then he signed one simple word by tapping his thumb and outstretched hand against his chin.

NOW

# NOW

## Thursday, October 31, 2024

Luna's mouth dropped open, her eyes bugging out of her head.

"What did he say?" Cole demanded.

But she didn't answer. Instead, it was Zanella who spoke. "He signed, 'Mom.'"

Cole stared at Luna in disbelief. "What is he talking about?"

"I-I don't know," she stammered. "I don't have any k-kids."

Cole looked from her to Zanella to the kid, and his anger rose as he tried to determine what was happening. "What the hell is going on here, Z? Why did this kid just fucking sign *mommy*?"

He had trusted Luna, more than he'd ever trusted anyone. He didn't know what he'd do if he found out the only woman left in his life lied to him.

"Enough with the theatrics, Cole," Z said. He cracked his neck and shoved his hands in his pockets before directing his attention to Luna. "You have to know I didn't plan for this."

She scrunched her face in confusion and horror as Cole's eyes ping-ponged between the two of them. "Didn't plan for *what*?"

"I would've never thought to check if you hadn't acted so strange when you and Cole went to the fertility clinic—yes, yes, I watched you two on the cameras

274

that day, don't act so surprised. But trust me when I say I was just as shocked as you are, really."

Confusion still twisted its way onto Luna's face—until it didn't.

"No," she breathed.

"Mhm," Zanella said, shaking his head. "I told you I had a surprise for you. Imagine my shock when I discovered that Miss Luna Monroe's egg had been fermented with a stranger's sperm to help a lovely local couple conceive a child."

The color drained from Luna's face.

*Oh my God,* Cole thought. "What did you just fucking say?" He jumped from his stool and took a step toward Zanella.

"You heard me correctly, I'm afraid. The boy is, genetically speaking, Luna's child." Z tugged at his hair, and the action gave Cole an odd sense of déjà vu. "He was born Deaf, and when the intended parents found out, they decided they didn't want him. The surrogate mother they'd selected to carry him couldn't afford to keep a child, so she gave him up for adoption. Jaxson here has been living in foster care his entire life, with frequent visits to the pediatric psych unit."

It was Luna's turn to vomit now. She ran toward a corner, and Cole heard her doubling over in agony as she emptied the contents of her stomach. He turned back to face Z and Jaxson again.

"I still don't understand." He pinched the bridge of his nose as the smell of vomit and blood curled in his nostrils. "How is that even possible?"

"I'm surprised she didn't tell you, Cole. Honestly, with the rate you two have been moving, I thought you'd know all of each other's deepest, darkest *secrets.*" He paused and then added, "Although, knowing you, she may have, and you were too consumed with yourself to notice."

The words stung and confused Cole. "Zanella," he growled, his patience wearing thin.

"Don't get your superhero panties in a wad, Cole." Z continued to walk in circles around the group, motioning lively with his painter's hands and playing into the theatrics of his orchestrated madness. "Luna darling donated her eggs about a decade ago while she was in college. Then, an infertile couple chose her eggs for their future child, and . . . well, you know that part of the story now.

"Anyway, the surrogate never signed the second contract that would've legally allowed the intended parents' names to be on the birth certificate, meaning they basically got off scot-free while she had to deal with the fallout. The state should really look into fine-tuning their assisted reproductive technology laws to prevent this type of thing from happening again."

Cole blinked, overwhelmed by the information.

"Yes, yes, it's a shame." Zanella sucked in his bottom lip and tsked.

Still dazed and perplexed by the increasing familiarity he found in Z's voice, Cole turned toward Luna, who was walking back now.

"Lu . . ." he started. "Is this really true?"

Her response was immediate. "No." She grabbed her hair and then laced her fingers behind her head. "I mean, yes. Ugh, I don't know."

Cole waited for her to find the words.

"I did donate my eggs in college. That part's true, but I don't know what happened to them after that." She looked at Jaxson again, her expression unreadable. "It's all confidential."

"But why?" Cole asked. Luna was the last person he'd expect this from.

"I told you about my sister." Her voice was barely above a whisper as she stared at the boy. "She was sick, and I didn't know what I'd do if I had a child who was sick."

She scrubbed a hand over her face as the tears slipped out. Cole closed the distance between them to comfort her, but she brushed him to the side and took a step toward Jaxson instead.

"Go on," Z said. "Ask him. He'll tell you it's all true, give you all the details."

Cole watched as Luna raised shaky fingers into the air and signed.

When Jaxson nodded and signed back, a futile cry erupted from her lungs. The tears flowed freely now, and Cole flew to her side, acting without thinking. She tried to speak, but the panic made her words come out broken.

"I—had—no—idea!"

"*Yeah, right,*" the boy signed, and Z interpreted, sending Luna into another fit of sobs. "*You never cared about me. You fucking gave me away before I was even created.*"

"Ouch," Zanella said, speaking for himself now. "Tell her how you really feel, Jax."

Z raised his hands to sign something to the boy, and when he did, Cole's eyes grew wide at the sight of his nautical star hand tattoo, a new revelation sinking in.

*No*, he thought, *impossible*.

He opened his mouth to speak, but just then Jaxson struck his lighter again, and Cole watched in slow motion horror as the child tipped it to his hair.

The panic in his voice rose like a crescendo. "Hey, hey, hey, what are you doing?"

He moved but wasn't quick enough. The spark danced slowly at first and then erupted all at once as the flame caught fire and spread to his entire head.

"NO!" Luna screamed in agonizing pain.

She tore her jacket off at lightning speed and flung it at him, trying to put out the flame before it caught further.

The boy deflected it with a quick move of his arm and cried as the tears consumed him, and he signed something else to her.

Flames exploded then on Jaxson's head, and something inside Cole snapped, rage taking over his body. "Get her out of here!" he yelled at Sol, who obeyed and scooped Luna up in his arms and ran toward the staircase. Her screams faded but not without resistance.

"That's my *child*! Somebody help him!"

Cole's brain snapped into focus. His eyes darted around, searching for Luna's jacket, and he grabbed it and attempted to wrap it around Jaxson's head again. But the boy threw it off, his throaty cries filling the air. Desperate and out of options, Cole launched for the child, grabbing him and ignoring the hot, searing flames that licked at his skin. "You," he barked at the only remaining male attendee. "I saw a fire extinguisher outside the door. Let's move!"

The man nodded quickly and moved without hesitation. Together, they barreled back through the maze of haunted bookcases until they reached the extinguisher.

"There," Cole shouted. The man shoved his foot into it, shattering the glass with force. Cole screamed as the heat from the fire breached his wardrobe. "Hurry!"

He held the writhing child and prayed to a God he hoped existed.

*Please . . .*

He struggled to breathe, and just when he thought the flames were going to consume them both, a blast of white foam shot through his midsection. His body buzzed from the electric jolt, but he held steady. Finally, the commotion came to a stop, and he opened his eyes.

Confirming Jaxson was no longer on fire, Cole shoved him into the guy's arms. "Get him to a hospital, now."

He turned back to face the door, red clouding his vision as his thoughts returned to that damn hand tattoo.

# NOW

*Thursday, October 31, 2024*

Without thinking, Cole raced through the web of shelves on the top floor, his body groaning in protest. The smell of burnt flesh invaded his nostrils, but he didn't care.

He had to see if it was true.

If it was really *him*.

He rounded the corner and found the door of doomsday once more, kicking it in. "Zanella!" he yelled. His eyes scanned the room, and he noticed that like Z, the other children were gone.

*Where are you?*

Something clattered behind Cole, and he spun around, his eyes wild as they finally landed on the now-familiar, unfamiliar face.

"Harley," he breathed.

Z took off the slim mask that covered his eyes and laughed. "Took you long enough."

Cole stared at him, stunned at the confirmation of his revelation—that Graham Zanella, the world-famous provocateur he'd chased for years, was his old college roommate.

"It's really you."

The artist offered him another dazzling smile. "I should've won an award for that performance." He tossed the mask aside and ran his fingers through his hair again. "All those theater classes finally paid off."

*Theater.*

Harley had been a theater major.

His mind swirled as he tried to piece it together.

"But you look so . . ."

"Different?" Z finished. "Yes, well, I was in an accident shortly after graduation, not that you'd bothered to check in, and it left me with this nasty scar. It's funny what a little cosmetic surgery can do."

Cole squinted, examining his scar in full now that the mask was off. Why did it still feel so familiar if he didn't get it until after college?

And his *name.*

"Your name," Cole said under his breath.

Zanella scoffed. "Harley Smith. I always hated that name. So *suburban.* Nobody would've taken me seriously with a name like that." He scratched his invisible stubble. "I needed something . . . enticing. Something people would remember."

"But *why*?" Cole asked, clearing his throat. "Why have you done—all of this?" He motioned his arms in a wide circle, looking behind him.

Z walked back to the fireplace and shook off his jacket, revealing a full sleeve of tattoos on his left arm. "Now, come on, Cole. You of all people should understand my intentions better than anyone."

Cole followed him and scrunched his face. "What are you talking about?"

"Who do you think I learned it all from?" His voice boomed in the now-empty space, causing a slight echo. "You were always going on about your journalism classes, and ethics this and ethics that. Honestly, I found it annoying at first, but I don't know. Somewhere around the eleventh or twelfth time you left *All the President's Men* playing in the background, I started to pay attention."

Cole still wasn't following.

"What do you mean?" he asked, ignoring Z's look of annoyance.

"I mean, Sloane, that all of *this*—all that I am and all that I do—is because of you."

*No.*

Cole shook his head.

That was impossible.

He wasn't the cause of the very thing that evaded him the most.

He couldn't be.

"That bullshit you spewed about uncovering the truth and acting as a *watchdog* over the government started to bleed into my thoughts." Zanella stretched his arms in front of him and then cracked his neck. "It was like a spider had crawled inside my veins, taking over my central nervous system and spinning a new web of ideas—ones I couldn't stop.

"I began to read your articles and became fascinated with them. I admired your willingness to challenge authority and seek the truth. Your writing was good, but you needed help in other areas."

"Help?"

Z gave him a rueful smile. "Does the name Carol Vance ring a bell?"

Cole's eyes widened. Of course it did. He remembered her well. Carol's body turned up dead the morning after a football playoff game during Cole's senior year. As the university's crime beat reporter, his editor had assigned it to him. He covered it for weeks, but it wasn't until provocative images of Carol and one of her professors landed on his doorstep that he went to the police and helped solve the case.

"I see you're remembering," Z said, bringing Cole back to the present.

"It was . . . awful." He stared into the fire, the hollowness in his chest growing weaker by the minute.

"Ah, but not for you." Z shook his head. "For you, it was the highlight of your academic career—the fuel that burned your increasing desire to be a reporter. And to think, it was all thanks to me."

Cole wanted to scream from all the mind games. "Just spit it out. What are you talking about?"

Zanella looked him dead in the eyes. "Who do you think sent you those photos?"

His words were like a lightning bolt to the chest.

"I went to great lengths to get you that information, and you didn't even care. You ran off with it straight to the cops and took all the fame, all the glory, while I muddled around our apartment—the true detective who'd solved the case."

*That doesn't make sense.*

Cole's head was spinning.

"And then," Z continued, "because that wasn't punishment enough, I came home one day and overheard you laughing about me to your friends."

*Oh, fuck.*

"'Harley's so weird, man.' 'Why do you room with this guy?' 'I think he's maybe, like, *into you*, dude.'" Zanella imitated jock-like voices for each quote.

"Harley," Cole started, "come on, we didn't mean the things we said back then—"

"Yes, you did, and you know it," Z spat, his voice turning lethal. "And it's Graham to you."

A hint of fear laced its way inside of Cole, and he tried again. "Graham, I'm sorry, man. I shouldn't have let my friends joke about you."

"Oh, boo hoo, you're *sorry*, Cole. Like that makes everything okay," he sneered. "You were a dick then, and you're a dick now. I don't know what Rose ever saw in you."

The sound of her name still sent daggers through his heart, but he grimaced nonetheless. "Don't bring her into this."

"Oh, but she's my favorite part! Her and that beautiful daughter of yours. It's tragic, really, what happened to her."

Something about the way he said that made Cole's pulse quicken.

"It's a shame about her accident, really. She looked so frail that day at the hospital."

*Hospital.*

Suddenly, Cole knew where he'd seen the scar before.

"You were there." He took a step forward, the beat of his chest rising. "You were there when she died."

"It makes you wonder if it was really an accident at all." Zanella winked, and that's all it took for Cole to snap.

He slammed his fists against Z's chest and shoved him into the mantle. "What the fuck are you talking about, *Harley*?"

Zanella's voice was a whisper. "It was so easy to convince her to pick . . . up . . . the knife."

Cole's body raged at Zanella's words, and he threw his fist back, punching the artist in an instant. Blood gushed out of Z's nose, but Cole didn't care. If what he said was true, then this asshole was responsible for his daughter's death.

The thought changed something in the very essence of Cole's DNA.

Before he could think, Zanella bashed his forehead against his, and he scrambled away. Cole screamed as pain and vengeance settled beneath his bones.

"Get back here, *you sick fuck!*"

A crash sounded from somewhere behind him, and he swung his battered body around.

"You've come out to play," Zanella yelled in a sing-song voice. "I must admit, Cole, I didn't think you'd have it in you."

Cole snarled. He'd blamed himself for River's death for years, but all along, it was this man's fault.

Anger boiled beneath Cole's skin at the revelation.

Zanella was the reason River would never breathe again.

And now he would pay.

Cole launched forward, weaving through the maze of old furniture and flinging his body when he spotted Z hiding behind a library cart, his fight or flight mode taking over. He wasn't quick enough, though, and Z kneed him in the groin and then threw Cole to the ground, pinning him down.

"I'm going to kill you," Cole gargled as he fought to break free.

Zanella laughed. "Good luck trying, Sloane. Tell me," he said, shoving Cole's head against the floor again with force. "Do you really think she would've had a different outcome if I hadn't been there to assist? Do you think she would still be alive, and that you would've changed? That maybe you would've gotten your priorities in order, and Rose wouldn't have cheated on you?"

Cole gasped as he fought for air.

"I hate to be the one to tell ya," Z said, a curl loosening and falling on his forehead, "but Rose was sleeping with David way before I stepped in."

Cole's vision blurred as he neared unconsciousness, but just then, he spotted a large, heavy book out of the corner of his eye. He willed his hand to move, and at the last possible second, his fingers curled around the edges and grasped it, allowing him to fling it at Zanella.

The spine of the century-old novel cracked Z square in the jaw, and air filled Cole's lungs as Zanella toppled over and ran. Cole took several deep, laboring breaths before rolling onto his hands and knees, steadying himself enough to stand. His body ached everywhere, but the adrenaline kept him pushing forward.

Slowly, he stood to his feet and squinted. His voice broke out in an earth-shattering yell that vibrated through the night as he took off once again after the artist. "Zanella! You can't escape me this time!"

Cole pounded his feet against the carpeted tile as he ran, in pursuit of Z's final story. He heard a manic laugh erupt from a lower level and cursed, realizing Zanella was already a floor below.

Cole chased the sound of footsteps and flung his limbs down the stairs. "Where'd you go, you FUCKING BASTARD?"

"*Shhhhhhhh.*" Cole heard the whispered hush bounce from the darkness. "We don't want to disturb the babies, now, Cole!" Z's voice echoed through the room, and Cole took off in the direction from which it came. He threw chairs, kicking anything and everything out of his sight.

All he knew was that Zanella had to pay for what he'd done.

To River.

To their family.

To Luna and Jax—

His thoughts were cut off at the sound of another crash. It sounded like it happened on the stairs, and Cole raced through the makeshift hospital wing, desperate to finally end this story. He reached the top of the next flight of stairs in record time and started barreling down them to the level where Nelson had been, trusting his adjusted vision to keep him from falling in the dim lighting.

And that's when Cole's body smacked against Zanella's once again.

The artist tackled him, but Cole quickly wriggled out of Z's hold and punched him. Zanella took the force of the blow, but that didn't stop him from fighting back. He kicked Cole in the ribs and scrambled to get away.

"Cock sucker!" Cole doubled over on the floor in pain and willed his body to continue. He was so tired, yet so wired.

A beat later, he rose from the floor and looked around, trying to see where his opponent had gone.

Then, out of the corner of his eye, he saw a spark.

Somewhere from deep within the library, a fire had started.

And it was getting bigger, quickly.

"Fuck," Cole breathed on an exhale. He had to get out of here fast—but not without Z.

"It should be illegal to have an open fire in a library," Zanella yelled.

Cole grunted and snapped his head, spotting him near the champagne fountain he'd first seen when they arrived tonight. He took off after him, this time desperate to catch him before his body gave out and the flames consumed him. He watched Zanella high-tail it down the stairs, and in a last-ditch effort, Cole made a snap-choice decision that risked the state of everything.

In one fell swoop, he took a running jump and lunged for Zanella, pummeling his body as they fell and hit the steps. The duo wrestled as they tumbled down the grand entrance together, and Cole felt one of his fingers snap.

They broke the landing, and Cole moved quickly, his body turning upright as he whipped his legs around the artist and pinned his arms against the ground with one hand while the other closed a fist around Zanella's neck.

"Go on, then," Z said, a crazed look in his eyes. "Kill me and prove you're just like the rest of them."

Cole paused, just for a moment to consider his words.

Z saw the opportunity and took it, spewing garbage from his mouth. "If you kill me, you'll be just like the filthy men and women you write about. And without me, who really are you, Cole? You need me, whether you want to admit it or not."

Cole's gaze lingered, his hand still firm around Zanella's neck. He could hear sirens in the background, meaning the others had escaped and called the cops. It was now or never.

"Just think about your daughter, Cole," Z whispered. "How would River feel knowing her daddy murdered the only man who offered her salvation?"

Cole's eyes blazed as the last restraint holding his wrist in place snapped, and he squeezed with every ounce of guilt and remorse he'd carried over the last two years.

"Don't you *ever* fucking say her name again."

*"Officials retrieved the body of underground artist Graham Zanella yesterday morning after sorting through the wreckage at Pugh Library. The fire that caused his imminent death is still under investigation."*


**—The Whetherington Post**

*"A series of unorthodox events occurred late Tuesday night at the old Pugh Library, which is seated on the outskirts of Springhill University's south campus. An underground artist by the name of Graham Zanella supposedly hosted a private gala there for a select group of individuals, one of which has an interesting take on the event. Here to share her recount of the night is artist Alejandra Winthrow."*


**—ZBD Live**

*"An official investigation is now underway at Honey Creek Fertility Clinic after a record-breaking number of women came forward about the mishandling of their embryos after the Monroe case broke. Officer Caden Ribyrd said he hopes the investigation can be wrapped up quickly.*

*'Of course, we hope to have answers sooner rather than later, but the problem with this sort of thing is you just never really know.'"*

**—The Ohio Province Papers**

# NOW

*Wednesday, January 15, 2025*

"Here," Cole said, shoving the paper across the table to Luna.

She stared at him, a brief hesitation passing across her face. "Are you sure?"

Cole nodded. "Just give it to Nate. Tell him it's all there." He looked at the guard in the corner before snapping his gaze back to Luna. "I had to handwrite everything, and I wanted it to be as accurate as possible—that's why it took so long."

Sighing, Luna nodded and took the envelope. "He's still harassing me to write mine, too, but I just . . ." She looked down at the scars that were permanently etched into her son's skull. "I can't do that to Jaxson," she whispered. "He's already been through so much. I don't want to draw more attention to us."

Cole felt Emmett nudging him, and he shifted to pet him, his wrists sore from the handcuffs. "I don't blame you." He scratched his dog's ears, a sense of warmth filling his chest.

He was so thankful Luna agreed to take him in. The pair felt like a natural fit compared to the other female in his life.

He waited for Em to lay down beside him, and then he looked at Jaxson and practiced the little ASL Luna had taught him. *"How are you doing, buddy?"*

The child stared at him for a minute before glancing back at the floor, not responding.

Luna gave Cole an apologetic look, but he waved it off. "It's okay. He'll talk when he's ready."

She smiled warmly and flipped her hair from one side to the other—a nervous tick Cole had picked up on during what he now called The Gala Games. "How are you holding up in here?"

"As well as you'd expect, I guess." He twisted his lips to the side, reconsidering his words. Prison wasn't as bad as he'd expected, and Luna visited often, always with Jaxson and Emmett at her side. Sometimes others came, too. Jayce, Nate, and even Greyson once. "Actually," he said, "I feel fucking great, all things considered. I just really miss you guys."

Luna smiled again, and he offered her a quick wink, making her blush.

"All right, visiting hours are over, folks," a security guard bellowed from behind them. "Let's go! Wrap it up, men!"

A series of eye rolls passed through the inmates. *How many times was he going to make that same fucking joke?*

Cole's expression changed, the same way it always did when he had to leave them. "Next Wednesday?" he asked.

"Next Wednesday," she said, smiling.

A guard swept an arm under Cole and pulled him up. "Let's go, Sloane."

Cole grumbled but obliged, allowing the man to escort him back through the visitor's room and into his cell. He stopped and held his arms out, waiting while the bailiff uncuffed him. "Thanks," he mumbled and then plopped down on his bed.

He closed his eyes, and a flame burned through his thoughts. He sat up straight, widening his eyes, but it was no use. His mind wandered back to that night again and again, no matter what Cole did to try and shut it out. He could handle the imagery if that's all it was, but it was the smell that haunted him.

Just as the illusion started to consume him, the same way the flames had lapped up the side of the library's infrastructure that night, the sound of his roommate bopping in and humming a familiar tune cut through his internal torment.

"What're you doing lounging around for, mate? The sermon starts in five minutes, and I want a good seat. You know Gran will have my neck if I don't go every week—and yours, too, for that matter." Sol grabbed a Bible from the top bunk and flung it at Cole. "I swear, I burn down one damn building, and suddenly the woman thinks I forgot who my Lord and Savior is."

Cole rolled his eyes but smiled, thankful for the distraction. It had taken Cole by surprise when he learned the rock star had been the one to light the match that night at the library, but Sol's fellow incarceration had been the best part of prison by far.

"Yeah, well," Cole said, standing from the bed and following Sol into the hallway. "I'm pretty sure the Bible says not to commit arson."

"It most certainly does not," Sol argued. "Thou shall not commit murder, though." He paused and gave Cole a knowing look before continuing. "I think you're the one who's got some repenting to do, mate."

"Yeah, yeah," Cole grumbled. "I know."

They rounded the corner and followed the guard to the makeshift pulpit. Once inside, he found two seats near the podium and moved toward them, his fear of sitting front and center long gone by now. He motioned to the seat beside him and waited for Sol to join. "If I can make it into Heaven after all that," he said, "I'm pretty sure anyone can."

He opened his Bible, the one he'd held onto since that awful night at the drive-in, and looked at the pastor, ready to study the Word and see if the concept of forgiveness really existed for a man like him.

THE END

*If you are experiencing suicidal thoughts, please call or text **988** for immediate help.*

# ACKNOWLEDGEMENTS

Holy crap. We've reached this stage of the book, y'all. I'm honestly still in shock, but I'm going to try and rein it in so I can thank all the wonderful souls who made this possible.

First and foremost, I want to thank God for placing this story on my heart. I will forever praise you for gifting me with this talent, and I pray this book finds those who need it most.

To my sweet, loving husband, Seth, thank you for taking care of our family and supporting me in this dream. I'm proud to say you can finally stop asking, "When are you gonna write your book?"

To my children, Willow and Ezra, while I know you won't read this for many years to come, thank you two so much for allowing Mommy to write in between our pockets of playtime and snuggles. I hope you both always find time to chase your dreams, no matter how big they seem.

To my mom, Susie, thank you for always being my biggest cheerleader in all that I do. You're the greatest mom a girl could have. (Sorry for all the curse words in this book.) And to my dad, step-dad, and uncle, thank you for your continued love and support.

To Madi, thank you for listening to my thousands of voice messages and being my Emotional Support Person. You're basically my Emmett.

To Alexis, thank you so much for helping me throughout this journey. I appreciate your friendship more than you know and can't wait to cheer you on as your backlist grows. (Go Eagles! #CTU)

To my beta readers, thank you for braving my messy first drafts. This book is one hundred percent stronger thanks to each of you.

To Mel, my designer, thank you for helping me update this cover! The journey to creation was quite unconventional, but you took charge and crushed it, per usual.

To my narrator, Steve, thank you so much for bringing my words to life! Hearing this story on audio was pure magic.

And lastly, to my readers, thank you for taking a chance on my debut novel. You guys are pretty freaking rad.

# ABOUT THE AUTHOR

Amy is a thriller author who was born in the heart of Appalachia before later relocating to the Midwest. With a Bachelor's degree in journalism and a professional background in content marketing, she has a passion for storytelling. When Amy's not writing, you can find her playing with her wild (lovable) children, hiding her book purchases from her husband, or rambling way too much on her Instagram stories. You can connect with her here: @authoramytackett.

## Also by Amy Tackett

*The Launch*
(The Art of Deception Book 2)

*Secret Santa*
*The Tides of Our Sins*